SHELTER BY THE SEA

ELENA AITKEN

Ink Blot Communications

Shelter by the Sea

ISBN: 978-1-927968-53-6

Also by Elena Aitken

Destination Paradise

Shelter by the Sea

Escape to the Sun

Hidden in the Sand

Ever After

Choosing Happily Ever After

Needing Happily Ever After

Wanting Happily Ever After

Fighting Happily Ever After

We Wish You A Happily Ever After

Keeping Happily Ever After

Finding Happily Ever After

Seeking Happily Ever After

Cherishing Happily Ever After

Ever After: Volume One (Books 1-4)

The Springs Series

Summer of Change

Falling Into Forever

Second Glances

Winter's Burn

Midnight Springs

She's Making A List

Summit of Desire

Summit of Seduction

Summit of Passion

Fighting For Forever

The Springs Collection: Volume 1

The Springs Collection: Volume 2

The Springs Collection: Volume 3

The Springs Complete Collection - Books 1-10

The McCormicks

Love in the Moment

Only for a Moment

One more Moment

In this Moment

From this Moment

Our Perfect Moment

Stand Alone Stories

All We Never Knew

Drawing Free

Sugar Crash

Composing Myself

Betty & Veronica

The Escape Collection

Vegas

Nothing Stays in Vegas

Return to Vegas

Timber Creek

When We Left

When We Were Us

When We Began

When We Fell

Castle Mountain Lodge

Unexpected Gifts

Hidden Gifts

Unexpected Endings - Short Story

Mistaken Gifts

Secret Gifts

Goodbye Gifts

Tempting Gifts

Holiday Gifts

Promised Gifts

Accidental Gifts

The Castle Mountain Lodge Collection: Books 1-3

The Castle Mountain Lodge Collection: Books 4-6

The Castle Mountain Lodge Collection: Books 7-9

The Castle Mountain Lodge Complete Collection

Bears of Grizzly Ridge

His to Protect

His to Seduce

His to Claim

Hers to Take

His to Defend

His to Tame

His to Seek

Hers for the Season

Bears of Grizzly Ridge: Books 1-4

Bears of Grizzly Ridge: Books 5-8

Halfway Series

Halfway to Nowhere

Halfway in Between

Halfway to Christmas

For mom and dad. Who never fail to support me and believe in my dreams. You have inspired my love for travel and without you this book would never have come to be. I think it's time for another visit!

Chapter One

BEYOND THE WINDOWS of the SUV, the dense trees of the Panamanian jungle whipped by. Cass Cutler had long since stopped trying to see anything of interest in the inky, black night. Once the bright lights of Panama City faded away, there'd been nothing except the occasional glow of what were probably homes in the distance and the glaring lights of passing motorists.

With a sigh, Cass closed her eyes. It was probably better if she pretended to sleep. There was no way she'd actually be able to, but maybe if she pretended it would be sort of the same thing. The last forty-eight hours had been a whirlwind of packing, booking a ticket and most unexpectedly, quitting her job.

Her job. Her nice, safe, secure job as an account manager for Munchies Food Distribution. Sure, it'd never been her idea of a dream career, but still. It was her job. Her temple throbbed, just thinking about the way she'd stormed into Jake's office, handed him her resignation and stood with her arms crossed to keep from shaking while he read through it.

As she typed it up, she imagined her boss of the last four

years—lover of three—reading the letter with disbelief. He would jump up from his desk with his perfectly pressed slacks and his neat white shirt becoming crumpled with the sheer stress of her resignation. He'd plead with her not to go and pull her into his arms for the public declaration of love she'd waited on for the last three years.

That's not exactly how it'd played out. In fact, he hadn't done any of that. Instead, he'd laughed.

Laughed.

His lip curled up, his eyes closed and he laughed. As if she was a big joke and she hadn't meant anything to him. And she, to her horror, had cried. Well, as close to a cry as she ever got. Cass never cried. Not when she'd crashed her brand new car and broke her arm, not when her best friend Angie moved to England, and not even when she was twelve and her father left. It was mortifying.

She'd blinked back the moisture in her eyes quickly, but it was too late. Jake saw it. And worse, he'd probably thought she'd been all teary over him. In reality, Jake wasn't worth so much as a sniffle. She'd known that for years, despite the fact that she'd stayed with him.

No, Cass's emotions finally boiled over because she realized how stupid she'd been for the last three years, letting herself be used with the promise of a promotion to senior account manager for Cheesy Bites, or worse—a real relationship with a man who was so uptight he'd never even let her see him naked. Not once in three years. That's not normal.

How she'd let herself be blinded for so long was beyond her. Never before had she been such an idiot.

And she'd never allow herself to be so stupid again.

Ever.

She popped her eyes open and stared once again into the darkness. Except, of course, for her present situation. It was possible that driving through the Panamanian jungle in the middle of the night with a complete stranger at the wheel, with no real idea where she was going or what she was going to do when she got there, might qualify as stupid. But it also—and more importantly—qualified as YOLO. A ridiculously childish notion her best friend Angie had explained when Cass had called overseas to tell her about the strange and unexpected letter she'd received only hours before.

"You only live once, Cass," she said. "You should go. YOLO."

"I don't know…"

"Why not?" Angie didn't wait for an answer before she demanded, "Read it to me again."

Cass looked at the letter in her hand, and did as requested.

"Dear Ms. Cutler, I am contacting you in regards to your father, Roger Cutler. As of October 13, it will be three years since Mr. Cutler's boat has been in our possession at Shelter Bay Marina. Repeated attempts to contact him have gone unanswered. As of September 1, 2014, Mr. Cutler has been presumed dead by authorities."

"God. I'm sorry, Cass."

She ignored her friend and the stab of pain in her chest and continued to read, getting to the part that really made her head spin.

"As you are the next of kin, his possessions become your responsibility. Please contact us with further instructions. Signed, Joe Holt. Shelter Bay Marina. Colon, Panama."

When she finished reading, there was a silence on the other end and for a moment Cass was afraid they'd been disconnected. "I'm really sorry, Cass." Her best friend's voice was soft. Angie was never soft and Cass hated the note of pity she heard in her friend's voice. Especially considering she didn't know herself how she was supposed to feel. "But you really should go."

"Of course I'm going to go." Cass hadn't known she was

going to go until that moment. But as soon as the words left her mouth, they made sense. Even if the letter didn't. She thought she should feel a little more emotion reading the words that her father was presumed dead. But how do you mourn for a man who hadn't been part of your life for the last sixteen years?

"Yes." Angie's voice went back to normal. "You'll go and you'll have a little break and maybe even some fun in the sun, and when you come back, you'll—"

"I'll what?" Cass could see her friend pacing the floor, maybe even waving her finger at her across the miles and time zones.

"You'll leave that wanker and move on with your life."

"Wanker?" Cass tried and failed not to laugh. "You've been in England too long."

"And you've been with that moron for too long."

It was true and almost impossible to argue. "Okay."

"Really?"

"Really. I'll deal with it tomorrow."

"With the letter or the wanker?" Angie laughed and it was a sound that made Cass miss her even more. Having an international best friend could really suck sometimes.

After they disconnected the call, Cass spent the rest of the evening booking a flight and after a few glasses of wine, drafting her resignation letter. Angie was right: she'd spent too long at that dead end job and with Jake.

Besides, surely he'd fight for her if he really cared. He hadn't. And now she was in a car headed toward what, she wasn't sure. But it had to be better than what she'd left behind.

Which was nothing, really. A boring job where the biggest benefit was as many Cheesy Bites and Twisty Nut Knots she could eat, and a relationship—if you could even call it that—with even fewer perks than her job. She'd been spinning her wheels for too long. It was way past time to move on. Which was exactly what she was doing.

. . .

A flash of light out the window caught her attention. The driver slowed as they passed through a guarded gate. He caught her looking in the rearview mirror and smiled a bright toothy smile.

"Almost there. It's late, and I do most of the driving for Shelter Bay, so I know the potholes to avoid, don't worry." His smile was proud and Cass couldn't help but grin. A grin that quickly melted away with his next question. "Joe expecting you?"

Crap.

She almost spoke aloud but caught herself just in time. The truth was, she didn't know whether Joe Holt was expecting her or not. She'd called and left a message, but when she hadn't heard back, she just continued with her plans and had completely forgotten that she'd never actually spoken to him. Until now.

Cass forced a smile to her face and nodded. "Of course." She hoped she sounded more confident than she felt.

It will all work out. It will all work out.

She chanted her dad's mantra—one of the few things she'd taken from him—in her head and tried to keep calm, but the panic must have shown on her face.

"Joe always has a spare room or two upstairs for surprise guests," her driver, Teddy, said. His voice was easy and friendly and not for the first time, Cass was thankful that she'd at least thought ahead to arrange a ride from the airport to the marina two hours away. She may have neglected to confirm some of the important details—like accommodations—but once the decision to go had been made, she wasn't about to put it off.

"Thank you."

Teddy smiled another kind smile as they pulled up against a long, low building. "I'll help you with your bags."

Her "bags" consisted of one duffel and a small backpack, but Cass wasn't in any mood to protest or declare her independence in some kind of girl power show. She was tired, it was late and as Teddy had more or less pointed out, she didn't really have a place to stay. She could use the backup, even if it came in the form of a taxicab driver she'd just met.

The moment she stepped out of the car, the heat and humidity hit her like a brick. Even in the middle of the night, it was hot. Really hot. The kind of hot that settled into your bones and made your whole body heavy.

Cass let Teddy take her bags and lead her across the pavement to the building where presumably Joe was. She had no idea what time it was but judging by the dark sky and thick carpet of stars, it had to be well past midnight. Living in Seattle, she wasn't used to so many stars. It had been years since she'd seen much more than the Big Dipper. Did they even have the Big Dipper in Panama? She tipped her head back and just for a moment let her senses fill with the wide openness of the night. She vowed to spend more time staring at the sky when she had a minute to breathe. Hopefully that minute would come soon.

Teddy opened a wooden door and waited for her to walk through it.

With a weak smile and a sigh to match, Cass went inside. The sky would have to wait.

Teddy led her through a tiny entryway to a small alcove where two offices sat. One door was open, with a sign on it that said: Registered Cruisers Only. Inside was a computer, printer, and two bookshelves full of books and maps with another sign: Take one—leave one.

However, it was the other office that had Cass's attention. The sign on the door said: Dockmaster. She presumed that meant it was Joe Holt's office, which was problematic because the door was locked and the lights were off.

"No problem," Teddy said.

Cass spun to look at him. How could it not be a problem? She was in Panama in the middle of the night with nowhere to stay and the only person who might be able to help her wasn't there.

"I'll make a call." Teddy pulled out a cell phone and grinned the wide, toothy smile that Cass was coming to think of as his trademark. She took another deep breath, because really there was no choice. While Teddy had a quick and quite loud conversation with someone in Spanish, she wandered into the open office and looked at the bulletin board and papers that were randomly stuck to the wall over the desk.

"For Sale—Wind Genny"

"Wanted—Crew for canal crossing"

"Missing—Roger Cutler"

Cass sucked in her breath when she saw the words peek out from layers of other papers. She reached out and pulled it free from the other ads that all but covered it. And there he was. Her father. Or his picture, anyway. The paper was yellowed and old, and in the photo he was older with a scruffy beard, a deep tan, and wrinkles that lined his forehead, but he was her dad. He smiled and looked happier in the picture than she'd ever remembered him. A female arm was draped around his shoulders, her hand resting on his arm, but the woman was cut out of the picture.

She didn't read the words; she couldn't. She was too busy staring into the familiar dark eyes, so much like her own. He looked so full of life, so—

"Miss Cass?"

As the paper crumpled in her hand, Cass spun to see Teddy holding a large anchor keychain; a single key dangled from it.

"Your room," he said proudly. "Joe will be here in the morning to meet you."

Cass could have kissed him she was so relieved to have a place to lay down.

"The rooms are right upstairs." Teddy pointed to a door farther down the corridor. "Would you like me to take you up?"

"No. Thank you, Teddy. You've done so much. I've got it from here." Suddenly, Cass wanted nothing more than to be alone. She shoved the piece of paper into her backpack and pulled out her wallet. "You've been fabulous." Cass handed him some bills. "I can't thank you enough."

Teddy winked and gave her the key in exchange for the money. "I'll see you soon. You enjoy Panama, Miss Cass."

When she picked up her duffel, it seemed much heavier than she remembered, but she heaved it over her shoulder as best she could and with a wave behind her, pushed her way through the doorway into the stairwell. The steel door clanged shut behind her, an ominous sound, but Cass was too tired to let it register. She took another few steps toward the stairs when there was a loud pop. Cass spun around at the exact second the lights went out and plunged her into darkness.

Chapter Two

THE DOCKSIDE INN was quiet for a Tuesday night. Beyond a few of the regular cruisers who never actually seemed to take their boats off the dock and sail them, the tables were mostly empty by the time Archer Wolfe was on his second beer.

Normally Archer enjoyed chatting to whoever happened to be in the Inn, but he'd heard most of the regular's stories already and he needed the time to think about his next move. A month ago, when he left his life in the Canadian Rockies for a two-week beach vacation that had been more or less forced upon him by his friends, he hadn't expected to enjoy the scorching temperatures, powdery sand that got into everything, and salty ocean water. Hell, he hadn't expected to like anything about Panama. He was a mountain boy. He needed cool temperatures at high elevations, pine needles under his feet, and a fresh glacier lake to swim in.

He'd been as surprised as anyone when he took one look at the Atlantic Ocean with water so blue he couldn't tell where it ended and the sky began, and known two weeks wouldn't be long enough. Where he felt comfortable and safe in the mountains, he felt free on the beaches of Panama. More than that, he'd caught the travel bug. He'd had a small glimpse of the world outside his safe Canadian town of Cedar Springs, and he was itching to see more. Now he just had the slightly problematic issue of figuring out how to fund those travels.

Archer rolled his almost empty bottle between his hands and considered his options. He didn't have many. He'd already cashed in his return ticket and enlisted his best friend back home, Samantha, to sell his truck for some extra spending money. But that might take awhile and if he wanted to keep traveling—and he did—he needed to figure something else out. The problem was, what?

He looked out over the masts of the many sailboats in the marina. Only a week ago, he'd been on one of those boats, along with a handful of tourists who came out from Panama City for the unique experience of sailing in the tranquil San Blas Islands. He'd spent most of his remaining money on that trip, but it had been worth it. And if he could have figured out a way to stay there for a few days, he would have. And he definitely wanted to get back there before he moved on to his next destination, wherever that might be.

But until he could figure out how to do that, his small room upstairs that overlooked the marina would have to do.

"Another beer, Arch?" Maria, one of the local waitresses, arrived at his table with a smile and a hand on the small of her back to support her growing tummy.

Archer instinctively stood and pulled out a chair for her. "Sit. You need it."

"I'm working."

He waved his arms to take in the mostly empty restaurant. "I'm sure you can sit down for a few minutes." She glanced around. "Besides," Archer said. "I could use a little advice."

She sat. "With what?"

"I need a job." He drained his beer. "Maybe you can put in a good word with Joe for me."

Joe was the dockmaster at the marina and pretty much ran every detail at Shelter Bay, which meant he was the man to go to if you needed anything. Including a job. Which was really too bad, considering he didn't seem to like Archer at all. It might have had something to do with the fact that the first night he'd arrived, Archer made the mistake of flirting with Joe's wife, Heather Okay, maybe it turned into more than flirting. Either way, it was a situation he never would have put himself in if he'd known she was married, which he certainly didn't. Nonetheless, it was a problem that was going to have to be overcome if Archer planned to stay at Shelter Bay, which he did.

Maria laughed, a deep, throaty, totally unabashed sound. "You want me to help?" she managed to say when she was done laughing. "What makes you think Joe will listen to me? Joe is Joe. That is all." She flipped her dark hair back over her shoulders and moved to push up from the chair. "And Joe will fire me if I don't get up and get moving."

Archer raised an eyebrow. They both knew it was a lie. Joe had a reputation for being stern, but fair. And the dockmaster seemed to have a soft spot for the young, pregnant Panamanian in particular. From the little Archer had seen, it was clear Maria could do no wrong as far as Joe was concerned.

"Now let me get you another beer. It's a hot night."

Archer silently calculated the money in his wallet. He shook his head. "I'm kind of tired." When he stood, his large frame towered over her. "It's a bit too quiet around here tonight." Another lie: he'd enjoyed the conversations he'd had with some of the regulars, but it didn't matter.

He handed Maria a few bills for the beers he'd drunk and thanked her before he made his way through the room to the back hallway that led to the marina offices as well as the stairwell up to the rooms over the restaurant. He'd been staying in one of those rooms for almost a week now and although it wasn't very expensive, Archer was pretty sure Joe had given him a special rate, and it definitely wasn't in Archer's favor.

He could afford a few more nights, enough time to figure out what to do. And he would. He always did.

Joe might be the best option for a job, but he wasn't the only one. Shelter Bay was full of people, all coming and going in a small cluster of buildings, and six large docks full of boats. But despite the non-traditional setting, it was a vibrant community and the people, although definitely a mixed bag, were genuine. He'd figure something out.

He pushed the heavy steel door to the stairwell open; it crashed behind him and left him in darkness.

Archer shook his head. If Joe wanted to save money, there were probably better ways than keeping the lights out in the stairs. And safer ways, too. He flicked the switch back and forth.

Nothing.

It took him one more flick that failed to produce light before he realized exactly why he stood in darkness. Again. The fuse must have gone. Archer rolled his eyes. Obviously Joe was saving money—by not hiring an electrician. It was the third time this week. Not that he minded too terribly much; the last time he'd been stuck in the dark, he'd had company. Although, Archer was pretty sure that Joe wouldn't appreciate the fact that it was his wife, Heather, who'd helped him find his way in the dark. He was also pretty sure that Joe would definitely not believe him when he told him he didn't know it was Heather he'd been kissing. No matter what Joe believed, or how good the kiss was, that information would definitely not help his chances of getting a job at Shelter Bay. As well as the information about what that kiss led to. No, that wouldn't help at all. That much Archer knew for a fact.

He picked his way through the darkness to where he knew from experience the fuse box was located. Too bad he didn't know more about electricity or he'd likely be able to convince Joe to hire him on as a handyman. Or not.

A shuffling sound and a slight cough, like someone tried to muffle the sound, caught his attention and he grinned.

Heather.

Another dark hallway rendezvous? He knew he shouldn't. It was a bad idea. A very bad idea. But what the hell? Joe already hated him and it wasn't his fault the woman clearly didn't care for her husband. He moved along the wall where the sound had come from and moments later, bumped into something, or someone, soft.

Without giving her a chance to speak, he reached out and pulled her head forward, finding her lips with his. Only she didn't yield the way she had in the past; this was different, more of a challenge. Archer used his free hand to find her cheek and stroked his thumb softly in circles as his mouth urged hers to open to him. And it did. She tasted different. Sweeter, hotter, and something else he couldn't quite identify. His body reacted hot and hard to her.

Archer's brain registered that it was not Heather he was kissing, almost at the exact second that she pushed him away and raised her knee in a sharp jerk, only narrowly missing his already extremely aroused jewels.

"What the hell do you think you're doing?" The voice was shaky, yet strong and definitely not Heather's.

Crap.

He stepped back to put a healthy distance between him and the woman he'd unintentionally accosted. "Whoa." He held his hands in front of him, although there was no way she could see him. "Just give me a second. I'll get the lights."

"Stay back."

"I intend to." There was no doubt about that. He felt his way along the wall until he reached the fuse box. Using a book of matches he'd taken from the bar, he used the glow of light to locate the right breaker and flicked it on, illuminating the tiny stairwell.

"Oh."

A female voice caught his attention; he turned around to see a very pretty and very startled woman in the corner, her hand over her eyes and her lips looking as if they'd just been thoroughly kissed, which they had. A fact his dick was still very aware of.

"Hey. About that—" He took a step toward her but she backed away and held her hand up in a pseudo-karate move. It was so cute that he would have laughed if she didn't look so terrified.

"Don't take another step." Her voice shook, but there was steel behind her words, too, and because Archer was no fool, he did as he was told. He'd been around enough strong women to know when to stand down. "I know self-defense and I'm not afraid to use it. One more step and I will drop you."

Then he couldn't help it. She didn't look weak or helpless by any means. In fact, she looked downright hot: her tank top clung to her breasts and her shorts exposed the kind of long, toned legs he could definitely imagine wrapped around him. But the idea that she could possibly take down all six one and at least two hundred and ten pounds of solid muscle honed from his days in the back country skiing, hiking, and hauling out game was laughable.

So he did.

A move his sexy companion really didn't seem to appreciate.

"What's so funny?"

"You," he managed to get out. "Obviously."

"You think it's funny that as I'm trying to get up to my room after a very long day, I'm thrust into darkness with no idea where I am or which way to go to get out and then assaulted by some beast of a man? The same big hulk of a man who continues to threaten me even though I've warned him to back the hell up? You think that's funny?"

She thrust her shoulders back and her chin out in a look of defiance that sent a spark of desire right through him. It was so unexpected, his laughter died on his lips.

"Look." He tried to soften his voice. He took another step toward her and although she didn't move away, she looked as if she might make good on her threat to drop him. "Okay." He held up his hands. "My name is Archer Wolfe and I'm a guest here. I won't hurt you, and I swear I didn't mean to kiss you. I thought you were someone else."

"You're a guest?" She narrowed her dark eyes at him. "Then how did you know how to turn the lights back on?"

"Practice. It happens a lot." He laughed again, but the look on her face told him in no uncertain terms that she was not amused, so he swallowed it. "I can show you how to do it if you like? I'd recommend it if you plan on spending any length of time here."

Suddenly, he wanted to know very badly whether she'd be spending any length of time at the marina and whether she might like to spend any of that time with him—perhaps revisiting that kiss, because damn if his body didn't react immediately and hard to the taste of her. Yes, he very much wanted to spend more time with her. Preferably not standing in the stairwell.

"I don't think that will be necessary." Something in her voice told Archer that she really wasn't so sure. In fact, something in her voice hinted at a lot more than uncertainty, so Archer forced himself to behave and not push the issue.

"Well, for however long you plan on staying, would you like me to help you with your bags? To make up for the kiss." Her fingers flew up to her lips as if she was only now remembering that little detail. "I promise," Archer continued, "I'm a really good guy. I have references."

That made her smile, at least a little. And just that sliver of smile was enough for Archer to know he wanted to see more. Much more.

"That's not necessary."

"If you're sure…"

"My name is Cass."

"Just Cass?"

She raised an eyebrow. "Just Cass."

To his surprise, she let him take her bag and together they walked up the stairs.

"So, what are you here for, Cass? Catching a charter?"

In the short time he'd spent at the marina, he realized that if you weren't a boat owner getting work done on your boat over in the yard, you were a traveler catching a charter out to the San Blas Islands. Not many people stayed long-term in the six rooms over the restaurant.

"Aren't you full of questions?"

"Questions are the only way to figure out the answer."

For a moment, she looked as if she was going to argue with him and Archer wanted nothing more. It had been a long time since he'd sparred with a woman and he liked it. And judging from the uncomfortable bulge in his jeans, his brain wasn't the only part of him that appreciated her sass.

Instead of saying whatever it was that was obviously on the tip of her tongue, Cass closed her mouth and nodded her head toward the door at the end of the hall. "I think that's me. Room three."

On the exact opposite end of the hall from him. He carried her bag the short distance and set it down. "So you're really not going to tell me what you're doing here?" He crossed his arms over his chest, in no hurry to let her go.

She must have sensed that he wasn't going to drop it; either that, or she'd finally decided he wasn't a threat to her. Cass sighed. "I'm here for a little holiday." But the way her eyes shifted made it obvious to anyone who paid attention that she was lying. And Archer was definitely paying attention. Before he could call her on it, Cass added, "And to sort out a few things of my father's."

There was more than what she was saying but it was clear she didn't want to talk about it and there was no way he could push without crossing a line. After all, they'd only just met; he couldn't expect her to spill all her secrets. Which was fine with him: he liked a little mystery in a woman. It kept things interesting. When she reached past him to unlock her door, her breast brushed against his arms, which sparked another reaction in his crotch. To keep his sanity, he stepped back to give her space and shoved his hands in his pockets to keep from reaching out to her when she picked up her bag, thanked him and walked into the room. Before she closed the door behind her, she turned and gave him the sexiest damn smile he'd ever seen, which just cemented her place as the star of his dreams for the night.

"Damn." He shook his head and walked back to his room with a smile on his face. Meeting Cass had just made things a lot more interesting in Shelter Bay. It was true he still needed a job to replenish his funds, but maybe, just maybe, he wouldn't be in such a hurry to move on after all?

Chapter Three

IT MIGHT HAVE BEEN the sunlight that streamed through her window, the thunk of the air conditioner in what had to be its death throes, or the shrill squeak from outside, but whatever it was that woke Cass, one thing was for sure—it was too early.

Reluctantly, she rolled over and grabbed her phone from the nightstand.

4:12.

Way too early. Four isn't even considered morning, or at least it shouldn't be. It was an unnatural time to get up. She pulled her pillow over her head to block out the sun.

The sun.

How could it be so bright if it was only four in the morning? It took a moment for the reality to set in.

Time change.

Cass groaned and reluctantly peeked out from the pillow at the wall clock across the room.

6:12.

It felt like only minutes ago she'd climbed into bed after leaving that smart ass in the hallway. Her dream rushed back in vivid detail.

Wait.

She flipped over and examined the rest of her small room to search for…what? The man? That was ridiculous. She wasn't the type of woman to go to bed with a complete stranger. Even one as tall, broad-shouldered, and totally manly as…Archer. His name was Archer. Of course it was.

With another quick scan of her room, Cass finally reassured herself that she indeed had not slept with him, despite what she may have done in her dreams. Her reality was still as boring and depressing as always. But her dreams…oh, her dreams. Clearly it had been too long since she'd been with a man. And Jake didn't count. Cass rolled her eyes. Not unless a five-minute quickie with his shirt left on counted?

No, he definitely didn't count.

With a groan of frustration, Cass threw back the blanket and stretched her arms overhead. She was way too tired for six, or four, or whatever time it was, but she had things to take care of. And besides, if she fell asleep again, she might dream about Archer. And from her limited experience, it was never a good idea to dream about strange men. Especially strange men she might actually run into.

Curious to see her surroundings in the daylight, Cass went to the window and pulled the flimsy drapes to one side.

"No wonder they didn't keep out any light," she muttered. "They're made of tissue." But the second the fabric was pulled aside, the brilliance of the tropical sun blinded her; her arm flew up to her face in a futile effort to block some of the intense light that now filled her room. "Okay, I was wrong."

It took a minute for her eyes to adjust to the light, but when she did, she took in the view. And what a view it was. The marina spread out before her. Six long docks of boats of every size, shape, and description. It looked like a forest of sticks and masts with a variety of colorful flags flying from them, and she felt the same familiar tug in her gut that she felt every time she looked upon a marina full of boats waiting to be sailed.

She shook her head and tried to squash the feeling as she looked beyond the marina to a breakwater of large boulders that created a protected cove for the boats within. It was easy to see why the breakwater was necessary. The Atlantic Ocean was vast and even from a distance, Cass could tell it was wild.

She drew in a sharp breath. It was so different from the Pacific Ocean. Not that she got much of a chance to sit and stare at the ocean, but even if she did—it was nothing like what she was looking at now.

The squeaking noise started up again, catching her attention and drawing her eyes away from the water and to the slope of the rooftop below her. A tiny black bird with a bright yellow head sat on the eaves. But that couldn't have been the squeaking that woke her. Birds didn't squeak. They chirped. She slid the window open to hear better. Startled, the bird flew off.

Cass shrugged but immediately heard the noise again. Her head swung around so quickly she almost hit it against the windowsill. It was definitely not a bird. It was Archer. Archer, with his giant biceps straining against the thin cotton of his t-shirt, pushing a large trolley loaded down with what looked like propane tanks. Somehow she wasn't surprised that he was responsible for her wake-up call.

"Figures," Cass muttered. There was no way he could have heard her, but at that moment, Archer looked up and instinctively she dropped to the floor beneath the window.

Maybe he hadn't seen her. There was pretty much no reason for her to be acting like a teenager, unless you considered the very private and very sexy things they'd done in her dreams, which would make anyone duck and hide. But of course, Cass couldn't consider any of that because it was ridiculous. She brought her palm to her forehead and squeezed her eyes shut. Twenty-eight was way too old for this type of behavior. Obviously she needed more sleep. But that was out of the question, so coffee…she had to find some coffee.

Her phone beeped and Cass crawled along the floor until she was out of view of the window.

Did you make it? Is it amazing?

Cass smiled. Angie always had the best timing. She quickly typed out a response, silently blessing the miracle of text message that made it seem as if her best friend were always in the same room as her.

I'm here. It's amazing but I haven't even seen it in the daylight yet.

While she waited for Angie to respond, Cass grabbed her toiletries from her bag and went into the bathroom. She was brushing her teeth when the response came in.

If you haven't seen it yet, what's so amazing?

She laughed with the toothbrush hanging out of her mouth.

What's his name?

Leave it to Angie to cut right through the bullshit. Cass took her time brushing and rinsing before she bothered to text back.

What makes you think there's a "he"?

The reply came back almost instantly.

God, there better be. For your sake. Have a fling. YOLO.

Cass laughed again and rolled her eyes. YOLO indeed. She'd wait to tell Angie about Archer. Mostly because there was nothing to tell beyond a few exchanged words and a dirty dream her subconscious created for her, but also because it would be fun to torture her best friend a little bit. She decided to skip a shower in lieu of caffeine and pulled her blond hair up in a ponytail. As an afterthought, Cass coated her lashes with a quick swipe of mascara and slicked a bit of lip gloss on her lips. There was no point going downstairs looking as tired as she felt.

Her phone beeped again as she tugged a pair of jean shorts on.

Seriously. Sleep with him. Whoever he is. It'll make you feel better.

She could only shake her head in response. Angie had no idea that the thought had definitely crossed her mind. Especially when his hard body had been pressed up against her. Clearly she hadn't been the intended recipient of the kiss in the stairwell, but her body hadn't known that and to even her surprise, she'd reacted so completely and kissed him back in a way that was completely out of character for her. Angie would have a fit if she heard about her wanton behavior. Cass giggled at the idea of telling her. But she swallowed it down when she saw her friend's next text.

What's the deal with the boat? What about your dad? Any news?

Despite the fact that she probably shouldn't feel any kind of sense of loss for her dad, there was a strange pang in her chest. It wasn't an entirely unfamiliar sensation; Cass had experienced it on and off ever since she'd read the letter from Joe Holt. And really, if her dad was actually dead and gone, she should feel some sort of loss, shouldn't she? That was normal, wasn't it?

Cass had no idea. Her dad had been out of her life for so long, it was almost as though he was already dead. But not really. In her memories, he was there and there'd always been a part of her that held onto the hope that one day he'd reach out and want to repair their relationship. She knew it was idealistic and somewhat foolish, but there'd always been a glimmer of hope despite her mother's best efforts to crush it. Even after remarrying and moving to Arizona almost ten years ago, her mother still harbored genuine resentment for the man who'd left her alone with a child to raise. It wasn't a subject they spoke about. Ever.

She went to her backpack and pulled out the crumpled paper she'd shoved in there the night before.

Missing.

Not dead. Missing.

There was a big difference. Cass trailed her fingers along the photo. When her phone beeped again, she snatched her hand back and tucked the paper away.

Cass?

She ignored the message. Angie was concerned, but there was nothing to worry about. Not until she knew something. And she wasn't ever going to know anything until she found Joe Holt. She stashed the paper in the top of her duffel bag and before she left her phone in the room, typed a quick response.

Gotta go. Need coffee.

She wasn't sure what she expected to find in the restaurant after she made her way, quickly this time, down the stairs, but whatever it was she thought she'd see, it certainly wasn't the packed tables full of happy people drinking coffee and eating what definitely smelled like bacon. It was so early. Didn't people in Panama sleep?

She scanned the room in search of an empty seat. Nothing. Not unless she wanted to sit at the very back by the bar, and she didn't. Cass wanted to be by the window or even outside. After living in Seattle her whole life, she craved the sun. Besides, the air conditioning inside was already making her shiver.

You'd think they'd wait until later in the day when it got hot to turn the A/C on. She shrugged and made her way to the door, hoping there'd be a seat on the veranda. The moment she pushed the door open, she realized why the air conditioning was already running full blast.

The heat hit her as if she'd walked into a wall and not out

onto the deck. Her hand flew to her chest and it took her a second to catch her breath.

"It takes some getting used to."

Cass dropped her hand and spun to see Archer watching her. He lounged with one leg crossed over the other at a nearby table. He looked just as freakin' good as he had the night before. Maybe better now that she could actually see him. He held a cup of coffee that looked ridiculously small in his big hands and a smile danced on his lips. It was the type of smile that suggested he knew something about her that she didn't want him to know.

There was no way he could know he'd been featured in her dreams, but nevertheless, a flush started at the back of her neck. With a lame attempt to cover her embarrassment, Cass snatched the menu off his table and fanned herself. "It is warm here."

Slowly, Archer took a sip of his coffee. It seemed to take forever for him to put it down and Cass did her best to act casual while he took his time. "I promise you won't even notice in a few days," he said. "Well, you will. But it'll be a bit more normal. Are you going to order breakfast?"

He pointed to the menu in her hands. The one that now hung lamely from her hand. "Oh." She tossed it back on his table. "Sorry about that. I will eat, but I need to find a place to sit. I can't believe how busy it is already. It's not even seven."

"You'll notice that people get up pretty early around here, what with the sun being so hot and all. Doesn't seem to be much point to waste the day in bed when you can be enjoying such beautiful weather."

He had a point. A point she hadn't bothered to consider. But as she looked around and took in the palm trees that lined the boardwalk next to the marina, the colorful birds that danced through the sky, and the pots of tropical flowers placed practically everywhere, it was easy to see Archer's point. She closed her eyes and inhaled deeply. As well as the lingering scent of bacon in the air, there was something else. Something she couldn't quite identify because she'd never before smelled anything like it. It was both deeply fragrant and yet, fresh and light at the same time.

"It's the smell of the tropics."

Cass's eyes flew open. She really must be tired if she forgot he was sitting there. She was losing track of the times she'd embarrassed herself in his presence and she hadn't even known him for a full twenty-four hours.

"There doesn't seem to be any other seats open," Archer said when she didn't respond. "Why don't you sit here?"

For a moment she was going to argue, but he had a small pot of coffee on his table and she was way too tired and under-caffeinated to protest. And really, there could be worse ways to spend her first morning in paradise. Cass sat, and as if by magic, a waitress appeared with a cup for her coffee, which Archer poured without asking.

"Are you ready to order?"

Archer looked at her with expectation, so Cass ordered the breakfast special, which she was assured came with bacon. After the waitress left, she sipped her coffee gratefully and gave herself a few moments to let the caffeine affect her brain. When she finally felt able to hold a conversation, she set her coffee down and looked at Archer, who watched her with an amused expression.

"Better?"

"Much." Cass smiled. "Sorry. It's been a long few days and I can't believe how badly I needed a little coffee."

"No problem." His smile was warm and despite the fact that he'd scared the hell out of her the night before, there was no reason why she shouldn't try to get to know him. No reason except for her total body attraction toward him that had clearly manifested itself in some sort of subconscious way. But that wasn't a reasonable reason to avoid him. Especially considering so far he was the only person she knew in Panama, and a little attraction couldn't be bad. Angie's text flashed in her memory.

YOLO.

No. She wasn't even going to think of that. She needed to focus and surely she could be mature enough to ignore her attraction. No problem.

"Did you sleep well?"

Cass almost spat out her coffee at the question. Instead, she managed to swallow the strong liquid and ignore the burn of her tongue.

"What were you doing this morning with that squeaky cart?" It was best to change the subject away from sleep and her bed altogether.

"So you did see me."

He wiggled her eyebrows and instantly Cass realized her mistake, but there was no help for it. "I did. You woke me up." It wasn't totally a lie. "So what were you doing? Do you work here?"

He took another sip of his coffee before he answered. "Not yet. I'd like to get a job, so I try to help out whenever I can. My theory is that maybe I can win Joe over by helping, but—"

"Joe Holt?"

"That's him." Archer cocked his head. "He pretty much runs this place. Which sucks for me since he hates me."

"Is he here somewhere?"

"Why? Is there a problem with your room?"

Cass didn't miss the edge that had appeared in Archer's voice, but it was easier to ignore it. She didn't need to get in the middle of anything going on between the two men. "No problem with my room. But I do need to talk with him. He wasn't in last night and…" She drifted off, not sure how much she should tell Archer. Or whether there was anything to tell at all. Her thoughts flashed to the piece of paper she'd taken off the bulletin board.

Was her father's disappearance well known around the marina? What did people think about it? It was better not to say anything until she knew exactly what she was dealing with and at that moment, the only thing she knew was that her father's boat was one of the many sticks out in the marina in front of her.

"I just need to ask him a few questions," she finished lamely.

The waitress bringing their food saved her from any further explanation. Cass didn't realize how hungry she was until the plate of eggs, hash browns, and of course, bacon, was put in front of her. There was also a dish of fresh fruit, and Cass dove into the food before the waitress had even left.

"Can I get you anything else?"

Cass looked up long enough to see the woman eyeing her strangely, so she slowed down and forced a smile. "More coffee, please."

"And can you see if Joe is around this morning?"

The waitress laughed. "You really want to try for that job, huh?"

"Yes. But not right now." Archer gestured to Cass, who had picked up a piece of pineapple and could barely concentrate on the conversation happening around her because of the burst of pleasure it had just created in her mouth. "Cass needs to talk to him. Maria, this is Cass. Cass, Maria."

The women nodded at each other and Cass tried to smile with her mouth full.

"I'll find him." Maria put a hand on the small of her back, emphasizing her pregnant belly. "You keep enjoying that fruit, eh? It doesn't get any better than that."

Cass could only grunt in agreement with a mouth full of papaya. She'd never tasted anything like it. Only once before had she bothered to try papaya, but it was nothing like this sweet, juicy goodness she now had in her mouth. In fact, none of the fruit she'd just eaten was like anything she'd ever had before. And she'd definitely had pineapple and mango before. But they had not tasted so amazing in her kitchen back in the States. It was as if she was discovering these tropical fruits for the first time and never wanted to eat anything else. She, in fact, pushed her plate of bacon and eggs away in order to bring the fruit closer.

"It's good, right?"

"I've never tasted anything like it," she said through a mouthful. "People back at home have no idea what they're missing. This is what it's actually supposed to taste like."

"It's even better when you're enjoying it on the beach, watching the sunrise."

Cass paused, another piece of papaya halfway to her mouth. "That sounds good. I'll have to try that tomorrow if I can get out of bed that early."

"Oh, not here." Archer shook his head. "There aren't any beaches worth waking up for at the marina. I'm talking about the San Blas Islands. The most amazing beaches in the world." He laughed. "Not that I've been around the world."

"Well, I'd love to see them. Hopefully I'll get a chance." She popped another piece of fruit in her mouth and chewed before she added, "The only beaches I would have for comparison are on the Pacific Northwest. And while they're pretty nice, I have a feeling the beaches here are a bit warmer."

Archer laughed but the smile quickly vanished and was replaced by a much less genuine one. His eyes locked on something beyond Cass's head. "That was quick." He nodded to the side; Cass spun around just in time to see an older man with a scruffy gray beard dressed in a Hawaiian print shirt and a large floppy canvas hat approach them.

"You must be Cass Cutler." He extended his hand in greeting. "Joe," he said. "Joe Holt." Cass quickly wiped her sticky hand on a napkin before she shook his. With a mouthful of food, she couldn't answer him but he didn't seem to notice. "I'm glad you got in alright. I heard your message a few days back but things have been very busy around here and by the time I went to return your call, you were already on a plane, I assume?"

She opened her mouth to answer, but Joe wasn't finished.

"We have a lot to talk about and I'm sure you'll want to see your father's boat. It's been sitting for quite some time, but I've had the guys go in once in a while to check for critters and mildew."

Critters? Mildew?

"It'll be livable, though. You can move in as soon as you like."

Move in?

"It's down on D dock. I can—"

"Mr. Holt." Cass finally managed to get a word in. "I don't—"

"Joe. Call me Joe."

"Okay, Joe." She took a deep breath and glanced over at Archer, who watched the scene play out with a look that was both amused and confused. "I'm still not certain what I'm going to do with everything."

Joe took off his hat, revealing a balding scalp with a longish gray ponytail that hung down his back. He wiped his brow and gave her a kind smile. Something about him was very comforting, despite his unorthodox appearance. "I'm sorry." He returned his hat to his head. "I didn't even think of what a shock all this must have been for you and there's no need to make any decisions right now. Why don't I show you the boat and we can start there?"

Grateful, Cass nodded. "That sounds like a good idea."

"I have a few minutes before I—"

"Now?" She glanced at Archer and her half-eaten breakfast.

He shrugged and nodded. "Go. I got this. Sounds like you have a lot to take care of." Was it her imagination or did she hear a note of regret in his voice? Even if she did, she had no time for it now. "Joe," Archer said. "I filled the propane tanks for you this morning. Brought them up to the shed."

Joe's friendly demeanor changed the moment Archer spoke. "Saw that." He extended a hand to Cass. "Ready?"

She ignored the tension between the two men and took Joe's hand. Right now, the only thing she was focused on was her father's boat and the answers it might hold for her. The sooner she figured out that little mystery, the sooner she could start to figure out what the hell she was going to do next.

It was less than twenty-four hours.

Less than twenty-four hours.

He needed to get her out of his head.

Archer increased his pace as he ran down the road that would take him away from the marina and into the park reserve. It was later in the day for a run than he preferred—the sun was up and it was already hot. The heat was steaming from the ground; ripples in the pavement shimmered as he ran through them and annihilated them as his legs pushed through each of them. He ignored the sweat that dripped in rivulets down his back and chest.

He needed the physical exertion to clear his head. He'd always needed it. Now that he was in the jungle, and couldn't hunt and hike the way he would have in the mountains to relive his tension, he needed to find his escape in other ways and since he'd been at Shelter Bay, the only way he'd found to release his stress was with a daily run through the jungle road.

Not that he had a lot of stress; how could you when you were in paradise? But from the moment he'd met Cass Cutler, she'd worked her way under his skin and into the very pulse of him. And tasting her…damn. It'd not only been unexpected but entirely welcome. He knew her kiss had come from a very different place than it should have. At least as far as a first kiss was concerned. But he didn't care.

She was tired, scared, probably excited to be in a new place. An exotic place. Maybe she didn't think she'd ever see him again. Who cared? He wasn't the type to overanalyze such a situation. Regardless, he may have initiated it, but she definitely kissed him back. At least for a moment. And it was that moment that Archer couldn't get out of his head.

Hence the run in the tropical heat of what was going to be another sweltering day.

The best way to work the heat out of his system was to work it out physically and if he couldn't have her underneath him, writhing and moaning his name—which really didn't seem to be an option—this was the only choice he had.

Archer pumped his arms, sucking the moist jungle air into his lungs, filling them with a heavy weight as he forced his muscles over the bridge that was usually his turnaround point. As a reflex, he stopped and put his hands on his legs, pulling air into his lungs and looking for relief from the burning torture he'd just put his body through. He waited a few minutes until his pulse slowed and stood up, slowly stretching, taking in the jungle around him.

The Panamanian jungle was the closest thing he'd found to the Canadian wilderness. The trees closed around him, encasing him in a protective cocoon that for some people created a sense of claustrophobia. For Archer, it had always been a safe place. A place he could be himself. Think about things and make sense of everything. The fact that the forest around him was no longer filled with pine trees and brown-eyed deer, but jungle trees and howler monkeys swinging from limb to limb was a minor detail he'd adapted to faster than he'd ever thought he would.

Born and raised a mountain boy, Archer had never expected that the rain forest would have the same effect, but now that he was here, he couldn't imagine any place else he'd rather be.

Unless it was a certain someone's bed.

Damn! That thought had hit him out of nowhere.

Cass.

God. Her tight little body, her full breasts pressed up against his. Had it really been that long since he'd been with a woman?

No. Not really. But with a woman that mattered…

And something told him, Cass mattered. He didn't know how, or why, but Cass mattered.

"Damn it."

He ran his hands through his thick, dark hair, stripped his t-shirt off and wiped the sweat from his face before he tossed it on the ground. He'd get it when he came back. Because there was no way he was stopping. Not with that woman occupying his thoughts.

Archer set off down the road, pushing himself through the burning muscles and past the point where he'd normally run, knowing he still had the return trip to make. He would not return to the marina until he had her out of his system. As long as it took, it had to happen.

The problem was, the more he pushed, pumping his arms harder and harder, the more Cass's face filled his thoughts. The taste of her on his lips. He couldn't escape it. What was worse was that he couldn't erase the image of her walking off with Joe. He'd probably filled her head with all kinds of poison about him. It's not as if it was Archer's fault that he'd hooked up with Heather, or that she'd made it clear she was available. Maybe if Joe took better care of—

No. It wasn't a train of thought he was willing to entertain. And for the first time, he didn't want to, because all he could think about was Cass and her—

"Dammit!"

The screech of a nearby toucan that erupted from its perch, disturbed by Archer's outburst, startled him enough to stop for a moment. God. When was the last time a woman got under his skin this way?

Never.

No. Not since Samantha, his best friend back home. But that was different. Very different. There was never anything romantic between them and even if he thought for the briefest of moments that there could have been, he was only fooling himself. She was too close. Like a sister. But that didn't mean he liked it when she hooked up with Trent Harrison, at least not until he got to know the guy. But Trent was good for her, which was a good thing considering he'd later become her husband. No. Whatever he'd felt for Samantha, as strong as it was, it was different. It was more like a brotherly concern. They worked way better as friends. Best friends.

He watched the brightly colored bird as it flew away, through the dense trees into the blue sky above the canopy. The world in the rain forest was a private little place. Sheltered, almost, from what was going on just beyond the thick branches. Those trees camouflaged a lot of things. Including what was really going on with the mysterious and extremely hot woman he'd shared his breakfast table with.

People didn't randomly show up at Shelter Bay Marina.

No. They turned up with a purpose. And it was one of two things: To find themselves. Or to find someone else.

Archer knew without a doubt, despite what Cass Cutler said, she wasn't there to find her missing father. She was there to find herself and Archer was the guy to help her along the road to discovery.

The idea gave him all kinds of mental imagery. Enough to finally fuel him back toward the marina.

As he retraced his steps, this time with a smoother gait, he let thoughts of Cass leave his head and focused on his greater problem. Because he did have one. He needed money.

And soon.

He didn't think it was possible, but in the short time he'd been in Panama, he'd fallen in love and he was in no hurry to leave. What was there to return to? Sure, he loved his small town of Cedar Springs, but it was long past time for him to face the facts. There was nothing for him there. And maybe there was nothing in Panama for him either, but dammit if he didn't feel that there was. He just hadn't found it yet and he needed time to figure it all out. Without a doubt, Archer knew he owed it to himself to give it a chance.

After all, he was already there. He had nothing to lose.

Surely he'd be able to figure something out.

He ran toward the bridge and bent down to grab his shirt without breaking his stride.

Today would be a good day. Things were different, and it wasn't just that Cass was there. For the first time in a long time, Archer felt like things would be different. And he couldn't wait.

It didn't take him long to make the return trip to the marina and instead of going straight to the shower, which was where he should have gone, Archer headed to Joe's office, or more specifically, the job boards outside his office. Every single day, he looked at the board and every single day, he dismissed the jobs that were posted. The problem was, he wasn't a sailor. Sure, he had a little bit of experience on boats, handling lines.

But he couldn't be considered a sailor, let alone a professional sailor or even someone who could fake their way through a real situation.

He leafed through the ads. More of the same. Not that he should have expected anything different. Being so close to the opening of the Panama Canal, most of the ads were for line handlers and skilled sailors who could serve as crew for people who wanted to take their boat through the canal. Archer had already tried to fake his way onto some of those jobs, but it didn't take long for the captains to figure out that his experience was sorely lacking, and when it came to a multi-million dollar yacht, no one seemed willing to take a chance on someone who didn't know what they were doing. Not that he could blame them.

He let the papers on the board slip through his fingers and he took a step back, swallowing the urge to express what he really felt.

"Hey."

Archer stepped aside as Samson, one of the head charter boat captains, entered the small space. His bulk sucked the oxygen out of the room but Archer was used to his presence after his time there. Most of the regulars at Shelter Bay gave him a wide berth because with Samson, it was a love-hate relationship: You either loved him. Or you loved to hate him.

Archer watched him post a paper on the board and before the bigger man even had a chance to step back, Archer reached forward and grabbed it.

"Whatcha got there, Samson?" Archer pasted a smile on his face and scanned the paper.

And then he scanned it again.

For the first time, he was reading an ad he was actually qualified for.

"Samson." Archer looked up and quickly shifted his body so he'd placed himself between the door and Samson. "I'm your guy. Why are you even posting this job?" He wiggled the page in front of the other man's face. "You should have just come to me."

"Why?"

It's not that Archer knew Samson well. In fact, he really didn't know him at all, except what Maria had told him. And there was a good chance that Archer had incorrectly assumed everyone knew what types of jobs he was qualified for, but as he looked at the other man's face, with his weathered, sun-beat skin and blank expression, he had the sudden realization that perhaps nobody knew.

"I'm a chef, Samson." He held the paper up again and looked over the qualifications. Basically, it was something Archer could do in his sleep. Samson ran a charter boat company that took tourists out into the San Blas Islands for a sailing holiday. He needed a chef to provide his guests with gourmet meals as he sailed the boat. If there was something Archer knew how to do, it was cook. "I ran a kitchen back home."

Okay, it wasn't a kitchen in the sense that it was a five-star restaurant, but Archer had not only run the kitchen at the Grizzly Paw pub back home, but he'd more or less run the whole place when Samantha wasn't there.

"You?" Samson ran a hand through his salt-and-pepper beard. "You're a chef?"

"Absolutely. I got this. I'm your guy."

"Sailing experience?"

"Enough."

Samson considered him.

"Can you cook fish?"

He'd cooked plenty. Never mind that it was cold, fresh-water fish from the mountains. Fish was fish. "Of course."

"We leave tomorrow morning." Samson looked more resigned than anything else. Given the timeline, he was likely out of choices. "Three-day charter. Two meals and a happy hour snack every day. The galley is stocked. Got it?"

Archer nodded, hardly able to believe his luck. Damn straight he got it. He didn't even need to know what was in the galley. But he did have one more request, and although he was likely shooting himself in the foot, he couldn't stop himself from asking.

"How many extra bunks do you have on your cat?"

Chapter Four

IT WAS HUGE. THE FREAKIN' boat was huge.

She'd had no idea what to expect, but it certainly hadn't been the fifty-foot yacht Joe led her up to.

"Here she is." He waved his arm dramatically, as if he were presenting a game show prize. "Isn't she a beauty?"

Cass nodded dumbly, and walked farther up the dock so she stood directly behind it and looked at the backside of the boat. She sucked in a breath, and stared at the name that had been painted on the stern.

Cassiopeia.

"Are you sure this is the one?" She swallowed hard, willing her voice not to shake. Her father couldn't have named his boat after her. It didn't make any sense.

Seemingly oblivious of both the connection of her name to the boat and her distress, Joe waved her over to the port side, where he climbed aboard. "It's the right one, alright. Come on aboard."

She did. And Cass did her best to listen as Joe rambled on about the boat, pointing out various features and explaining the basics. Of course, none of what he said to her sunk in, and she knew she'd have to get him to come back and go through everything again. She couldn't help it; there was no way she could focus.

When Joe unlocked the door to the companionway to go below deck, Cass begged off and walked the length of the deck for what had to be the fourth time. At least. She couldn't bring herself to go below deck yet. It was all too much. This was her father's home. He'd lived on the boat for years. Longer than he'd lived with her. There was more on board the *Cassiopeia* that was Roger than there'd ever been back home.

The idea was a lot to process.

A lot.

She sank onto a cushion in the cockpit and dropped her head into her hands.

"She's a beauty, isn't she?"

Cass jerked her head up to see Joe in front of her. She'd forgotten he was there. He'd been so accommodating and generous as he'd shown her the boat for the first time. No doubt, he was just happy to have someone claim the thing. But still, as much as she wanted to curl into herself and think on everything that had just happened, she owed it to him to at the very least not be rude.

"What do you think?"

She smoothed her hair back from her face and joined Joe on the foredeck.

"She's lovely," Cass said. And she really was. If Cass was honest with herself, the *Cassiopeia* was more than lovely. The boat was downright gorgeous and from the moment she'd set foot on it, she'd been overwhelmed with memories of being a twelve-year-old girl, all wide-eyed and innocent in the open ocean with her father at the helm of their sixteen-foot Hobie Cat while Cass manned the sails. She'd pulled the lines as he barked out orders and when the boat came about, the boom swinging over her head as she ducked and the sails filled with wind once again, set on course, her father would hold his arm up and cheer. The best feeling in the world was knowing she'd done it right and he was proud of her.

Those days sailing with her father along the West Coast shoreline, with Seattle in the distance, were some of her favorite memories. No. They *were* her favorite memories. Feeling the wind in her hair as the boat cut through the waves, watching the dolphins dance in the froth of their wake: there was nothing like it in the world. It had been over a decade since she'd even set foot on a boat, let alone sailed one. Just being on deck of the *Cassiopeia* made her feel different. Alive. Her body thrilled at the idea of the deck moving beneath her with the rocking of the waves; her fingers instinctively curled as if she were gripping a line and hauling a sail up the mast. Instinctively, her gaze drifted up the mast. She'd never sailed such a large boat. Could she handle her? Did she even want to?

"So?" Joe stood in the gangway and peered up out of the boat at Cass. "Ready to come on down and check her out?"

Suddenly, it didn't feel right for her to see, for the first time, what was essentially her father's private space with a relative stranger. Even if Roger had been friends with Joe. It didn't feel right. It felt like something she wanted—no, *needed*—to do on her own.

"If it's alright with you, I'd rather check it out later."

The older man nodded and gave her a friendly smile before he joined her in the cockpit. He sat next to her and put the key in her hand. "It must be a lot to take in."

Cass nodded. That was an understatement for sure, but no other words felt adequate.

"Not to worry, you'll get acquainted with her soon enough." He patted her on the leg in a gesture that instantly made her think of her father, although she really had no idea if it was something he'd do. "Make yourself at home." Joe pushed up. "After all, she's all yours."

The thought struck Cass for the first time. She owned a boat. A yacht, really. What the hell was she going to do with a yacht?

"I never asked." Cass looked up at Joe, who watched her with a question in his eyes. "Do you sail? I guess I just assumed that Roger's daughter had to be a sailor like him. One of the best, too. Just a real instinct for the sea, and…hey. I'm sorry. I didn't think. This must be a lot to take in and here I am just rambling away about—"

"No." Cass got to her feet and smoothed down her shorts. "It's fine. My dad and I…we weren't…you know what? It doesn't matter." There was no point getting into the complicated relationship with this man, who no doubt knew her father better than she ever had. "And to answer your question, I haven't sailed a boat in years." She walked over the teak deck to the helm and ran her hand over the wheel.

"Well, you look like a natural and I'm sure it will all come back to you in no time."

"Like riding a bike?" Cass laughed.

Joe's smile was friendly. "Only better."

She stroked the wheel again and looked the boat up and down. It really was beautiful and so much larger than anything she'd ever taken to sea. But the mechanics were the same, just on a larger scale. After her father had left, the urge to sail had completely disappeared. It had been years since she'd felt the familiar itch in her fingers to haul up a sail, and feel the movement of the ocean under her feet. Maybe it was feeling her father's presence on the boat. Maybe it was just being on a vessel again. Maybe it was that she had nothing else to lose. Whatever it was, at that moment, more than anything, Cass wanted to be out on the water.

As if he read her mind, Joe added, "Anytime you want, kiddo. Say the word and I'll take you out so you can get to know her. I think you two are going to get along really well."

He patted her arm and crossed the deck to climb down to the dock.

She watched him make his way down, moving with confidence as he made the slight hop from boat to dock. "Thanks, Joe. I'll get my bags out of the room and check out right away."

"No rush." Joe adjusted his hat. "I'll just add the cost of the room to your bill."

"My bill?"

"I didn't have time to get it ready before you got here, but I'll get it printed out and bring it down to you."

Cass shook her head. "I don't understand. My bill for the room?"

Joe's face twisted in confusion, and something about the way he slowly came to a realization had Cass worried. And with good reason, because as soon as Joe spoke again, she'd wished he hadn't.

"Your bill for the dock fees, Cass. She's been occupying a slip for three years now and while I don't have the exact figure on me, I estimate it to be around thirty grand."

A sound that was something between a choke and a cough came out of her mouth. Cass waved her hand around next to her as she looked for something to hold onto. "I'm sorry," she managed to get out. "Thirty grand?"

Joe nodded. "'Fraid so. But don't worry; we can work out some sort of payment plan."

Payment plan? Only if there was some kind of plan that involved her not paying anything at all because she didn't have any money.

She forced a smile and nodded. "Sounds good."

If Joe noticed any strangeness in her voice, he did a good job ignoring it. To her relief, the older man gave her a wave and made his way down the dock toward the restaurant. She watched him go, waving at sailors who puttered about on the dock or cleaned their boats. Some sat in their cockpits, having breakfast, but mostly people were up and doing things. So much for a more relaxed lifestyle in the South. If Cass had her way, she'd still be in bed. Or lingering over that delicious fruit at breakfast. And the even yummier company.

An image of Archer's face filled her memory.

True, he was delicious to look at, and maybe their totally unplanned, yet totally fantastic kiss the night before had made her stomach flip in a completely unexpected way, but that wasn't why he popped into her head now, when she should be focusing on her current problem. Of course not. It was because he was interesting and funny and…hotter than the sun that currently beat down on her head.

Cass mentally chastised herself and ducked down into the cockpit, where she was sheltered from the already scorching sun. Whatever the reason for thinking about him, it had to stop. She had bigger problems. She let her eyes travel over the beautiful boat.

Yes, much bigger.

Men, even incredibly hot ones who kissed like the devil himself had taken up residence, had to wait. No matter what her body was telling her.

Or what Angie would say.

Angie.

Maybe she should text her; maybe Angie would—no.

Cass straightened her ponytail, pulling it higher on her head to get it off her neck, and headed below deck to see what state the galley was in.

An hour later, Cass had done a quick check of the inside of her new, very expensive piece of property. Not that thirty thousand dollars was a lot of money for a fifty-foot yacht; in fact, it was a steal. But when you'd just spent most of your money on a ticket to Panama after spectacularly quitting your job, it might as well have been two million. Because she didn't have either amount.

The finishings of the boat were nice, nothing too elegant, and of course there was a mustiness in the air which she'd expected considering it hadn't been aired out in years. It was easy to tell it had been a man's space. There were barely any personal touches, and really nothing to give Cass any indication of what type of man her father had been.

From a cursory glance, there were three bunks: two in the stern and one in the bow. The main salon was more spacious than she would have expected, with the galley kitchen running along one side, and a table with wrap-around seating on the other. Another couch separated the two spaces, but it didn't feel claustrophobic or small the way she would have thought. The two bunks in the back of the boat appeared to have been used for storage, which meant the one in the bow must have been her father's room. She poked her head in, but didn't investigate further.

As she walked through the boat, she made a mental list of what she'd need to pack up, if anything, before she sold the boat. Because selling it would be the only option. What the hell was she going to do with a fifty-foot yacht? Let alone one that came with an insurmountable bill. It was really too bad, too, because the urge to take her out onto the ocean had only kept growing instead of diminishing.

She pushed open the hatches in an effort to let some air flow in because she had no idea how to operate the air conditioning, or even if it had air conditioning. There had to be a manual somewhere. The nav station, the built-in desk area nestled into the back of the main salon, seemed like a good place to start the search. Even if she was going to sell the *Cassiopeia*, she had a lot to learn, especially if she planned to live on it in the meantime. And at the moment, it seemed like as good an option as any. She'd just started to dig through the stack of papers and books that lined the shelves over the desk when she heard the familiar voice call out.

"Ahoy."

It both irritated and excited her the way her stomach flipped at Archer's voice. She'd known the man less than twenty-four hours and already she was acting like a schoolgirl around him. Maybe Angie was right and she should just sleep with him to get it over with.

She left the mess of the desk behind and headed above deck. She saw Archer on the dock, shirtless, his ridiculously hard chest glistening with sweat.

Jesus. It shouldn't be legal to walk around looking that hot.

Cass ignored the tightening in her core and waved him aboard. "Hey. Come on up."

He jumped aboard easily and joined her in the cockpit.

"I'd offer you a glass of water, but…" She trailed off as she realized that she didn't have anything to offer him. "I haven't really had a chance to provision or anything yet."

"Not a problem. I can't stay."

A wave of disappointment washed through her. Not like she expected anything else to happen between them. The kiss had been…well, it had been amazing. And definitely felt as though she'd enjoy a repeat, especially one that might be intended for her. But she didn't have time for a man. Even a really hot, half naked one who was currently less than a foot from her, his muscles glistening and…no. She shook her head and wrapped her arms around her waist to keep from grabbing him. An urge she couldn't explain if she'd tried.

"What's up?" She went for casual, but was pretty sure it didn't come off. Nothing about the situation was casual. Hell, nothing about anything that had happened since she'd hopped on the plane was casual.

"I just wanted to stop by and see how you were doing with

the boat." He ran his hand through his dark hair, smoothing it back on his head. "You ready to take it out yet?"

"Yeah right." Cass ran her hand along the top of the stainless-steel covered compass and tried not to notice how bad it needed a polish. Everything on the *Cassiopeia* needed a polish. She looked away before she could dwell on it. "But I really would like to," she confessed. "As soon as I take care of a few things."

"How about going out for a sail on a different boat?" She swung her head around to stare at him. "It won't be the same, but it could be better," he continued. "At least in some ways. Besides, it'll give you a chance to check out the San Blas Islands I was telling you about. I know you'll love them."

"Wait? What are you talking about?"

He smiled and her stomach would have flipped again if she wasn't so focused on trying to understand what he was talking about. "I just picked up a cooking job with Samson; he's one of the charter captains here. Anyway, I got you a bunk on the trip."

"A bunk?"

"A room."

"I know what a bunk is." She shook her head. "But why?"

"I told you, so you can see the islands. It doesn't mean anything, okay? I just thought you might like it."

She stared at him and tried to figure out his angle. He did seem like a genuine guy, but those were few and far between, it seemed. What were the odds she'd found one in Panama? Besides, she did want to see the islands and if she couldn't get the *Cassiopeia* in shape, she might not get a chance. And the lure of the open water, the wind in her hair… "Okay."

"Okay?"

"Yes, thank you," she corrected herself. She was being spontaneous and probably more than a little irresponsible, but she didn't care. Cautious and boring hadn't been working for her, so why not try something new? Besides, Angie would most certainly approve. "It sounds good. I'd love to."

Archer's face transformed into a smile that made her want to kiss him again. "Perfect. We leave in the morning, about seven so the wind will be with us. You can meet us at the restaurant and—"

"Wait. Tomorrow?"

"Is that a problem?" Archer took a step toward her. "Did you have something else to do?" He reached out and for a split second, Cass was positive he was going to kiss her. A move she would have been totally okay with. But he wiped his thumb across her cheek. "You have a bit of dirt…"

She released the breath she'd been holding and tried to shrug casually. "No problem. Tomorrow works fine."

He put one hand on the edge of the sunshade and swung himself casually out of the cockpit and out to the deck. "I'm looking forward to it." Archer waved and hopped down off the boat. Almost as soon as he hit the dock, he broke into a slow, easy jog.

She watched him go until he disappeared out of view and then she sank down onto the cushion again. If she was leaving in the morning, she better get started on her to-do list. But first, she had to text Angie. Her best friend was not going to believe it.

Chapter Five

THE NEXT DAY dawned bright and cloudless, not that Archer noticed. He'd only managed to grab a few hours of sleep and had been up for hours before Samson left the *Seaduction* to head up to the Inn and collected his charter guests. Archer put the finishing touches on a fresh breakfast of island fruit and yogurt that he'd serve as soon as they were underway and out into open water, and put it back in the refrigerator. He wiped down the counter and made sure everything looked perfect for the guests.

The *Seaduction* was a well-appointed sixty-foot catamaran, which meant it had almost a full-sized kitchen. Archer had never been on a cat so large and had been expecting to cook in a much smaller galley. After he spent most of the night investigating and categorizing what he had at his disposal, Archer was more than impressed and he was fairly sure Samson and their guests would be equally impressed with the menu he'd designed.

Of course, the fact that Cass had enjoyed the fruit so much the previous morning had nothing to do with his decision for the breakfast menu. None at all. Although, he certainly wouldn't mind watching her suck the juices off a piece of papaya again. Okay, *maybe* she had something to do with his decision.

He wanted to be up at the Inn to greet her, but Samson had given him the rundown on what was expected of him while they were out on the charter, and a lot of the expectations involved Archer in the galley. It was a job, and he wasn't going to complain, but as long as Cass was going to be on board, he was going to make damn sure to find some downtime to spend with her.

Voices from above deck cued him. It was show time. He took a quick glance down at the khaki shorts and orange polo shirt embroidered with the boat's name on the chest. He picked two orchids out of the vase of island flowers and made his way out to the deck to greet their guests.

"And this is our chef, Archer Wolfe." Samson waved his hand in his direction and Archer nodded. "This is Harriott and Donald Winchester, and their daughter Brittany."

"Nice to meet you." Archer shook Donald's hand and presented both Harriott and their very attractive, probably barely twenty-year-old, daughter with an orchid. "Welcome aboard the *Seaduction.* Let me take care of those bags for you." He scanned the dock behind them for Cass and lit into a smile when he saw her. She looked amazing in only cutoffs and a tank top. The strings of what was probably a bikini top peeked out of the top of her tank and Archer felt a tug low in his belly at the thought of those luscious breasts showcased in only a scrap of bathing suit.

"Archer."

He turned to see Samson glare at him. "Sorry, I got distracted for a second."

"I noticed." The other man had followed his gaze to Cass. The Winchesters had wandered up to the bow of the boat, but still Samson kept his voice low. "Don't let it happen again. I only agreed to this deal because it—"

"Meant you didn't have to pay me as much," Archer said with a forced grin. *Cheapskate*, he wanted to add, but bit his tongue. "Cass!"

"Hey. I hope I have the right boat."

"You got it." Archer took her hand and helped her aboard. Once she was next to him, he reluctantly released her hand but kept her near. "Let me introduce you to the captain of the ship. Samson, this is Cass Cutler. Cass, Samson."

Samson almost choked at the introduction. "Cutler?"

"That's right."

"As in Roger Cutler?"

The smile slipped from Cass's face and her hand dropped to her side. Archer's fingers inched to grab it. "As in Cass Cutler," she replied calmly. "Thank you for having me aboard." She recovered easily and forced a new smile; this one didn't reach her eyes and her voice had a false ring as she continued to compliment the boat.

Samson looked as though he was going to push the issue, but then the Winchesters returned from their investigation and joined them on the large back deck. "How long until we're ready to shove off?" Donald asked.

"As soon as everyone's ready to go." Samson gave Cass one last sidelong look, before he set off to make the final preparations. Archer did the rest of the introductions, took the bags below and before anything else could go amiss, they were ready to set sail.

The *Seaduction* moved smooth and steady through the channel. It was a large yacht. Much bigger than any Cass had been on before, but compared to the large container ships anchored throughout the channel, it was completely dwarfed.

She couldn't be sure what the deal was between Samson and Archer in regards to having her aboard the boat, and she was pretty sure she didn't want to know. Whatever it was, Cass got the impression that the captain wasn't entirely pleased with having her there. Or maybe it was her name he took offense to? It wasn't hard to see there was some kind of reaction when he'd heard her last name. Probably because everyone in Shelter Bay had heard about Roger Cutler going missing. From the short time she was there, it was easy to see that although his story was almost infamous, and everyone knew him or knew of him, nobody knew anything about what had actually *happened* to him.

Cass had spent the rest of the previous day either trying to figure out her new boat, or trying to find someone to help her figure it out. She hadn't made much headway with either project, but she had managed to meet and talk to a lot of nice people. Her head was still spinning with information about refrigeration systems, generators, and sewage tanks. There was so much to know. It was much more complicated than the actual act of sailing and that's all she wanted to be doing.

Now, aboard the *Seaduction*, she was finally getting exactly what she wanted. The sea breeze whipped her hair off her face; the smell of the ocean, that was indescribable to anyone who'd never actually been on the ocean, washed through her. She closed her eyes and let each of her senses fill her heart with the sensation of being at sea.

"Coffee?"

Her eyes snapped open to see Archer, looking sexier than should be allowed in his bright orange polo, with two cups of coffee.

"Can I join you?"

"Yes. Of course." She remembered herself and slid over on the deck to make room for him.

"I thought you might like a coffee. Black, right?"

She took the steaming cup. "Right. How did you know?" She inhaled deeply. The promise of caffeine hitting her system in short order was more than welcome. There hadn't been any usable provisions on board the *Cassiopeia*, and she hadn't had any time to get any.

"I remembered from yesterday." He sat next to her and his arm brushed against hers. He didn't move away, but stayed close enough so his arm rubbed against hers.

She hid her smile behind her coffee cup. "Thanks. And thank you for this. I don't know how you managed it, but I didn't even know how badly I needed this. It's been a long time…"

"Since you've been on a boat?"

She nodded and glanced at him out of the corner of her eye. He wasn't looking at her, but gazed out at the horizon. There were fewer large ships as they got away from the mainland and headed toward the islands. Without even trying, this man, whom she'd only just met, got it. He got *her*. Cass didn't know how or why he would arrange this trip for her, but all she did know was that she was determined to just go with it and not overthink it, the way Angie told her to in a text the night before. And Angie was right; she had enough to worry about with the *Cassiopeia* and the little matter of the hefty bill that Joe had delivered to her the day before. Not only was the bill not going to go away, it was only going to get bigger the longer she stayed on the dock. But no. She couldn't think about it. No. She *wouldn't* think about it. Not when there were dolphins dancing with the bow. Dolphins?

"Archer! Look." She jumped to her feet and coffee splashed all over her toes. "Dolphins."

Cass ran to the rail and looked down at the pod. They dove

and jumped alongside the boat, dancing in the froth of the waves. "Oh my God, I've never seen that before." She turned to look at Archer. She'd somehow known he would be there, standing next to her, just as taken with the sight as she was. "They're playing."

Soon the Winchesters were there, too, watching the dolphins. They all pointed and cheered as they jumped high in the air. There must have been at least ten or twelve of them in the pod. She'd seen dolphins on the West Coast before, but never so many all at once. It was a sight like she'd never seen before. They were so free and wild and…

Archer held her hand. All of her senses were diverted to the feel of his fingers laced through hers. She tore her eyes away from the pod and looked up into his dark eyes but didn't move her hand. She smiled, squeezed his hand and looked back at the dolphins.

"See that bay over there?" Samson pointed to a space with three or four islands that formed a small private bay. Archer nodded dutifully. After he'd served the simple breakfast, Samson had set up Donald Winchester with a deep sea fishing pole off the stern, while his wife and daughter had retreated to the bow of the boat and the net trampoline that spanned the two keels between the catamarans. It was the perfect place to sunbathe and enjoy the fresh air. Cass was still on the foredeck, with a floppy hat to shield her face from the hot sun. Archer couldn't tell, but it looked as if her eyes might be closed. He'd made the right decision in bringing her on the trip. Sure, he barely knew her, but there was something about the woman. And it wasn't just the fact that every time he looked at her, his dick twitched a little. As much as there was a physical response, it was so much more than that.

"It's called the Swimming Pool," Samson continued, and Archer refocused. "There are four islands. The guests can go to three of them."

"What about the fourth?"

"Barbecue Island," Samson said by way of explanation. "Stay away from it and make sure the guests stay off as well. When we get close, I'll need you to watch the depth meter." Samson changed the subject. "I'll drop the anchor, and set it, but the moment we're settled, I want you to have the kayaks and snorkel gear ready. Got it?"

"Absolutely." He turned to clear the breakfast dishes and started to get ready.

"And don't forget to give the girl some attention."

Archer froze, two plates in his hand. "Pardon?" He might have guessed that the captain was telling him to flirt with Cass, but something told him that wasn't the case at all.

"The Winchesters' daughter."

"Brittany?"

Samson nodded. "Make sure you show her a good time."

There was no way. The girl was barely legal. "You want me to—"

"Hell no." Samson had the decency to look taken aback at least. "Do you want to get fired?" The captain glared at him. "You never sleep with guests. Do I make myself clear?"

"Crystal." Archer nodded. He definitely wasn't thinking about sleeping with any of the guests. The only one he wanted to get naked was Cass and as the day passed, it became less of a want, and more of a need.

"Just flirt with her a bit. It's part of the experience. Make the female guests feel like they could have the ultimate vacation experience, if you know what I mean?"

"Got it."

He shook his head, finished wiping down the table in the cockpit and was about to head into the galley when Samson called his attention again. "Just so you know, if I'd known you were bringing Roger Cutler's daughter aboard, I wouldn't have agreed."

Archer turned, ready to ask him what the problem with Cass was, but the man's steely eyes stopped him. There was no point poking what was obviously a sleeping bear. Nothing was going to get in the way of Cass enjoying her trip. Especially if it meant he had a shot at enjoying Cass. And judging by her reaction with him, and the way she'd looked him straight in the eyes while she enjoyed her breakfast papaya, he was pretty sure they were on the same page.

But first, he had work to do and there was no better way to pass the time between now and when he could get her alone than by keeping busy.

As it turned out, the chance to get her alone didn't come until later. Much later. The afternoon had been spent with the guests of the *Seaduction* swimming off the boat, exploring a nearby reef with their snorkels, and kayaking to one of the small deserted islands they were anchored next to. Archer was kept busy in the galley, serving snacks and making slushy drinks. Finally, when the Winchesters went for a siesta, Archer had a moment to breathe and search for Cass. He hadn't seen her in a while, and assumed she'd taken a kayak out for a ride.

"She went for a swim." Brittany noticed him scanning the horizon.

Remembering that he was supposed to be flirting and seeing Samson watching them, he gave her a wink that made the girl blush. "Thanks. Did you see where she went?"

Brittany pointed to the island farthest away. The one they'd all been told to stay away from. Of course that's where Cass would go. He quickly glanced at Samson and held up one hand to ward off the captain's anger. "I got it," Archer told Samson. "I'll get her. Is there anything I should be worried about on the island?"

"Just the old bat." Samson shook his head and went into the cabin.

Archer was left to wonder what he was getting into as he got the dinghy ready and motored over to the island to fetch Cass.

Chapter Six

THE MOMENT SAMSON told them they couldn't go to Barbecue Island, Cass knew that was exactly where she was headed. It was an easy swim and with no current, it didn't take her long at all to reach the sandy bottom. From the boat, the island looked like all the others in the beautiful bay: White sandy beaches. A spattering of palm trees. Surrounded by turquoise water. Beautiful. Just the way Archer said they'd be.

He was right.

She walked through the shallows as tiny reef fish danced around her feet, and out onto the soft sand beach. The sun heated her skin and dried her quickly as she wandered down the shoreline. She was supposed to be clearing her head, trying to figure out what to do with the *Cassiopeia* and subsequently, the rest of her life. Or at the very least, the next few months. But being on the *Seaduction*, feeling the wind through her hair and the familiar thrum of the boat beneath her that vibrated throughout her entire body as it cut through the water, had only complicated things.

She knew she had to sell the boat. There was no other choice. How on earth was she going to come up with the kind of money she needed to pay the bills? The short answer was, she wasn't. She couldn't. She had to sell it, and it's not as though she was connected to it or anything. She'd barely even spent time on it. Yet, the idea of not being able to take it out on the open sea caused her breath to hitch in her chest. It was too much to think about.

For the first time, Cass looked around at the island beyond the beach. There wasn't much to it. At least not that she could see. Of course, palm trees dominated. But they seemed to grow thicker farther down. Maybe there was something at the other end?

"Hello there."

Cass jumped and flipped around to see an older woman, tanned deeply by the sun, wearing a floppy hat, tank top, and some sort of skirt covered in elaborate embroidery. Her wrists and ankles were decorated with thick strands of beaded bracelets.

"I didn't mean to scare you." The woman smiled, the skin around her brown eyes wrinkling as she did so. There was something almost familiar about the woman, but Cass was sure she'd never met her before. She would have remembered.

"You didn't," Cass assured her. "I guess I just thought I was alone."

The woman laughed. "A safe guess for sure." She held out a beaded arm. "I'm Josie. Nice to meet you."

"Cass." She shook her hand.

"You're from the *Seaduction*?" Josie gestured with her head and Cass nodded her affirmation. "Then I guess we should keep walking." The older woman looped her arm in Cass's and started to walk. It felt natural, so Cass went with it. "Samson usually makes a point to keep his guests from visiting my island."

"Your island?"

"Well, not really mine. All these islands belong to the

Kunas. They're the local indigenous tribe, but they let me live here. We kind of have an agreement."

Cass was sure there was more to that story, but she went back to the first part of what Josie had said. "Why doesn't Samson like his guests coming here? It's a beautiful island."

Josie had led her up off the beach and into the shade of the palm trees. The grass beneath her feet tickled, but it was soft on her bare feet. Now that they were inland, Cass could see there'd been pathways beat into the grass that crisscrossed the space.

"He has his reasons, I guess."

She didn't offer any more information and Cass didn't pry.

The island was bigger than she'd thought, and as they crossed through the palm trees, to the opposite beach, Cass could see what looked to be like a little village, or at least a collection of huts. They entered the clearing of what was obviously Josie's home. "Would you like a drink?"

Cass nodded and Josie produced a can of remarkably cold beer from a small refrigerator. "I have solar panels," she said by way of explanation as she handed it to her.

"You live here?"

"Not only do I live here, I run a bed and breakfast."

Cass raised an eyebrow and glanced around at the rough accommodations.

"I know it doesn't look like much." Josie laughed. "But you'd be surprised how little you really need. My guests come to reconnect with themselves and sometimes each other. You don't need anything for that except sun, sand, and a little serenity."

As she spoke, Cass took in the space and looked out through the trees to the beach, where the water gently lapped up onto the sand. Josie's words made sense. She nodded slowly and a smile grew across her face. "Yes."

They sat in silence for a few moments as they each sipped

their drinks. Finally, Josie spoke again. "You remind me of someone I knew once."

"From back home?" Cass didn't know where home for Josie was or might have been, but she was definitely North American, despite her appearance that led Cass to believe she'd been here awhile.

"Oh, no, dear. This is home. And the man you remind me of was here with me."

Something about the way Josie looked at Cass while she spoke, looking straight at her, gave Cass the impression she was searching for something in her eyes. "Where is he now?"

Josie laughed, but it was a sound tinged with sadness. "He was the love of my life, but life called him on."

"I'm so sorry." Cass's hand flew to her chest. "I didn't mean to—"

"Oh no." Josie laughed; this time it was a lighter sound. "He's not dead. But he is gone. His life called him in a different direction, and I never saw him again."

There was no reason she should think anything of what the older woman was saying, but yet, there was a sense Cass got from Josie. A sense that they were connected somehow. She couldn't explain what made her ask, but yet she couldn't seem to stop herself. "Was his name Roger Cutler?"

The look on Josie's face answered her question for her. The instant tears that shone in her eyes confirmed it. "I'm sorry," Cass said quickly. "I shouldn't have asked. I didn't mean to—"

"You're his daughter."

It wasn't a question, but Cass nodded anyway. "And you…you…"

"Loved him," Josie answered. "I still do. Our souls are connected. I feel him." She tapped her chest. "In here."

Talking to Josie was easy, comfortable as though she'd known her forever. Josie filled her in on everything she knew about her dad and their relationship, and it didn't take long for

Cass to realize that whatever they'd shared together, it was special. They'd met almost ten years previously, fallen in love instantly, and had the perfect life in paradise until he'd gone missing three years ago. Josie seemed to have made a strange peace with it, assuming Roger had been called to some other path in life. But even if the other woman was okay with it, Cass was instantly fueled by anger on her behalf. She knew exactly what it felt like to have her father leave without a trace. They definitely had that in common.

"You don't think he's dead?"

"No." Josie smiled sadly. "I mean, it's possible. But men like Roger, they have a traveling spirit. They need to follow their spirit, wherever that takes them."

"But, he's been missing for years and his boat…I mean, I have his boat now—why would he—"

"The *Cassiopeia*?"

Cass nodded.

"He told me all about you and why he named the—"

"It doesn't matter." Cass was not in the mood to relive memories. "Either way, I have the boat."

Josie let her head fall back, and she gazed up at the sky through the palm frond canopy. "Oh, we had some good memories on that boat. Did you know your father used to run a little charter business on the *Cassiopeia*?" Cass shook her head. "He did. Just like Samson. In fact, that's part of the reason Samson doesn't like me or want anyone on the island."

"Oh?"

Josie waved her hand, dismissing the conversation. "It's a story for another day, my dear."

She was disappointed, but Cass had the distinct impression she wouldn't discover anything more if she pushed. "Another day, then." Cass tipped the can back and finished her beer.

"Cass!"

She turned at the call of her name. "Speaking of

Samson…" The women got to their feet. "I should probably go." Cass could see Archer making his way down the beach. "But it was so nice talking to you, and I have so many questions still."

The smile Josie gave her was warm and full of love. "You know where to find me, child."

They exchanged a quick hug and before Josie released her, she gave her a tight squeeze and whispered in her ear. "You're here for a reason, Cass. I can feel it. Please don't worry too much about anything. Just go with your gut and trust your instincts." She kissed her cheek and pulled back.

Stunned and slightly thrown off by Josie's words, Cass stared for a second until Archer's voice split the air again.

"Thank you," was all she could manage to say before she turned and ran through the trees in Archer's direction, Josie's words ringing in her ears.

Go with your gut.

Archer was thankful Cass was far enough away that she wasn't likely to see his mouth hanging open at the sight of her jogging down the beach toward him. Let alone the tent he'd unwillingly and almost instantly pitched in his shorts the second he saw her breasts, only barely contained by the scrap of blue fabric, bouncing as she moved toward him.

It was the last thing he wanted, but he looked away in an effort to put a lid on his growing desire for the woman. He took a few deep breaths and tried to get his lust for her under control, at least a little bit. He was pretty sure it was a losing battle—and one he wouldn't mind losing—but despite their one kiss, and the connection he knew she felt too, he needed to pull himself together.

"Where've you been?" He turned to face her; she was only

a few steps away, still running. Damn, there was no way he'd be able to pull himself together. Not with her in that bikini.

She came to a stop only inches in front of him. "Hey. Sorry, I didn't know you were looking for me."

"Samson warned everyone not to come to this island." He tried to look over her shoulder at the ocean beyond, anywhere but directly at her and her mostly exposed body. "I came to get you."

"To rescue me, you mean? From the terrors that lurk here?" He couldn't help it; he met her eyes that glinted with mischief. "Samson's an idiot," she added. "There's no reason we shouldn't be coming to this island."

"Well, he said to stay off, and since he's signing my check… come on, let's go."

"What's your rush?" There was a challenge in her eyes. "You're not scared of Samson, are you?" She took a few steps backward, dragging her feet in the sand in a way that made her legs look even longer and sexier than they already did.

He stepped slowly toward her to close the gap. "I would like to keep my job."

"Come on." Her mouth curled up into a grin and she crooked her finger, beckoning him forward. It was an invitation no red-blooded man could turn down, and there was no way he would, especially when she turned and jogged down the beach.

"Oh hell," he muttered and shook his head. The bulge in his shorts made itself known and he set off after the chase.

Cass turned to see whether he was following her—as if he wouldn't—and squealed with laughter when she saw him behind her. She didn't make it easy for him to catch up with her, twisting and darting around the beach, finally heading for the trees in the opposite direction from which she'd come.

"You don't stand a chance, woman!" He'd closed the gap between them, but still she managed to elude him.

She laughed in response and broke out onto the beach on the far side of the island. The sand caught her feet, slowing her down just enough for him to lunge forward and grab her around the waist. In a move he'd be forever impressed with, he managed to wrap his hands around her and pulled her tight against him as they fell to the soft sand. He broke her fall, but he didn't loosen his hold on her.

Her breasts were pressed up hard against his chest, heaving with the deep breaths she was taking. Having her up against him did nothing for his almost painful erection, except make it pulse with his need for her. Her eyes darkened with lust the moment she realized his heavy breathing wasn't just from the exertion of chasing her in the hot sun.

He released one hand from the small of her back where he had her pinned and threaded it through her hair, pulling her head down toward him until their lips met in a crush. His other hand slid down to her perfectly round ass and slid beneath the scrap of fabric she called a bathing suit to squeeze her flesh and pressed her hard into him.

She pulled back slightly. "I thought you said we needed to get going."

Archer could only grunt in response and flip her, so she was totally pinned under his much larger frame. "I'm not going anywhere."

"What about your job?"

Thoughts of getting fired, and once again being jobless, flashed through his mind for only half a second until he realized the only thing he needed at that moment was the amazing woman beneath him. And *damn,* how he needed her. "I don't care," he grunted. "I have got to have you, Cass."

Her tongue traced her lips. "Then what are you waiting for?"

That was all the invitation he needed. Archer sat up on his knees, straddling her, and in one smooth motion, pulled his polo shirt off his head. She reached up and traced his chest and abs with her fingers. He gave her free rein of his body, but only for a moment before he pulled the tiny piece of fabric from her breasts to expose the milky white skin beneath and bent his head to taste her. Her skin was salty from the sea, but also sweet. He pulled her breast into his mouth; his hand squeezed the other, his fingers rolling her nipple between them, eliciting a long, low moan from her.

Her hands threaded in his hair as he turned to give equal attention to her other breast; his tongue flicked the nipple before he bit down gently.

"Archer." His name escaped her lips like a sigh of pleasure. He would have liked to spend hours worshipping her breasts and the rest of her body the way it deserved to be worshipped, but as much as he wanted to, he was also painfully aware of their location and the fact that if they didn't return to the boat soon, not only would he lose his job, but they'd have an audience.

Reluctantly, he lifted his head and looked in her eyes. "Cass, we should—"

"No."

"No?"

"If you're going to tell me that we should stop," the words came out in short bursts heavy with need, "the answer is no. There's no one on this side of the island." He glanced around. It was true; they were alone. "Don't stop."

Two little words and his dick twitched against her core. And then reality crashed down once again. "I don't have protection."

"I'm safe."

"You're—"

"Do you trust me?"

Without a doubt he trusted her, despite the fact that they'd only just met and he had a personal rule to never, under any circumstances, go without a condom. He answered her with a deep kiss.

What the hell was she doing?

The little voice in the back of Cass's head—the one that usually kept her in her safe, boring little bubble—demanded to be heard and for once in her life, she ignored it. Never in life had she had been so reckless and there was no way she'd ever even contemplated having sex with someone she barely knew. Maybe that was the problem. She'd totally stopped listening to her instincts and just going with what felt right. Hell, maybe she never had. And what had playing it safe ever gotten her?

Nothing. Because never, ever before had she ever felt like a situation was completely right.

If she'd been asked to explain why she trusted Archer so completely, there would be no way she could verbalize it. And it didn't matter, because at that moment, all she wanted was to feel his body against hers, his lips on hers, and have him inside her.

Feeding the urgency they both felt, she trailed her hands down his incredibly hard body; her fingers rippled over his abs as she made her way to the button of his shorts. With deft fingers, she slipped the button out and pulled the zipper down before she plunged her hands inside.

The size of him took her breath away momentarily. His entire body stiffened when she wrapped her hands around him. As his need throbbed in her hands, a rush of warmth pooled between her legs. She needed him just as badly.

"Cass. I…" He reached down and gently removed her hands. "I need you, now."

She bit her lip and nodded slightly; she let out a gasp as his fingers slipped under her bikini bottoms and up her crease, before he found the bundle of nerves, where he pressed just hard enough to curl her toes and tip her head back with want.

As much as she'd be happy to lie in the sand all day, exploring each other's bodies, there wasn't time for it, and Archer agreed, because as soon as she felt the pleasure build within her, starting in her toes, he removed his fingers and tugged her bottoms down. He looked up, his cock poised at her entrance, and locked his dark eyes on hers.

Never before had she been with a man who knew her needs as if they were his own. Cass threaded her hands through his hair and pulled his head down to her mouth right as he entered her with one solid thrust. His mouth still on hers, she took in a sharp breath, breathing him into her. When he was buried to the hilt, he paused to let her adjust to his size. Her body fit him perfectly and almost at once, she reached around him to grip his firm ass in both hands and urge him on.

"You. Feel. So. Fucking. Fantastic." He punctuated each word with a thrust. Each one hit a spot deep inside her; sparks of pleasure radiated from her core to her entire being, until all at once, her muscles tightened as her orgasm came hard and fast and she shattered beneath him. Archer was right behind her, his body stiffening on top of her as he groaned out his own release.

No doubt they each had sand in places they'd be rinsing out for days, but Cass couldn't care less. He rolled off her, and pulled her up against him, so her head rested on his chest. She would have happily lain there all afternoon, but she couldn't let Archer lose his job because of her. "We should probably go."

He groaned and squeezed her tight. She loved the fact that he didn't instantly let her go, even if it didn't make any sense. "Come on," she tried again. "I don't want you to get fired."

"I can think of worse ways to lose a job." He kissed the top of her head. "That was…that was, God, Cass."

"I know." She lifted up on one elbow and grinned down at

him. "I absolutely agree. But I can't let you lose your job because of me."

He pulled her down on top of him. "It's just a job." He kissed her slow. "But this…this—"

"Was fun." She wriggled out of his arms before she said something she didn't want to say. There was no doubt in her mind that he felt the same connection she did. How could he not? "And just so you know, I don't usually do that type of thing." Cass tugged her bikini top back into place and pulled her bottoms up before she got to her feet. "I mean, I do *that*—just not…you know…"

He laughed as he did up his shorts and stood next to her. "I know."

She turned away, but Archer grabbed her hand, spun her around and kissed her thoroughly. "And just so you know," he said when he released her. "I don't normally do that type of thing either, but I'd do it again. I can get another job."

His words were meant to spark something in her, and they resonated with her, certainly. But more importantly, as they headed back to the *Seaduction*, Archer's words sparked something else in her. An idea of how she might be able to save her boat.

Chapter Seven

SAMSON WAS DEFINITELY NOT IMPRESSED when they got back to the boat, but Cass ignored him. She didn't really care whether he was upset. He'd known Josie was on the island, and by the sounds of it, he knew exactly who she was and what she meant to her father and therefore, likely her. And he hadn't said a word.

There was no doubt that Archer was going to get in trouble. But boats were small places, and Samson was obviously smart enough not to give him shit in front of the guests. Instead, the moment they returned, Cass made her apologies for delaying dinner and settled into the cockpit to play a card game with the Winchesters while Archer prepared their meal. It was easy and fun to spend time with the family, and despite her issues with him, Samson was a gracious host. He kept them all entertained with stories of the islands and what she was sure were exaggerated tales of adventures he'd been on with the *Seaduction.*

When Archer came out carrying beautifully plated dishes of sea scallops in a passion fruit sauce with a bed of coconut rice, the aroma made her mouth water, almost as much as the sight of him standing in front of her, looking down at her with that sexy smirk on his face.

"Thank you." She took the plate and winked at him before she dove into her meal. She'd worked up quite the appetite with her afternoon activities. "Archer, this is delicious," she said with her mouth full.

The rest of the group agreed wholeheartedly and heaped him with praise. After sneaking a peek at Samson, from the look on his face, there was no doubt Archer had job security aboard the *Seaduction.*

Cass peered at him over the top of her wine glass. The sun had set and the lanterns they'd lit around the cockpit for ambience cast a glow over his face. She took her time and looked around the group; her eyes landed back on Archer. When he looked up and met her gaze, his lips curling up in a smile, her stomach fluttered as if she were a teenager again.

"How about some music?" Samson's booming voice broke the spell between the two of them. He disappeared inside the boat and returned a moment later with a guitar in hand. "Anyone up for a sing-along?"

Brittany rolled her eyes the way teenage girls do, but Cass saw her singing along just like everyone else. The entire night was easy and fun and only helped to solidify the idea Cass had earlier on the beach. It was still only an idea, but the more she thought about it, the more plausible it seemed. By the time everyone was ready for bed and disappearing into their bunks, she was positive it could be something.

"Hey there." Archer joined her on the deck, where she was staring up at the stars. Everyone had gone, and it was only the two of them. "I didn't have a chance to show you your bunk earlier." He didn't sit, but instead extended a hand to her. "I hope it's okay."

She took his hand and let him help her up. "I'm sure it's great. This boat is beautiful. It seriously has five bunks?"

"Well, that's the thing." Archer led the way into the boat, and down the small stairs to the lower level where the rooms were. There were two bunks in the front, one larger state-room that Archer pointed out as Samson's room. And then… "I hope you're okay to bunk with me." He looked at her with a question in his eyes. More than a question, passion lurked beneath his gaze as well.

"Are you kidding me?"

"I swear I didn't know when I invited you." He held up his hands in defense and looked genuinely concerned that she'd be upset. "I'll sleep on the couch in the salon; it's not a big deal. I—"

"No." She took his hands in hers and closed them before she leaned over to kiss him softly on the lips. "This is perfect."

And it was. It was a small room, as all bunks on a boat tended to be, and she was pretty sure it was the smallest room on the boat. But it didn't matter. It was more than enough. The double bed filled most of the space, with a door leading to a bathroom, or head as they were referred to on boats. There were cupboards and bookshelves lining the walls, and that was about it. All they needed. Not that they were a *they*, but maybe for the night they were. Angie was not going to believe a word of it when Cass finally got the opportunity to text her. But she didn't care. Josie's words about going with her gut replayed in her mind. So far, her gut had led her to the beach with Archer and that had turned out very well.

Maybe she should trust her gut about more things.

"So this is okay?"

"Better than okay." Cass jumped up on the bed, and scooted to the center of the mattress.

He stepped in the room and closed the door behind him. When he turned, Cass could see his passion-filled eyes darken again and her body reacted appropriately. Yes, the sleeping situation was definitely going to work out okay. She'd have no problem with a repeat performance of earlier; after all, it was only temporary, so she might as well enjoy it as much as possible.

Archer pulled his shirt over his head and tossed it on the ground before he crawled up on the bed toward her, like a lion stalking his prey. She fell back to the mattress as he straddled her and looked down at her with a look on his face that made her body quiver with the expectation of what was to come.

He lowered his mouth to her neck and trailed soft kisses down to the top of her tank top. "So, did you have a good day?"

Really? He wanted to make conversation? *Now?* Two could play at that game.

"Actually, I did." She pushed herself back, so she sat up and faced him. "I had an idea today."

"So did I." He slid down her body, pushed the fabric from her shirt out of the way and trailed kisses along her stomach; shots of pleasure went straight to her core.

"I like your idea."

He lifted his head, tormenting her. "Tell me about yours." He really was going to mess with her.

"I was thinking how this was fun earlier, but it was a one-time thing."

The look on his face told her that her words had exactly the effect she had hoped for. He shot up so he was once again directly over her. "One time?"

She nodded, playing her role to the hilt. "Absolutely. I'm not the kind of girl who does this kind of thing at all, so I figure that once is enough."

"Oh no." He shook his head. "Once is definitely not enough."

She pretended to mull over his words, enjoying the

payback. She wasn't lying about one thing. She was definitely not the type of girl who had random flings with men she met on holiday, but it's not as though it was going to turn into anything anyway. She needed to focus if she was going to keep her boat, and there was no way she could focus with a man. Especially one who had pushed her tank top up and had her nipple in his mouth.

"Hmm..." She tried to sound casual, but was pretty sure the sound that came out of her was closer to a groan.

"So just the one time, huh?" He looked at her with those eyes, and Cass knew she'd been bested.

"Well, maybe just one more time."

Archer didn't need any more invitation than that. In one quick move, he had her tank off, taking the bikini top she still wore with it, and his hands and mouth were back on her, kissing away any doubts she'd had, both real and imaginary.

Conscious of the thin walls on the boat, Archer and Cass were as quiet as they could be. She buried her face into his shoulder as she came undone beneath him, and he was right behind her with his own intense release. When they were both spent, and slick with sweat, he got up and opened the hatch to let some fresh air in while they lay together under the sheet.

She felt so good curled up in his arm and Archer planned to enjoy every moment while it lasted. And it wouldn't last. Neither of them wanted that. Cass had made it clear that whether it was once, twice, or hopefully at least once more, that's all it would be. And Archer was more than happy with that. The last thing he wanted was a relationship of any kind. His plan for the immediate future involved traveling wherever and whenever he felt like it. No ties. He'd seen all his friends back home in Cedar Springs settling down, having kids and getting married. Sure, they seemed happy but they didn't know what they were missing. There was a lot of world out there, and now that he'd experienced a taste of it, he wasn't in any hurry to quit.

"Didn't you say you had an idea, too?" He smiled wickedly and she flipped around in time to catch it.

"I did before I was distracted." She narrowed her eyes and he smiled innocently.

"Will you tell me?"

She shifted and took the sheet with her, wrapping it around her full breasts. The same breasts he'd only very recently been selfishly enjoying. She blushed a little when she saw where he was staring.

"I'll tell you if you pay attention."

He laughed and sat up, tugging the thin blanket over his own nakedness. "I'm listening."

"Okay." She took a deep breath. "I know how I can keep my boat."

"What?" On the sail this morning, she'd filled him in on the situation with Joe and the huge amount of money she owed. He didn't know everything about the situation, but from what he did know, it didn't look good. What could possibly have changed in such a short time? "How?"

"I'm going to do this."

"Do what?" He glanced around the small room, from the bed where they'd just had sex, and back toward Cass, still wrapped in a sheet.

"No." She reached forward and smacked him playfully. "Not *this*." She waved her arm between them. "This." She waved her arm around. "A charter business. My boat is big enough. I have sailing experience. I mean, how hard could it be?"

Archer stared at her for a few moments, trying to figure out whether Cass was serious.

A charter business? That was her plan?

It actually wasn't a bad plan at first glance. And there probably wasn't any good reason why she couldn't do it. He shrugged. "Why not?"

"Really? You think it's a good idea?"

"It's not a bad one."

"No." She nodded and sat up straighter. "It's not. I'd have a lot of work to do on the boat to get it ready, and of course I'd need to advertise and figure out a bunch of things, but there's no reason I can't do it. And Josie, she's the woman I met on the island, said my dad used to run a charter business on the *Cassiopeia*, so it's almost like the boat was destined for it."

He listened while she rattled on, her excitement growing the more she spoke. It really was a good idea. Probably the only idea that could give Cass what she wanted. And from the short time he'd known her, it was clear that if anyone was going to turn an abandoned boat into a charter sailing holiday business in paradise, it was her. Hell, Samson did it and Cass was a heck of a lot cuter than Samson.

"Who's going to be your chef?" He interrupted her in mid-sentence.

"My what?"

"Your chef." He repeated himself. "Your crew. I mean, you can't do it all yourself. You'll need someone to boss around."

She laughed and her sheet slipped a little to reveal the swell of her breast. He felt his dick twitch to life again.

"I'm sure I'll find someone. How did Samson find you?"

"This isn't what I do," he said. "I'm just filling in. I needed the job. He put up an ad and I answered."

"Then that's what I'll do." She shrugged, as if it was no big deal to hire a stranger to live with her on her boat. Did she not realize the dangers of what she was thinking of? He didn't know her well enough to know whether she was inherently a risk-taker or not, and despite the fact that she'd agreed to come on the trip with him, a virtual stranger, she certainly didn't seem like the type of woman who would take unnecessary risks. "I should write some of this down." She crawled over him, still holding her sheet in place, to grab her backpack from the cupboard. Her body hovered over his; little more than a thin piece of cotton separated them from nakedness and his body responded appropriately.

Oblivious of the effect she was having on him, again, she continued to rummage through her bag.

It was probably the fact that they'd just had amazing sex for the second time in the space of a few short hours, and his brain was muddled from the current lack of blood as it all rushed south, but whatever it was, he couldn't believe his own ears when he heard himself say, "I'll do it."

She froze. Still on all fours over his body, she twisted her body so she looked back at him. "You'll do what?"

"I'll be your chef. Your crew."

Cass's beautiful face twisted with confusion. She abandoned her search for the notebook in the depths of her pack and sat down next to him, her bare legs draped over his lap. "You'll be my crew? I don't understand. Why would you want to do that?"

It was his out. His chance to take back what he'd said and continue on with his plan of moving on. When they returned to the dock and Samson paid him, he'd have enough money to get to the Bocas Islands and then go on to Costa Rica. He did not need or want to stay in Shelter Bay. His whole plan had been to move on and explore as much of the world as he could. He didn't want to work with or for Cass. "I can help you get the *Cassiopeia* shipshape, too. You might need someone around to do some heavy lifting."

What was he saying? The words that kept coming out of his mouth were completely unexpected and unplanned. Yet they kept coming. "You liked the food tonight, didn't you?" She nodded and continued to stare at him. "Well, there's more where that came from," he said. "Wait until you taste breakfast. I've got a veggie frittata planned that will—"

"Archer."

He stared at her and waited for her to finish.

"I don't understand." She shook her head. "I mean, I'm… it's not that I don't want you to…but you were going to…"

"I know." He didn't. He really didn't know at all what he was saying. "But it sounds like a great opportunity, and ultimately I do need a job and I can think of a lot worse places to work. You don't think I'm any good at it?"

"I think you're great at it."

He ran his hands up and down her toned calves and squeezed gently. "I'm really great at it."

She yanked her legs away and her face shifted. Not at all the reaction he was looking for. "You're not just offering because of what we…us…not that there is an us, because there's no us. I don't want an us. I mean, it's not that I don't want an us. I just—"

He laughed, hoping it sounded a hell of a lot more casual than he felt. "No." He shook his head. "The only reason I'm offering is because I need a job and I happen to like sailing. That's it."

It was a lie and it burned his tongue. Somehow, in the last few days, whether he knew it or not, he'd really started to like Cass. Not in any serious way, but in a way that made him hate the idea of moving on and never seeing her again.

"Good." Her face changed again, this time into a look of relief. "Because I couldn't work with you if you were staying for any reason other than that. I was serious when I told you this was temporary. The last thing I need in my life is any more complications than I already have. But if you're serious about staying and helping me, then I think that would work really well."

He nodded. There was no doubt about what she was saying, and he'd respect it. In fact, the situation worked perfectly for him, too. Yes, the sex was great. But that's all it was. Sex. "I totally agree."

"Okay." She nodded a few times as if she was working things out in her head. "Yes. This could work really well. Okay." She must have reached a decision in her head because she nodded one more time and then slid off the bed.

Archer watched while she shimmied into her shorts, still holding the sheet around her. She turned her back to pop her tank top on. "What are you doing?"

Cass grabbed her backpack off the cupboard and stuffed her bikini in the pocket before she tossed the sheet back on the bed. She hefted the bag over her shoulder. "I'm too wired to sleep. I'm going to go sit under the stars and make plans. Besides, I can't stay in here, Archer. Not now."

"What? Why?" He patted the mattress next to him. "It's late. Come on."

Her pretty face wrinkled up in worry. "No. If we're going to work together, this," she gestured between them, "us, this thing between us. It can't happen anymore. I told you, no complications. You feel the same way, right? Because otherwise this isn't going to work."

He knew what he should say. He should tell her that he thought they could handle both: a no-strings, sex-only relationship while they worked together. But he knew that was the wrong answer. She was dead serious about the charter business, and he was smart enough to know how much she was putting on the line. If what she needed was space between them to make it work, that's what he'd give her. At least for the time being. His lips crept up into a smile. "Of course," he said, with a casual shrug. "Consider us totally professional. No complications here."

Relief washed over her face and the sexy smile he loved to

see returned. "Thanks, Archer." She blew him a kiss and left him sitting alone in the middle of the bed with a raging hard-on, completely bewildered by how quickly things had changed.

He'd let her go. For now. After all, there would be plenty of time to change her mind later.

Chapter Eight

CASS HADN'T BEEN PROPERLY PREPARED for exactly how much work it would be to get the *Cassiopeia* ready for charter in the days and weeks after she made her decision. But once she'd decided on her course of action, there was no going back, particularly after she'd talked Joe into not only giving her an extension on her debt, but adding a small loan onto it. It seemed like an insurmountable sum, but she didn't have any other options, not if she wanted to stay on the boat. And with all the unknowns in her life, that was the one thing she was sure of.

She looked up from the stainless-steel metal she was polishing to see Archer on the bow of the boat, working on the stainless up there. One thing she'd learned over the last month of work was that there was a never-ending amount of stainless on a boat, and the only way to keep it sparkling was a continual circuit of work.

The other thing she'd learned was that the only thing worse than polishing metal was watching a shirtless Archer doing it, his tanned muscles glistening with the heat of the day, rippling with the work and causing all kinds of heat within her that she absolutely could not act on.

She'd meant what she'd said that night on the *Seaduction*. She couldn't sleep with him and work with him, and she still felt that way. If she let herself, she could quite happily, and without a doubt, most satisfactorily have a wicked love affair with him. But she couldn't let herself because that would mean losing him as a first mate. No doubt things would get messy. Someone's feelings would get hurt and then what? At the moment, she needed him on the boat a lot more than she needed him to satisfy the never-ending ache in her core. And she needed that pretty bad.

Angie couldn't understand why she didn't just go ahead and sleep with him. They'd had more than one conversation that focused solely on that particular topic.

"How bad would it be?" Angie had asked the last time Cass called her. "I mean, you said yourself the sex was fantastic. Seems like a no-brainer to me."

Cass rolled her eyes and sighed. "I'm not talking about this again."

"Why not? If you're not *doing* it, you might as well talk about it." Cass could picture her friend thousands of miles away, giving her that little smirk that basically let Cass know she wasn't dropping the subject.

"Okay, fine," she'd relented. "I'm not sleeping with him again because I need him."

"Well, I know that you *need* him." Angie's laugh came across the line.

"I don't mean like that."

"Oh yes you do."

"Do you want to talk about this or not?"

Angie's laughter cut off and when she spoke again, her voice was serious. "What I want to talk about is what will make my best friend happy and quite frankly I don't understand why some good-old toe-curling, hair-raising orgasms aren't on that list. It seems to me that's exactly what will put a smile on your face."

Cass couldn't argue with that.

"Trust me," she said. "I totally agree with you and maybe…no. Archer is too important right now. I can't tell you how helpful he's been helping me out. I would be months away if it wasn't for him and all the work he's put in, and I've barely even had to pay him. It's really been a godsend."

"Right. I'm sure he's doing it to be charitable."

"What's that supposed to mean?"

"Don't go getting all defensive and cranky with me," Angie said. "All I'm saying is if this man is selflessly donating all his time and energy, it's most definitely not out of the goodness of his heart. He totally wants something in return. Or should I say, a little somethin' somethin'?"

"It's not like that."

"Sure it's not." Angie laughed again. "Look, you said yourself that he's a traveler and that means he's not likely to stick around for long anyway, right?"

It was a worry Cass tried not to think about. "That's true," she said reluctantly.

"So give him a reason to stay. That's all I'm saying and I'll say it again, too. But not right now. I've gotta run. Text me later. I miss you."

"I miss you, too."

Long after she'd hung up, Cass replayed her friend's words in her head. Maybe Angie had a point. It was entirely possible that Archer would stick around if he had more of a reason than just helping her with the boat. But that would mean a relationship, the idea of which made her stomach twist. The last thing she needed in her life was any relationship besides the one she had with her boat and the never-ending work it required.

Like the stainless she was still polishing. Remembering where she was and what she was doing, Cass shook the memory of the phone conversation away and focused on the present.

"Hey," she looked up and hollered at Archer. He turned and when his eyes met hers, the lazy smile that crossed his face made her stomach flip, just the way it was designed to. He hadn't come right out and said anything, and on the outside, there was no reason for her to think that he wasn't respecting her rules. But there was no doubt that Archer would be more than happy to not only break every single one of the rules she'd created, but to absolutely shatter them. "When you're finished there, I think we should get ready to take her out."

"Today?" He stood from his crouch, lazily stretching his arms overhead in a way that made his chest look particularly yummy, and started an unhurried walk over to where she sat. "You think we have enough daylight to get to Barbecue Island today?"

"I don't, actually." That was the point.

He narrowed his eyes, but didn't question her. He rarely did.

"We don't have enough experience dropping anchor at night, and I think it's better to gain that experience without passengers, don't you?"

He nodded and she did her best to ignore the way he smiled at her.

"I do." He slapped the rag against his bare hand. "I'll get everything ready—shouldn't take more than thirty minutes."

She nodded, totally aware of what was going through his head. For the last month, they'd made day-trips out to sea while Cass refreshed her memory when it came to sailing. It hadn't taken long for it all to come back to her, and soon she maneuvered the *Cassiopeia* as if she'd been sailing the boat all her life. Despite all the trips, Cass had mostly managed to avoid spending much time off the dock alone with Archer. She'd designed it that way, and they both knew it.

Days were spent working, polishing, sailing, cleaning, and provisioning. Nights were spent at the Dockside Inn, getting to know the locals and other cruisers who spent their time at the marina, making friends and hearing sailing stories. In a few short weeks, Cass had managed to learn about the best snorkeling spots, dangerous bays to drop anchor in, the prettiest beaches—although arguably they were all the prettiest beaches—and where the best fishing was.

Not only had the evenings surrounded by people been beneficial, they'd also kept her from being alone with Archer, which was her number-one priority. And they both knew it.

"Good," she said. "I'm going to go check out with Joe." She got to her feet before she realized that the only way past him was right next to him. No matter; she was the captain: it was her ship and she would not let him—or her insane attraction to his sexiness—distract from that. She took a breath. "I'll meet you back here and we'll get moving then." With a curt nod, she took two steps toward him and steeled herself to slip past.

Archer grabbed her arm and spun her around so she was inches from him. Her chest rose and fell and she cursed herself for stirring up any kind of feelings in her.

"Archer, I—"

"Just wanted to know if you needed anything from the store." He grinned down at her, and she'd slap him if she could, but that would only prove that he was getting to her. Even if they both knew it, she didn't need any more reason to show him.

She forced herself to keep her voice level despite the fact that every nerve ending in her body lit up at his proximity and the urge to touch him was strong. Too strong. "I'm good. Thanks."

"Not even some of that bubbly water you like?"

"No, I'm—yes, that would be nice. Thanks."

He nodded, winked and let go of her arm, but didn't back away.

It was Cass who narrowed her eyes and squished past him. Her breast rubbed against his arm in a way she knew would make him crazy. There. Let him have a taste of his own medicine. She wasn't the only one fighting their attraction, and two could play at that game.

She was making him crazy and she damn well knew it. He knew she wanted to keep it professional between them and he respected that. Or at least he thought he did, which was why for the first few weeks of their working arrangement he'd tried to keep his distance. He really had. It hadn't been nearly as easy as he'd thought it would be. A boat, even a fifty-foot yacht, wasn't a big place, especially when you were trying to avoid close contact with a woman who made him want to rip her clothes off, press her up against the wall, and kiss her senseless while he drove into her and made her scream out his name.

No. A boat was a very small place.

He knew he could change his mind at any time and continue with his travel plans to move on to Costa Rica and then, wherever the wind blew him. He had a bit of money saved up now that Cass had been paying him. He could leave. No, he *should* leave. She was getting under his skin in a way he both loved and hated at the same time. He shook his head and laughed under his breath. Who was he trying to fool? He wasn't going anywhere.

He'd pulled a t-shirt on before he headed up the dock to the small store they used for provisioning. For bigger trips, they took the bus into Colon, which was the closest city—a trip he volunteered for whenever possible, because it got him off the boat and away from the temptation of her. But if Cass wanted to set sail, there was no time for a bus ride into the city. Besides, he didn't need much. Mostly, he just wanted to get off the boat for a few minutes, long enough for his hard-on that seemed to be ever present around Cass to simmer down. He grabbed a few tins and packages as well as a bottle of the sparkling water Cass liked so much that he liked making fun of, charged it all to the *Cassiopeia* account and headed back to the boat.

"Ready, sailor?"

Cass stood on the bow of the boat; one arm gripped the jib sheet. She let her body swing slightly as she watched him walk up the dock. Damn, she looked good. The last month in the sun had turned her milky skin into a delicious warm tan, which only made every luscious curve on that body of hers look even more amazing. Her blond hair was almost always up in a ponytail, and she seemed to permanently live in some combination of a bikini, tank top, and cutoff shorts. All combinations were absolutely acceptable to him, although he would much prefer her to not be wearing anything at all.

Damn.

So much for putting a lid on his desire. He couldn't help the way his body reacted to her. Lord knew he'd tried. Or at least he *had* tried. When it became clear staying away from her wasn't going to work, Archer had decided on a new approach, one he was enjoying a lot more. The new strategy involved wearing her down and he would, too. She wanted him just as badly as he wanted her; she couldn't fight it forever. "I was born ready." He hopped aboard and instantly pulled his shirt off again. The reaction on her face was exactly what he was looking for. Even from the distance they stood, he could see her chest rise and fall as her breath came a little faster, the way she dropped her arm and ran her hand through her hair.

Oh yes, his plan was working just fine.

Cass picked her way through the lines, and joined him in the cockpit. "We're going to have to talk about uniforms," she said with a smirk. "And actually wearing them." She gave him a wink and turned to fire up the boat. "Go stow the supplies, and we can shove off."

Chapter Nine

THERE WAS nothing better than getting off the dock and using a sailboat for the purpose it was created for. As soon as they were clear of the breakwater, Cass hauled up the foresail, set a course and let her go. She sailed beautifully, slicing easily through the swells. While Cass consulted the maps, and busied herself tidying the lines on deck, Archer set a fishing line out in an effort to catch dinner.

She didn't mean to pay him any attention, but soon the maps and tidying were forgotten as she sat back and watched the way he handled the fishing pole, casting it out to sea before he let just enough line out so the lure was far enough from the boat, but not too deep as to not catch anything.

"Have you ever been deep sea fishing before?" She startled herself with the question, but Archer seemed to know she'd been watching. He turned his head to give her smile before he finished what he was doing.

"Besides out here, with you?"

She nodded and he laughed. "Just once but that was only a few weeks before I met you. I'd jumped onto Samson's charter—that time as a guest, not a chef." She blushed with the memory of him working on Samson's boat as a chef. He'd brought her along, and that was when they'd had sex for the first time, and not too long after that, the last time.

She tried not to think about it, and chose to focus instead on watching how comfortable he was with the fishing rod. "Well, you look like you've been doing it your whole life."

"I have." He let the rest of the line go and locked out the rod before he returned to the cockpit and the little bit of shade it afforded. "Just not like this. I guess it's not too different than fly fishing in the rivers back home. A fish is a fish." He shrugged and his casual indifference just made him even more attractive. Damn.

"So besides fishing, what else did you do back home?"

He leaned back and stretched his arms overhead. Cass looked away. "I spent a lot of time in the mountains. Fishing." He nodded to the rod he'd just set. "And hunting, of course."

"Of course." Cass tried to sound as if it was no big deal, despite the fact that she'd never even fired a gun, let alone shot an animal. To her surprise, the thought didn't disgust her the way she'd expected it to.

"Basically, I just liked to be in the woods. Camping, hiking, skiing: you name it. If it was outside, I was there. After all, if you're going to put up with the cold, you might as well get all the benefit from the mountains that you can. There's something special about mountains, don't you think?"

Cass shrugged and immediately felt guilty. Living in Seattle, the mountains were close enough to admire in the distance, but far enough away that she'd have to get in a car and drive to them. Something, she was embarrassed to admit, she didn't do nearly often enough.

"So did you do those things in the mountains alone?"

She could have smacked herself. What kind of stupid question was that? If she was trying to be disinterested in him in a romantic way, which she was, she certainly wasn't doing a very good job of it.

If Archer thought anything of the question, he didn't say so. Instead, he gave her a sly smile and shook his head. "No. There was no one at home." Much to her annoyance, she blushed and glanced away before he could notice. "Why do you think I'm here?"

Cass whipped her head around. She'd never bothered to ask, but of all the reasons she could think of for Archer leaving the mountains he obviously loved so far behind, love wasn't one of them. "You're here for a woman?" Just asking the question made her feel as if she'd done something wrong by being with him. But what did that say about him if he'd come to Panama to be with a woman? What the hell was he doing on a sailboat in the middle of the ocean with her?

"Really?" He challenged her with his eyes. "That's what you think?"

She shook her head. "I don't know what to think. I realized I actually don't know all that much about you."

He leaned forward and crossed his arms over his legs, bridging the gap between them yet still managing to keep distance. "Well then, I think we should change that. Don't you?"

She nodded. It was almost impossible to maintain any kind of professionalism between them when he sat across from her half naked and looking like a god of the sea. But she'd try. Oh yes, she'd try.

Cass sat back against the cushions, scooting herself away so she was at least an arm's length away and wouldn't be tempted to reach out and touch him, or pull him in for a deep kiss.

"Good," he said with a sexy smile. "I'll go first. I did not come here for a woman; I came here because I'm not in a serious relationship. But no, before you ask, it was actually not my idea at all."

"Really?" This was getting interesting.

"I actually had no plans to go anywhere. Why would I? I love my town. The mountains are amazing and full of things I love. I have a lot of friends back home. A good life, really. Why would I leave?"

"Why would you leave?"

"Because they bought me a ticket and a backpack and told me to go."

"Seriously?" She couldn't imagine under any circumstances forcing her best friend to leave town. Hell, it sucked bad enough when Angie fell in love and moved to England. And she'd wanted to go. Cass certainly couldn't imagine a scenario where she'd tell Angie to leave. "Why would they do that?"

"Because they care about me." She cocked an eyebrow, so he continued. "I know it sounds crazy, and I'll be honest. At first I wasn't sure either, but you have to understand, all my friends were pairing up, falling in love and having kids."

"And you weren't?" She hated herself for hoping that was true and his heart hadn't been desperately broken by some woman back home.

He shook his head and her spirits lifted a little. "Nope. They wanted me to go out and experience life, so on my birthday, they all chipped in and bought me a gift that more or less forced me out. I thought I'd hate it and be back in a week. Turns out I kinda love it here." He waved his arms around. "Who wouldn't?"

"Wow." Never in her life had Cass had friends who would have thought to do something so unselfish and totally thoughtful as what Archer's friends had done for him. Not even Angie would have thought of that. "Those are some great friends."

"They really are. I wish you could meet them."

Cass froze. Had he really just said that?

Before she could say anything or analyze anything further,

a loud zipping noise pierced the air. Archer jumped up and was at the back rail, his fishing rod in hand before Cass even knew what happened.

"Ease the sheet, Cass! Slow the boat!"

Woken from her stupor, Cass hopped up and released the main sheet. The effect on the boat was immediate. As the wind fell from the sails, the *Cassiopeia* slowed dramatically.

As focused as she was at bringing in the sails, she couldn't see what was going on behind her, but she could hear Archer cursing and yelling with excitement.

"I almost got her. Just a bit more."

Cass finished with the sail; with the boat turned to wind and barely moving in the water, she turned her attention to Archer.

His back and arms strained with the pull and tug of what had to be a large fish on the line. She tried not to stare, but there was no way she couldn't appreciate those fine muscles at work as they brought in the catch.

"There she is!"

Cass ran to the rail and spotted the large fish, jumping in the water, still a good distance away from the boat. "Are you sure you got it? It looks like it's swimming out to sea."

"I'm sure she'd like that. But not today. Not today."

"What makes you think it's a she? Why can't it—"

"Get the net, Cass, and the gaffing hook."

Cass stared at him, her mouth hanging open. Did she even *have* a net and a gaffing hook? She must. Too bad she had no idea where they might be.

"The net..." she mumbled uncertainly. "Right. I'll get the net."

"In the aft hatch, Cass. Hurry."

If she hadn't been so amped up with the excitement of it all, she might have been impressed that he actually knew where the supplies were and she, the captain, did not. As it was, there wasn't time to think about it. She moved quickly and sure enough, the supplies were right where Archer said they were.

"Here." She held out the net but he only glanced at it.

"That's for you. But you're probably going to want the hook instead."

"The hook?"

"Yes. She's thrashing pretty hard." He heaved and reeled with remarkable skill while she watched, trying to take in everything that was happening. "I'll need you to use the hook and try to get it in the gills, so we can haul it aboard."

"The gills?" The reality of what she was going to have to do sank in. Despite living next to the ocean her entire life, she'd never actually been out fishing. When she was a kid, they'd been too busy sailing to throw a line in, and after her dad took off, she hadn't wanted to be on the water at all, for any reason.

Archer stared at her for a moment. "You can do this, Cass. I know you can."

She met his eyes, and she actually believed him. She could do it. So what if she'd never tried before. How hard could it be?

For the next few minutes, Cass watched Archer work to bring the fish close enough for her to reach out with the hook and she was ready when he yelled. With a firm grip on it, lest it fall overboard, she reached out and—almost blindly with all the splashing and thrashing—thrust the hook into what she hoped was the fish's gills.

"I got it."

"Pull."

She did as she was told. Crap, the fish was a lot heavier than she expected it to be, but she put all her strength into it. Soon Archer abandoned the rod and joined her in using the hook to bring the fish aboard.

The second the fish hit the deck and started thrashing wildly, Cass automatically jumped into the cockpit to avoid getting hit while Archer dove into action. He pinned it with one arm, and mercifully and skillfully took care of it.

Cass watched in fascination for a few minutes before she turned her attention back to the sails that still luffed in the wind. She hauled the main sail and set a course for Barbecue Island. It looked as though Archer had a few hours of work ahead of him with the fish. They might as well get moving.

He hadn't been sure how she would react to the fish. Hell, he wasn't sure how he would react to the giant yellowfin tuna he'd hauled aboard—with Cass's help, of course. It was a whole lot bigger than the trout he routinely caught in the streams of the Canadian Rockies; the few times he'd gone salmon fishing off the coast of Vancouver, he'd landed a few beauties, but none of them compared to the beauty he'd brought aboard that afternoon.

Cass had handled it all like a pro. Especially when she'd turned around and noticed the mess he'd made of the deck. Fish were messy. There was no doubt about it. But once he had it all filleted and packaged for the freezer, reserving two choice steaks for their dinner, he'd made sure to clean everything up. Not that she'd complained. She hadn't. Not one word. His respect and desire for the woman grew by the day. Heck, it grew by the minute.

The day went quickly, and by the time they began their approach into the bay where they would anchor, the sun was disappearing behind the horizon quickly. Cass flipped on the nav lights and Archer stood at attention. It wasn't a tricky bay to anchor in, but any anchorage at night could be problematic, particularly when they didn't really have much practice.

"Get ready on the anchor," Cass hollered to him. Archer

had made his way to the bow of the boat so he was ready when she'd found the perfect place. "Do you see anything?"

"It's all good from up here." He turned and yelled so she'd hear him. He probably should have turned around and kept a lookout, but he didn't. At least not right away. Instead, he kept his eye on her. Lit by the cockpit lights, she looked incredibly sexy at the helm, but he could see the steel of strength that ran through her as well. The firm set of her jawline as she focused on what she was doing.

"Archer!"

It took him a moment to realize she was calling his name. He snapped to attention.

"What?"

"I told you to drop. Drop now."

He shook his head. Not that he didn't think she should drop anchor where they were, but as an instinct so she wouldn't realize he'd been daydreaming. "No."

"What do you mean, no?"

"Not here." He quickly pointed to a spot a few feet away, and silently cursed himself. "There. It's better there."

"I told you to drop, Archer. Drop."

There was something about the way she commanded him. He knew he shouldn't be turned on by it. It's not as if she was taking control in the bedroom, telling him to do all kinds of dirty things, none of which he'd object to. It was a very different situation, but he couldn't help it. His mind went firmly to images of her standing over him, naked and demanding all kinds of things that made his cock grow hard in his shorts. With all the blood flowing south, he wasn't listening or paying attention the way he should have been. It wasn't until Cass flew up the side of the boat, deploying the anchor herself by stepping on the foot pedal, that he took notice.

"I said, drop. The. Fucking. Anchor." She spoke each word carefully, clipping the ends as she glared at him before she ran back to the helm, where she put the boat in reverse and set the anchor. All with very little help from him.

Archer took his time tidying up the deck before he returned to the cockpit, where no doubt Cass was waiting for him, more than likely pissed off. Finally, he couldn't wait any longer and he made his way to the back of the boat.

"Hey. I thought I'd get started on dinner," he said cautiously. She didn't look up from what she was doing, so he continued. "You must be getting hungry and I have a great idea for the tuna we—"

"Do that then."

Archer had been around women enough to know when they were pissed off and when he should back off. Which was exactly what he did. He made himself useful in the kitchen, preparing the fish and a delicious meal to accompany it. There was nothing better than freshly caught fish, no matter where in the world you were, and he was happy to use the delicious protein to create a spectacular meal that would blow her away. Archer's original plan had been to keep it really simple by searing the fish and serving it with rice. However, given Cass's mood, he decided to try a more impressive approach.

He knew exactly what was in the galley and set about preparing an Asian slaw salad with rice noodles before he crusted the tuna in black sesame seeds and seared it. The smell was phenomenal and Archer's own mouth watered. He could only hope Cass would react the same way.

When he went above deck to set the table, he took a bottle of wine and two glasses. It was an assumption for sure, but he needed to make things better, and wine made everything better. Plus, if he was lucky…nah…he couldn't even let himself think of it.

"Dinner will be out in a second." He set down the glasses. "I thought maybe the fish called for a celebration." He nodded toward the wine and Cass stared at him for a minute before she finally nodded her approval.

"It smells great."

He smiled and gave her a wink before he disappeared inside to grab the prepared plates. He was hoping for a smile when he brought out the black sesame seed seared tuna on a bed of Asian slaw, and he got one. It was easy to see that Cass was trying not to look impressed, as she was clearly still upset with him. But the delectable aroma must have gotten to her, and if it wasn't the smell, it was the first bite that she put in her mouth. Her eyes shut as the flavors hit her tongue and Archer watched with pleasure and a touch of jealousy for the fork that got to languish between her lips as she savored the first bite.

Finally, she opened her eyes and looked at him. "Archer, this is…it's…wow."

He smiled, trying not to look too satisfied with himself. "I'm glad you like it." It was lame, but it was all he could say. Especially when what he really wanted to say involved telling her how hot she looked earlier, helping him bring in the catch, and how much he wanted to abandon the fish and take her instead. He shoved a bite of his own into his mouth and concentrated on chewing and counting slowly, willing his body to calm the hell down. He'd never wanted a woman as badly as he wanted her. And as much as he wanted to shove the dishes aside and pull her into his arms, showing her exactly how much he did want her, it wasn't an option.

Archer watched Cass enjoy another bite and relished each second with the type of passion he wished—with a ferocity that scared him—was directed to him.

No. He forced the thought to the forefront of his mind. It wasn't an option.

At least not yet.

Chapter Ten

"ARCHER, WE NEED TO TALK."

He'd been awake and out of bed for less than fifteen minutes when she called down to him. Hardly even time to put the coffee on. He'd barely slept the night before. After they finished every bite of their dinner, and drank the bottle of wine he'd chosen and half-expected Cass to object to, they hadn't fallen into each other's arms the way he'd hoped they would.

Hell, who was he kidding? He may have hoped for it, but it wasn't going to happen. At least not over tuna. Not even freshly caught tuna. And long after Cass had excused herself and gone to bed, Archer had lain awake, tossing and turning. Thoughts of the woman haunted him every time he closed his eyes. It was almost worse once he'd fallen into a restless sleep, as his dreams had gone straight to a very sensual, very naked Cass. Her full breasts dangled over him while she straddled him, her head thrown back in ecstasy as she rode him to—

"Archer! Are you awake?"

He shook his head and tossed back the glass of orange juice he'd just poured. "Yes. I'm here. I'll be right out." For his own mental health, he was going to need to get thoughts of her, especially thoughts of her naked, out of his head.

He pulled a shirt over his head and headed out to the back deck, where Cass paced. Archer tried not to notice how cute she looked in her signature cutoff shorts and a tank top; a few strands of her blond hair escaped the messy bun she'd piled at the back of her head. Her skin was sun-kissed, and freckles that hadn't been there a few weeks ago were now smattered across the bridge of her nose. Every time he looked at her, it never failed to amaze him how one woman could look so bloody cute and so goddamned sexy all at the same time.

"Morning."

"Archer. Hi." She stopped pacing and crossed her arms over her chest, which had the delightful effect of pushing her breasts up so he could see the swell of them peek out of her tank top. His cock twitched in his shorts. How could she have no idea the effect she had on him? No doubt, she knew exactly what she was doing. "We need to talk."

He tilted his head. "About what?"

"About the way you disregarded my command last night."

"Your command?" He shook his head a little. Had he heard her right? "What are you talking about?"

She stiffened her spine and if she didn't look so serious and slightly pissed off, Archer might have laughed at her effort to look tough. He was smart enough to know that would probably be a bad choice. "Yes," she said. "My command. I told you to drop the anchor and you said no."

"I didn't say—"

"You did. And you need to understand that it's not okay for you to disrespect me like that."

"But I wasn't. I was just…" His mind raced while he tried to remember the circumstances of the night before. It was true: he hadn't dropped the anchor the way she'd said. And he may have suggested another spot, but that was only because he'd been caught daydreaming. About Cass. There was no way he could tell her that. "I just didn't think it was a good spot," he finished, trying his best to look confident in his answer.

"That's not your call."

Something about how indignant she looked sent signals to his dick and at the same time, kind of pissed him off in a way he couldn't explain.

"I was just trying to—"

"Well, don't. I am the captain and you're not."

"I know that. I was just—"

"You need to remember your place."

"My place?" Okay, now he really was getting pissed off. She was taking her little power trip way too far.

"Yes." There was a bit of a shake in her voice, but she stood firm. "I'm the captain of this ship and you are the cook. The hired hand."

The what?

"I know that might be hard for you to accept," she continued. "But I demand a certain level of respect and if you can't give it to me, then—"

"Then what?" He was all for letting her blow off steam, but this was too much. The *hired hand?* That's what he was to her? He'd put his whole goddamned life on hold for her. Not that she'd asked him to, but still. He was more than just a fuckin' hired hand. A lot more. "Are you going to fire the *help*, Captain?" He obnoxiously emphasized the word.

"Archer." Her uncrossed arms dropped to her side, but she didn't back down. "Don't be like that."

"Don't be like what?" He hopped out of the cockpit to the back deck. "I'm just trying to understand my role here on the *Cassiopeia*." He was well aware that he was being a jackass, but he couldn't help it. He'd busted his ass for her over the last few weeks for a pittance. They weren't making any money, and didn't expect to be paid much when he knew full well she didn't have much. But he'd obviously wrongly assumed he was, if not a partner with Cass, at least somewhat more of an equal than simply the hired hand. It both pissed him off and hurt to hear her refer to him that way. "You know what, Captain?" He stripped off his shirt and threw it in her general direction with more force than was probably required. She caught it before it hit her in the chest; the look on her face almost broke his resolve, but he was too fired up for that. "It's time for a break."

He didn't say another word before he turned, climbed the side rail and dove off the back of the boat into the crystal-blue water.

She watched him swim away with strong, sure strokes. They were anchored in almost the same place as they were the first time they'd been on the *Seaduction* together. That large catamaran had been able to anchor much closer to shore, and when Cass had swum from the boat to Barbecue Island, it wasn't nearly as far.

But she needn't have worried—not that she was really worried; he was obviously a confident swimmer. She watched as Archer reached the beach. She willed him to turn around, to look in her direction, or make any kind of show that he wasn't completely pissed off with her. But he didn't. As soon as he reached the sand, he took off in a jog, going in the opposite direction of where she'd met Josie. He headed directly to where they'd made love for the first time.

"Ugh." Cass threw his shirt that she was still holding and looked for something else she could throw or hit, or...she was being stupid. And she was being really stupid when she'd pulled her whole power trip business with him. It's not as if she'd meant what she'd said. Not really. Whatever feelings of insecurity she was having about being able to captain the

Cassiopeia, they weren't Archer's fault. It was true she'd been pissed off when he questioned her the night before, but that did not warrant her little outburst. Not even a little. Archer had been amazing the way he'd been helping her out with the boat and getting everything ready. It was almost like it was his future on the line, too. Like he really cared. Like he really cared about *her*.

"No." She shook her head and went below deck to grab something to eat. She couldn't let herself think about Archer like that. No matter what Angie said, Cass couldn't afford for her relationship with Archer to be anything more than it already was. She grabbed a banana, unwilling to make any more of an effort for breakfast than that, and headed back up to the deck.

There was still no sight of him on the island. Not that she was looking. Because she wasn't. Well, maybe she was. There was no getting around it; just being around him made her body sing. Her skin still flushed, remembering the touch of his hands on hers, the heat from his kiss, the feel of—

No.

It had to stop. She couldn't let herself be so affected by him. He said himself that he'd caught the traveling bug. Archer wanted to see the world because he didn't have anybody—or more specifically, any woman—tying him down. Sure, he might be a big help to her right now. Almost indispensable, really. But he would leave. There was no doubt in her mind he would leave and just like her father had, he'd probably take off right when she needed him the most.

Cass spent the rest of the morning busying herself with the never-ending chores around the boat. She tried to force herself not to think of Archer, and why he still wasn't back yet. Maybe she'd done it? Maybe by freaking out on him, she'd pushed him over the edge and he was done with her and her boat. It wasn't totally inconceivable.

She paused in her scrubbing of the deck and laid the brush down where it couldn't be kicked overboard. She couldn't lose him. Not yet. Not before she'd even had a chance with the *Cassiopeia*. She needed Archer. He couldn't leave. More than that, she really didn't want him to.

Angie's words flashed through her head. *Give him a reason to stay.*

Her body thrilled at the idea of giving in to Archer's incessant flirting. She wasn't a fool: he'd been trying to wear her down, convince her that they could both work together and sleep together. She didn't agree. It was risky and it would put their business relationship in a precarious position.

Not that it wasn't right now. Really, what did she have to lose? Except, of course, for the continual sexual frustration and tension between them.

And that, she could stand to have a little less of.

A decision made, smart or not, Cass readied the dinghy at the back of the boat that would motor her toward Barbecue Island and Archer. Assuming he was still there and hadn't convinced Josie to take him somewhere else.

It hadn't taken Archer that long to cool off from the argument with Cass. He'd been fired up, but his anger had burned out quickly on the swim and subsequent jog that led him around the small island, past the piece of beach where he'd made love to Cass for the first time, and right around to a cluster of grass buildings. In his anger and need to get away, he'd forgotten about the woman Cass had told him about who lived on the island. Josie, if he remembered correctly. She was the woman who seemed to have inspired Cass's desire to run her own charter company and try to hang on to her father's boat.

He'd forgotten all about her until he'd literally stumbled upon her camp. It was a decent little setup on the south end of the island with a collection of grass huts and one main, slightly larger hut that he took to be Josie's. He wasn't really in the mood to have a conversation with anyone, but before he could turn around and head in the opposite direction, a woman dressed in an embroidered skirt, billowy blouse, and beads lining her arms and legs appeared, holding a mug.

"Good morning." Her voice was melodic and oddly soothing. It instantly put Archer at ease, as did her warm, welcoming smile. He paused, willing to put his plan to retreat on hold. "It's a beautiful morning in the islands, isn't it?"

"Aren't they all?"

She laughed and took a sip of her coffee. "You speak the truth, son. You do speak the truth. Won't you have a cup of coffee with me?"

He tried to think of a reason he couldn't, but he wasn't in a hurry to return to the boat just yet—not if it meant dealing with Cass, who was likely either just as pissed off as she'd been, or even more so. Not that he couldn't handle her angry; without a doubt, he could. The real problem was hearing all her talk about who was in charge and how she was the captain of the ship made him want to throw her over his shoulder, take her into her bunk and show her exactly who was in charge. At least when it came to the bedroom.

But it wasn't an option. And with things the way they were between them, it was definitely safer to stay on the island for a bit.

"That sounds good." He smiled. "I could use a coffee."

Once the introductions were made and Josie went to prepare him a cup of coffee, the two sat comfortably in Josie's lawn chairs that faced out to the ocean and the gently rolling surf as it washed up on the beach.

"It's a beautiful spot you have here."

"I like it. And it's quiet today."

"Quiet?" Archer took a sip of his coffee. Looking at the small house, he could only assume she had some sort of open fire or something inside to do the cooking. He made a mental note to ask about it later. "Wouldn't it be quiet every morning?"

She nodded, a sad look in her eyes. "Lately it is. You see, I used to operate a sort of bed and breakfast type of thing on the island. Something for those people who wanted to get away from it all and sleep under the stars. A few years ago, it kept me pretty busy but these days, the guests are fewer and fewer. It's hard when I don't have any way to advertise."

"How did you do it before?" Archer was fairly sure he already knew the answer, as Cass had filled him in on how the older woman knew her father. It was likely Roger Cutler brought the tourists to her, and her answer confirmed as much.

"But since Roger left, the other charter boats brought a few from time to time, but now it's mostly dried up."

He made a sympathetic noise, but something she'd said caught his attention. "What do you mean, since he *left*? Pardon me for saying so, but he's presumed dead, is he not?"

"The seasons of the world ebb and flow, my friend, and people change like the tides. No doubt Roger's journey simply took him somewhere new."

"Without his boat?"

She smiled and nodded, giving him he sense that she saw a lot more than she was letting on. "You never know what drives people, Archer. Roger had a wandering soul. Much like you, I suspect."

"I don't know about that." He laughed and looked at his

feet shuffling the sand. "I've lived in one place my whole life. Until now, that is."

Did he have a wandering soul? He thought it over and rolled the idea around in his head. He was born and raised in Cedar Springs. It was a small town with a big heart, that's what his grandmother had always told him. Despite the size, he never felt trapped or cornered, and he'd never felt the urge to travel before. In fact, there was no doubt he'd still be there if his friends hadn't bought him the ticket and basically forced him to take this adventure.

Aware that he hadn't said anything for a few minutes, he looked over at Josie, but she didn't seem to be in any hurry to continue the conversation, giving him plenty of time to mull over the thought. And the more he mulled it over, the more it made sense. Despite never actually leaving Cedar Springs, he did leave. All the time. It was true that he escaped into the backwoods, up into the mountains to hunt, fish, and camp. If he stayed down in town too long, he started to get itchy feet, and needed to get away.

"Maybe you're right," he finally said.

It didn't seem to require any further explanation, and Josie didn't press. She simply nodded, so he asked, "Will I ever stop wandering?" It seemed like a silly question to ask a complete stranger about his life, but there was something about the woman. Something comfortable and knowing that reminded him a lot of his grandmother.

"Yes." She reached over and patted his knee. "For you, it will take the love of a good woman."

It was his turn to laugh. The idea was preposterous. Love? A woman? Somehow that would make him want to settle down? Or at least stop wandering? The idea was ridiculous. Even more ridiculous was the fact that Cass's face popped into his head. "I don't know about that."

Josie leaned back in her chair and took another sip of her coffee. "You'll see, Archer. You'll see."

"What about Roger?" The question popped out of his mouth before he realized it. He wished he could take it back the second the words were spoken, especially when he saw the look on her face. The smile melted into a quick grimace of pain. "Oh, Josie. Forget I asked, okay?"

"No." She waved him away. "It's fine." She straightened her back and forced a smile. "Roger was a wanderer and despite our love, he had to leave. It was what his spirit called to him. I have to accept that." She shook her head and stood. "No. I *have* accepted that."

She collected his now empty coffee mug and disappeared into her hut. He waited a beat before he got up, unsure whether he should follow her in or whether she'd come back at all. Before he could make any decision, a figure walking down the beach caught his attention.

Cass.

He glanced toward Josie's cottage and then back toward Cass, who was almost upon them. She didn't look angry anymore, but they still had a lot to talk through and it was probably best if they didn't have that discussion in front of others.

"Josie? Cass is coming and I—"

"Oh, good. Cass. I wanted to talk to her about something." The older woman appeared and before Archer could say anything else, Cass walked into the camp.

She smiled, a move that lit up her face. No, she was definitely not still angry. "Oh good, you two met."

"Not only did we meet, we had a lovely chat." Josie walked over and pulled Cass into a familiar hug. "He's perfect."

If she meant to whisper the last bit into Cass's ear, she sure didn't try to do it very quietly.

He watched Cass carefully for her reaction. Would she agree?

Cass pulled away from the embrace and looked directly at Archer. Her smile was small, but it was there. But it wasn't the look on her face that captivated him; it was her words when she said, "Yes. He is."

Chapter Eleven

SHE'D MEANT what she'd said. Archer was perfect. He was absolutely the perfect companion for her when it came to running the *Cassiopeia*, and the plans she had brewing.

He was perfect in other ways, too. But there was a time and place for all of those things, and she wasn't sure this was the time for any of them. Although, thinking of his perfect hands on her—*no*. She couldn't go there. Not now.

Cass focused her attention back on the other woman. "I'm glad to see you again, Josie."

"And I, you, dear. I've been thinking a lot about you. You've been in my dreams."

"Really?"

"You have." Josie took her hand and together they walked through the palms toward the water's edge. "I think we can thank destiny for putting you in my life. Roger's daughter. After all these years, there's a reason you're here, my dear."

She laughed. "Yeah, a boat with a big bill."

Josie gripped her hand and Cassie was spun to face the older woman. "No, Cass. There's a bigger reason. A much bigger one. That's how destiny and divine intervention works."

"Divine intervention?"

Cass turned to see Archer had joined them on the beach.

"Yes," Josie answered him. "I was just telling Cass there was a reason she was brought to my island after all these years. Not to mention brought into yours."

"Mine?"

"His?"

"Yes. This is not coincidence," Josie said. Cass tried not to laugh, and she almost did. But the look on Archer's face, and the way he so intently stared at her, stopped her.

"Maybe…" she said, desperate to change the subject to something a bit more tangible. "I was thinking about something that could benefit both of us."

"Having you in my life is the benefit, my dear."

Cass shook her head but forced a smile. The woman's spirituality was refreshing, but it also made it incredibly difficult to have a serious business discussion, which was exactly what she had hoped to do.

"Well, obviously," Cass said. "But besides that, I've been thinking now that I'm getting the charter business up and running again—with Archer's help, of course." She glanced at him and gave him her best smile, which he returned with only an eyebrow lift. She'd deal with him later. She turned back to Josie. It was safer to focus on her, at least until she knew where they stood. "Anyway, I had an idea that maybe could help you out, too."

It was an idea that came to Cass while she was cleaning and trying to get her mind off Archer. Josie hadn't said it in so many words, but it sure didn't seem to Cass that she had many paying guests; maybe they could incorporate a sailing charter holiday with an island escape. She told Josie her idea while Archer listened in silence. When she finished, Archer laughed.

"What's so funny?"

"Were you listening to our conversation?" he asked.

Confused, she looked to Josie, who grabbed her hand and squeezed. "It wasn't an accident that brought you to me, Cass. This was meant to be."

"So you think it's a good idea?" She looked between them, still not sure what Archer was talking about.

"I do." Josie released her hand and bent to pick up a shell. "I was just telling Archer how your father and I used to have a similar arrangement."

"You were?" She tipped her head at Archer, whose face was still impossible to read. "What a coincidence."

"Nothing in this world is a coincidence, my dear." Josie pressed the shell into Cass's hand—only it wasn't a shell: it was a stone in the shape of a heart. She squeezed her fingers around the smooth surface. "Take the two of you," Josie continued. "The two of you on the *Cassiopeia* together is far from an accident. You two were meant to be—"

"I don't know about that."

Archer didn't say anything either way, which frustrated her a little more. Cass didn't know what the two of them were meant to be, but she wasn't about to assume a damn thing. She'd be lucky if she could hang on to him as her chef after the little stunt she'd just pulled.

"Anyway, we should probably get going." It was safer for her to change the subject completely. "I think Archer and I have a few things to discuss and we really should get some work done. But maybe we can work out the details later?"

Josie patted her hand. "You two go *talk*, dear. I'll be here." She turned and walked in the opposite direction with a swish of skirts, leaving Cass and Archer alone.

"So…" She kicked her feet in the sand. "About earlier…"

Archer didn't say anything, just annoyingly, frustratingly stared at her with a cocky smirk on his face. And dammit if he didn't look gorgeous. She hated the way he stirred so many conflicting emotions in her. Yet she loved it at the same time.

She waited another beat and when he still didn't say anything, she cracked. "Okay, I'm sorry."

"You're sorry?" His words were slow and sexy. "For what?"

He certainly wasn't going to make it easy on her.

"Come on, Archer."

This time when he smiled, it reached his eyes and she could see the mischievous glint there. "Okay, I accept your apology."

"And?"

He tipped his head in question. "And…you want me to drive the dinghy back?"

"No!" Cass turned and walked as quickly as she could along the beach. If she could get back to the boat before him, he could swim back, the cocky bastard.

She heard Archer's laugh behind her but she didn't turn. Instead, Cass broke into a run. There was no way he was going to get back to the dinghy before her.

It only took her a second to realize Archer was right behind her, still laughing, and despite the adrenaline that flowed through her at the sense of competition, Cass started to laugh, too.

Only a few steps away from the rubber dinghy, Cass felt Archer's hand grab her arm, and before she knew what happened, he'd pulled her back and somehow the two of them were tumbling on the sand. His strong arms around her broke the fall. They rolled through the soft sand before they finally came to a rest.

Cass opened her eyes tentatively, unsure of what had just happened. Archer was beneath her and she stared directly down into his dark eyes.

"Well, Captain." His voice was playful, matching his sexy smile. "If you wanted to prove to me who was in charge, I can think of easier ways to do it."

"What?" She squirmed, but he held her tight. "You did this. It wasn't my—"

He pulled her head down to firmly meet his lips and shut her up with a kiss.

Archer couldn't think of a better way to make Cass stop talking. And by the feel of her body and the way it first tensed, but then relaxed and sunk into the kiss, there was a good chance that she agreed with him.

Sure, he was still upset with her for their fight earlier, but damn, there was something about her that he couldn't get enough of. It had been a month since he'd had her. A month since he'd tasted her sweet lips on his. A month of pure torture. He was done. A man could only take so much.

The kiss was over way too soon, and Cass pulled back, at least as much as his tight grip on her waist would allow. "Archer," she began. "I don't…I mean, I don't think…"

"Good." He slid his hand down her bare back and gently cupped the swell of her ass. "Don't think." He kissed her again, harder this time. She groaned in response, but kissed him back.

Archer easily rolled over, putting her beneath him, never breaking the kiss. He braced his body weight with one hand and used the other to slide down her smooth skin, dusted with the fine sand. He found the heat between her legs, and slipped one finger under the scrap of swimsuit she wore. Just as he'd expected, she was wet and ready for him. She could try to pretend she didn't want him just as bad as he wanted her, but she wasn't fooling anyone.

"Archer." Her hands were between them, and she pushed on his chest. "We can't do this—"

Somehow, he controlled his voice. "Cass. We can."

"No, really." She laughed, and pointed over his shoulder. "We can't. Not here."

Archer looked over his shoulder, although he was already

fairly sure what he'd see. Sure enough, a small dinghy loaded down with snorkelers was headed toward them. He groaned and rolled to the side, sitting up next to her.

"I didn't think it would be a good idea to put on a show for everyone." Cass laughed and adjusted her bikini before she leaned back on her arms next to him. "I mean, there might be kids on board." She laughed again and Archer thought it might be one of the sexiest sounds he'd ever heard—besides making her scream out in pleasure, of course.

"You think this is pretty funny, don't you?" He crossed his arms over his knees and willed his hard-on to go away. He hadn't planned on it, but maybe he should swim back to the boat to give his body time to cool down. It was as good of an idea as any. "Right," he said, his decision made. "I'll meet you back there."

"You don't want a ride?"

"I think it's best if I swim." And it was, too. There was no way he'd be able to sit next to her in the tiny boat while her breasts jiggled with every wave. Not in the current state he was in, anyway. He needed to cool off. He got to his feet and tried to adjust his shorts as best he could.

"Okay, but Archer?"

He glanced at her, still sitting on the sand.

"When you get back, we need to talk."

He blinked in acknowledgment, turned and ran into the water, arcing into a perfect dive before he broke into smooth, strong strokes. They needed to do something, but as far as Archer was concerned, it would have very little to do with talking.

He got back to the *Cassiopeia* before she returned with the dinghy, so he was there to catch the rope, tie it off and give her a hand up onto the deck. The exercise had tempered his desire slightly, but the moment he felt her soft hand in his, all the blood rushed south again. He didn't let go, but led her into the cockpit to sit on a deck cushion.

"You wanted to talk."

He'd had enough time to think about what exactly Cass was going to want to discuss and he'd prepared the answers he knew she'd want to hear.

She glanced down at his hand still grasping hers, but didn't comment on it. "Yes," she said slowly. She looked him in the eyes. "I wanted to apologize for what I said earlier. You aren't just a hired hand, Archer. You have to know that."

He nodded.

"You're so much more," she continued. "I couldn't be doing this without you and I didn't mean those things I said."

"Any of them?"

She hesitated and finally pulled her hand out of his and back into her lap. "Well, I did mean what I said about listening to me."

He sat up with interest. This was the part of the conversation he'd prepared for. He knew her well enough by now to know exactly how she'd reacted to their power struggle.

She stood, making herself taller than him. "I'm the captain of this ship, Archer. You need to understand that."

He nodded and kept his face carefully neutral.

"When I give you an order, I expect you to follow it." She took a deep breath to fortify herself. "If you hesitate, even for a second, that could mean the difference between life and death, and if we have guests aboard—well, I don't think I need to tell you how dangerous that could be."

"No ma'am."

She took a second take at him but still Archer kept a neutral face. "When it comes to the *Cassiopeia*, I'm in charge. I make the rules here, Archer." He nodded and she continued.

"If you have a problem with a woman being in charge, then perhaps this isn't the place for you." She let out her breath and looked hard at him. It took everything he had not to smile. She'd never looked sexier than that moment. Her entire body blushed, even through the golden tan of her skin, and her breasts heaved with the deep breaths she took. "Do you have a problem with anything I said, Archer?"

He shook his head. "No ma'am."

"Do you understand everything I'm telling you?"

Archer stood and put his body only inches from hers. "Let me see," he said, his voice low. He gazed deep into her eyes, daring her to look away. "You're saying that if you tell me what to do, I must do it."

"Yes." Her voice shook under his scrutiny.

He used one finger to trace a line from her collarbone, slowly down between her breasts. "And it could be dangerous if I disobey one of your commands," he repeated. His finger slid just inside the fabric of her bikini top to graze the swell of first one breast, and then the other; each nipple peaked into hard nubs.

She nodded, the movement slight. "That's right."

His finger continued the journey, moving down her belly, his eyes never breaking contact with hers. He could see the desire she held there, barely in check. "You're also saying that on the *Cassiopeia*, you're in charge." Her body shuddered as his finger reached the edge of her bottoms and moved around her hip to tease the strings that held the tiny bit of material in place. "You were also saying," he continued his slow torture, his fingers abandoning the knot and sliding inside the fabric, to her heated core. "That if I have a problem with a woman being in charge…" He slicked his finger through the moisture pooled there, up to the tiny bundle of nerves, where he pressed just enough for Cass to let out a moan. She quickly swallowed the noise, but the heat in her eyes gave her away. To punctuate his point, Archer slid first one finger inside her, and then another. "Perhaps this isn't the boat for me," he finished, repeating her words while his fingers slid in and out of her and his thumb put steady pressure on her clit.

He was suitably impressed that she still hadn't looked away from him. Her eyes were dilated with passion so completely, they were almost black, but still they held his. "Did I miss anything?" He subtly increased the pace of his fingers.

Cass's body trembled around his fingers, and he knew she was close to a climax, but still she wouldn't give in to it. Damn, this woman was incredible. Just watching her was making him harder than he thought possible. If she didn't give in soon, he might explode from the intensity of it.

She shook her head slightly. "No." She managed the word.

With his free hand, he cupped one breast, sliding the fabric down and trapping her peaked nipple between his thumb and forefinger. "So, just to be clear." He squeezed her nipple; his other hand maintained its relentless rhythm inside her. "When it comes to the *Cassiopeia*, you're in charge?"

"Yes." The word was a moan. Her body constricted hard on his fingers, stilling his actions and she finally closed her eyes, as her orgasm crashed through her. "Oh God, Archer. Yes."

He let her ride out her orgasm before he kissed her hard.

Archer once again looked in her eyes when he said, "As long as we're clear about who's in charge."

Chapter Twelve

GIVE HIM A REASON TO STAY.

Angie's words replayed over and over in her head for the rest of the afternoon. What had happened between her and Archer on the deck of the boat had been…well, it had been fantastic. But had it been smart? Probably not. No. Definitely not.

She needed to maintain control of the boat if she was going to make everything work out and what Archer had done…well, it was far from staying in control.

When it was over, she'd tried to pull herself together as much as possible. It had taken all of her self-control, and she didn't have a whole lot left at that moment, to walk away from him then. Having sex with him would just make everything even more complicated, not that what he'd done hadn't just complicated things. It had. A lot.

Cass's head spun with it all. She'd somehow managed to avoid him for a while by working on the computer, answering a few responses to their ads, but now that they were both lounging in the cockpit in an effort to get out of the heat of the day, she couldn't ignore the fact that he sat only a few feet away from her. Shirtless. His legs propped up on the bench next to her as if the space wasn't enough to contain him. She'd been peeking at him over the top of the book she was pretending to read, trying to see whether he was watching her. He wasn't. He seemed intent on the cookbook he was browsing through.

Undetected, she let her eyes travel up his legs, across his shorts, only lingering for a second at the bulge there before moving up his rock hard abs and chest. He hadn't shaved in a few days—the resulting scruff, sexy. His mouth, so kissable; his eyes…staring directly at her.

Damn.

She snapped her gaze back to the book, totally aware of the heat in her body. No doubt she'd turned a totally unattractive shade of red that had nothing to do with a sunburn.

She needed to get off the boat and away from him.

She lifted her head from the book, hoping he wasn't still watching her. "I'm going to go…"

Where?

Archer looked up, a question in his eyes along with something else. Humor?

"I'm going to go snorkeling," she announced, making a split-second decision. "There's a reef I want to check out to see if it's easy enough to anchor the dinghy and hopefully the snorkeling will be good for the guests. I thought I should go and see for myself before we put it on the list of—"

"Sounds good. I'll go with you."

Wait. What?

Cass shook her head. "You don't have to. I know you're busy menu planning and that's important, too. It'll only take a few minutes and I'll be back before you know it." She was aware she was rambling but she couldn't seem to stop herself. Needing distance, she moved to the back deck and the aft hatch where they kept the snorkel gear. She bent to open the hatch, but Archer was right there next to her and lifted it before she could.

"I've got it."

"I'm sure you do. I was just trying to help."

"Well, I don't need it." She instantly hated herself for sounding like a bitch. He was just trying to be nice. "I'm sorry," she tried again. "Thanks."

Cass leaned into the hold and pulled out the mesh bag that contained her mask, snorkel, and fins. Before she could close the hatch, Archer leaned in and grabbed his bag.

"I told you, I've got this. You don't really need to—"

"I want to." He looked at her in that way that made her shiver all over despite the heat of the sun, and she couldn't say no. "Okay." She nodded. "Let's get going."

They locked the door that led to the main salon, but left the boat unattended. There was no real need for security in the San Blas Islands. It was a very safe island chain. There usually weren't many people around, and the ones who were, were friendly sailors like themselves, or the even friendlier Kuna Indians who still inhabited the islands.

The snorkeling site wasn't far from the anchorage. Cass drove the dinghy around the tip of the small island, navigated a shallow area of reef, and when they found a sandy bottom, Archer dropped the small anchor. They didn't speak until they'd donned their fins and masks.

"I'm going to head that way around the reef so I can circle back toward the boat," Cass told him. She didn't expect him to come with her, but somehow she knew he probably would.

"Sounds good."

Cass didn't bother to protest. Instead, she popped her snorkel in her mouth and flipped backward into the ocean, kicked hard and blew the water from her snorkel as she swam away from the boat. The water beneath her was alive with an entire underwater world that burst with color and movement.

Cass sucked in a breath before she remembered to breathe slowly and evenly as she slowed her pace and took in everything around her.

It was amazing. Schools of yellow and blue fish darted in swirls through the coral and a stingray floated by in big, broad strokes. She felt Archer next to her before she saw him and not only did it not bother her, it surprised her how pleased she was to share the moment with him. Together, they kicked gently through the water, over and around the reef, and watched the secret world beneath them. With her head under the water, it was serene and peaceful and strangely, the time allowed Cass to put all her muddled thoughts and feelings aside and focus on nothing but the fish below them.

By the time they circled around back to the boat, Cass had completely forgotten about the tension between them. They climbed into the dinghy and removed their gear, the entire time talking about what they'd just seen.

"That was the most beautiful reef I've ever snorkeled on."

Archer nodded and took her fins from her while Cass removed her mask. "Me too. It was amazing. Did you see that barracuda that escorted us through the back half of the reef?"

"No!" Cass looked up from shaking out her hair. "Really? And you didn't say anything?" Barracudas weren't likely to attack humans, but their quiet, ominous presence was intimidating nonetheless. It was probably best that she hadn't noticed. There was no doubt it would have freaked her out.

Archer must have seen the look on her face. He reached across the boat and grabbed her hand. "I wouldn't have let anything happen to you."

She looked in his eyes, held by the intensity there. Without a doubt, she knew it was true. Archer would have protected her if anything threatened her. Not that it would have been the barracuda, but…she shook her head and looked away before he could pull her in. "What about the angel fish? Did you see them? With the yellow and the—"

Cass broke away mid-sentence because Archer was still looking at her. She refused to fall into the trap that was quickly becoming Archer Wolfe and the way he made her feel.

"The parrot fish were my favorite." She changed the subject and looked away, busying herself getting the engine ready to fire up. "They're probably my favorite. So many pretty colors and the way they look so gentle. What are your favorites?"

He didn't answer, so Cass turned around again. Water droplets glistened on his hard, tanned chest; her body responded the way it always did at his nearness and it took a lot of willpower to resist reaching out and wiping the water from him. "Archer?" Cass swallowed hard. "What's your favorite?"

"You."

Heat shot through her at one simple word. But it wasn't just the word. It was the way he looked at her with his dark eyes, hungry for her, promises of the pleasure they could have together. It was too much. "Archer, stop. Please."

"You weren't telling me to stop earlier."

She shook her head, trying in vain to keep the memory of what they'd shared earlier from her head. "That was different."

"How?"

"It shouldn't have happened."

"I don't think that's true."

Turning, Cass pulled hard on the starter cord and the engine roared to life. "Lift the anchor please."

For a moment, Archer looked as if he was going to object. Although the urge to reach across the small boat and kiss him while his hands traveled the length of her was tempting—oh, so tempting—she couldn't let it happen. As it was, she could barely concentrate with him around. If she gave in to him again, it would be disastrous. In more ways than one. Ultimately he was going to leave. All the men in her life did, and Archer had already told her that was his plan. It would be hard enough to lose him; she didn't need to make it any harder by letting him into her bed and her heart.

Saving her from asking again, Archer lifted the anchor and secured it in the front of the boat as Cass slowly navigated her way out of the reef. As soon as they hit open water, she opened up the throttle, drowning out any more opportunity to talk, and they cruised back toward the *Cassiopeia*.

It didn't matter what Angie said. Even if she gave him *a reason to stay*, there was no guarantee that he would. Look at her father. He'd left her and her mother. And maybe he hadn't loved Cass's mother, but he should have loved his daughter. A *traveling spirit*, Josie called it. But he'd left Josie, too. And Cass hadn't missed the pain in the older woman's eyes as she spoke of him. It might have been true love that they'd shared, but it hadn't kept him from leaving her, too.

Archer was no longer looking at her, a fact Cass was thankful for as she could watch him undetected. Yes, he was built like some sort of outdoorsy god, but the more time she spent with him, the experiences they shared together, it was becoming a lot more than lust that she felt for him. And that's what scared the hell out of her.

Snorkeling with Cass had been perfect. She'd been so relaxed and at ease in the water, pointing out the various fish and interesting things she'd seen; it had been good to see her let her guard down around him long enough to experience that together. For a moment, Archer thought maybe it meant she was going to let her guard down completely, but the second they were back in the dinghy, the walls were back up and she pushed him away again.

He couldn't figure out why she was fighting it. It didn't make any sense, and he was getting tired of playing along with whatever game she had going on. It was growing old—quickly.

They raced toward the *Cassiopeia.* Any chance at all of conversation was lost due to the noise of the engine, which was fine by him because he was running out of things he could say to her. He'd tried to keep it professional; Lord knew he'd tried. It was time to get to the bottom of things with her.

Cass pulled the little boat up along the stern of the *Cassiopeia* and Archer jumped out with the line. He tied it securely and held his arm out for Cass to take. She shoved the snorkel equipment at him instead and scrambled aboard next to him. They stood inches apart on the small platform over the water. Without taking his eyes off her, he lifted the snorkel equipment to safety and once his hands were free, he took her face in his grip and held her.

Before she could object, he kissed her thoroughly, leaving no question as to what his intentions were with her. She didn't push him overboard, which was a good sign, but when he finally pulled back, reluctantly leaving her lips, she wasn't smiling.

"Archer, I—"

"Cass, this thing between us, it's—"

"Not happening."

"Why are you fighting it?"

"I'm not." She looked down so he couldn't see her eyes. "There's nothing between us, Archer."

She was lying. There was no doubt about it, but despite the fact that he knew it, her words felt like a shot in the gut.

"Look at me." She looked up, but her eyes didn't quite meet his. Instead, they were fixed on some point just over his shoulder. "Now tell me there's nothing between us. Tell me you don't feel the same way I do. Tell me that your body doesn't—"

"Nothing." She shook her head slightly. "We're just friends, Archer. We work together and that's it."

"Bullshit."

She looked at him then, her eyes wide with surprise at his vehemence.

"What about earlier?" He needed her to admit to the lie. He needed her to admit that when he'd been kissing her, touching her, making her moan in pleasure, there had definitely been something there between them. They both knew it; he just needed to hear it from her. "You weren't faking one second of that, Cass. You know there's something between us and—"

"That shouldn't have happened. I'm sorry." Again, her voice was practiced, almost clinical. "Just friends, okay?"

He tried to take a step backward, but was quickly reminded of their location on the tiny transom at the back of the boat. There was nowhere to go. He searched her eyes for some sliver of the truth that had to be lurking there. The only thing he saw reflected in her beautiful eyes was a pleading look of what was almost desperation. Damn. He couldn't figure this woman out for the life of him, but if she thought she didn't need him, he'd play along for now. But just long enough to prove to her how wrong she was.

He swallowed hard and gave her his most charming smile. "Just friends. Sounds good." Archer turned and climbed up the short ladder to the deck of the boat without waiting for her response.

She didn't come up right away, even more proof that the only one she was fooling with this *just friends* business was herself. And even then, she wasn't doing a very good job of that.

Archer's stomach growled to remind him he still hadn't

eaten anything. Food was a good distraction for him, so he might as well go try out a new recipe for his *boss* to test over lunch. Before he could unlock the companionway, a small wooden box with a roughly engraved word, "Dad" on the lid, caught his eye. A napkin stuck out from underneath it. He pulled the napkin free to see it was a note.

Cass,

I thought this might look familiar. Roger left it on the island with me. I thought you should have it.

~Josie

Archer flipped the box over in his hand. It was locked, but didn't seem to have any place to put a key to open it.

"Cass," he turned and called to her. She'd made her way up on deck and was rinsing their snorkel gear with fresh water. She looked over at him at the mention of her name. "I think Josie must have come by for a visit while we were gone."

"Really?"

He held up the box. "She left this."

She dropped the hose and made her way to where Archer sat, and took the box from his hands. By the look on her face, it was clear that she knew how to open it. But she didn't. She stared silently at the box for a minute before she handed it back to Archer.

"It's just an old box."

"But it belonged to your dad. And…did you give it to him?" The answer was obvious, but he needed to hear her say it.

"It doesn't matter." She stood and looked away. "Can you put it below deck? I'm going to get us ready to go."

"Go where? I thought we were going to stay out in the islands for a few days."

Cass wouldn't look at him. "I forgot it was Joe's birthday tomorrow, and there's going to be a party on the dock. We should leave at dawn if we want to make it back in time."

"Joe? Really?" The dockmaster was definitely not one of his favorite people, and Archer could have thought of a few dozen things he'd rather do than go celebrate the man's birthday. Particularly when Joe clearly felt the same way about Archer.

"Yes, Joe," Cass said. "He's been good to me, and I think that getting back to land would be a good thing right now."

She didn't add that she was looking for a way to escape Archer. She didn't have to.

"What about Josie?"

"What about her?"

"Are you going to talk to her about the box?"

"It's just a box, Archer." The sad look on her face gave away more than her words ever could. "It doesn't mean anything."

He watched her go to the bow of the boat and fiddle with the lines, before he headed below deck. Watching her, and the demons she was clearly struggling with, Archer would have bet everything he owned that Cass was trying desperately to run away from the lies she continued to tell herself. The problem with living on a boat was there was nowhere to run.

Chapter Thirteen

BY THE TIME Cass and Archer docked the *Cassiopeia* in the slip at Shelter Bay Marina, Cass wasn't any further ahead in forgetting about the box that had been sitting on the nav station next to the computer where Archer had put it the day before. She knew she should look at it. She knew there was a reason Josie had given it to her, but she couldn't bring herself to even look at it. She wasn't ready.

"I plugged us into shore power." Archer climbed aboard and wiped his hands on his shorts. "I'll connect the water in a minute. I'm just going to—hey." He sat next to her. "Are you okay? You look a little worried. Is everything okay?"

Cass forced a smile to her face. The one thing the appearance of the box had done was distract her from the more immediate problem of Archer and the whole *just friends* thing that had spewed out of her mouth the day before. Of course, with him sitting so close she could smell him—a combination of pure manliness with a touch of something citrusy—the boundaries she'd placed between them suddenly seemed like a bad idea. A really bad idea.

"I'm fine," she lied. "I was actually just thinking that I

didn't get Joe a present. How can we go to a party without a present?"

Archer laughed and pushed up to stand. "Well, I don't know about you, but I'm pretty sure the only present he'd want from me was my absence at his party. We're not exactly the best of friends."

"What happened between you guys anyway?" Cass was glad for the distraction, even for a minute.

"Let's just say, I didn't realize Heather was his wife. And if you ask me, I don't think I'm the only one who's made that mistake. She seemed pretty happy to—"

"Whoa. That's all the detail I need, thank you very much. I know we said we were friends and all, but I don't need to know the details of your conquests." Especially considering the idea of Archer with anyone besides her made her positively green with jealousy. She may have said they were just friends, and that's all they could ever be, but not only had she opened her mouth before she thought it through, she also couldn't seem to convince herself.

"Look, I really didn't realize—"

"It doesn't matter." She shook her head, trying to appear casual when she felt anything but.

"Besides, friends talk." Archer crossed his arms over his broad chest. "And you were the one who said we were just friends. I didn't."

"Archer."

"I just wanted to be clear. It was your idea, not mine."

She almost took it back. She almost told him she was being an idiot and she didn't mean any of it. Instead, she said, "I know. And I still mean it. Just friends."

"So you won't mind if I meet a girl tonight?"

She shook her head. "Of course not."

"And you won't mind if we hit it off and I kiss her?"

Her gut twisted into a hard knot. "No. Why should I?"

"And if I don't come back to the boat tonight and spend the night in her room, that'll be okay with you?"

She shrugged despite the lump in her throat that made it hard to swallow. "Yup."

"It won't bother you one bit to think of me kissing her neck, my hands sliding down to her breasts, cupping them, while I—"

"No." She jumped up and flipped her hair off her shoulder. "It won't bother me at all." The lie tasted bitter on her lips. "What you do on your own time is your business." She couldn't look at him. "We should get going. I need a drink."

She pushed past him, trying to ignore the shocks of desire that raced through her when her arm brushed his. With her shoes in one hand, she climbed down to the dock below. Archer stood on deck and watched her.

"Are you coming?"

He looked at her and opened his mouth as if to say something before he changed his mind and nodded. "Right behind you, boss. You're not the only one who could use a drink."

She was definitely trying to drive him crazy. Archer had thought for sure he could break her with that talk about hooking up with another woman, and he almost had. He wasn't stupid; he could see the way she reacted to his words: the way her body stiffened, the way she couldn't look him in the eye. He knew he was getting to her. Damn stubborn woman. She wouldn't admit it, but she wanted him just as badly as he wanted her. Maybe more.

There was no way she'd admit it, though, and that made him crazy. Maybe what he really did need was a distraction. He hadn't meant what he'd said to Cass about hooking up with anyone else. But maybe it would help. Something to get his mind off her. To let off a little steam.

It wasn't a bad idea. And by the looks around the Dockside Inn, and the crowd gathered for Joe's birthday, there were definitely some options. Not a bad idea at all.

Leaving Cass to talk with some of the regular cruisers who always seemed to be on the dock, Archer went directly to the bar to get himself a beer and with any luck, the name of the hot brunette sitting there. Not that she even came close to being as gorgeous as Cass, but with that option firmly off the table, maybe a little female attention from someone besides the one woman he really wanted would be exactly what he needed. Even if it wasn't, he had nothing to lose. Not according to Cass, anyway.

"Can I buy you a drink?" He didn't even bother with a line. The way the woman looked at him told him he didn't need to bother. She'd be his if he wanted her to be.

"I'd love a margarita," the woman purred.

A margarita? Seriously?

She wasn't an unattractive woman. Far from it, especially if you liked oversized breasts popping out of a too-small top. But he didn't. He glanced across the room at Cass, whose simple sundress showcased her well-proportioned curves perfectly. No, he definitely didn't want what this woman was putting out there. What he wanted stood across the room from him, looking perfectly luscious and ball-breakingly beautiful. She glanced over and caught him watching her.

He knew it was childish, and totally counterproductive to what he wanted to achieve with Cass, but he couldn't stop himself. He turned, flashed his best panty-melting smile and leaned into the woman who stood in front of him. "I'm Archer."

"Brooke."

"Well, let's get you that drink, shall we, Brooke?"

He ordered her drink and a beer for himself, and when he looked over again to where Cass had been, she was gone. His heart dropped a little and he felt like an ass. He looked back to…the woman whose name temporarily eluded him…Brooke. He shook his head, doing his best to focus on her. She leaned enticingly across the bar toward him, her breasts busting out of her dress. She was a sure thing and she was beautiful. There should be no problem.

Except there was.

He knew it was a bad idea. An idea he really didn't want any part of, but…

"So, what brings you to Panama, Brooke?"

Archer spent the next few minutes trying to make conversation with the woman who really wasn't very interesting at all. She was there visiting with her sister and…whatever else she'd said, Archer hadn't remembered. His mind was across the room with Cass, whom he'd spotted again talking to a group of cruisers, only a few who he recognized. She laughed at something someone had said. Her head thrown back in laughter, a smile lit up her beautiful face.

"So what do you think?" Brooke grabbed Archer's arm and he turned back to focus on her, totally aware he hadn't heard a word she'd just asked.

"I think…" He racked his brain for some clue as to what she was talking about. A familiar face popped into his line of sight. "I think I'll be right back. I just spotted someone I need to say hello to. Will you excuse me?"

He didn't wait for an answer before he removed her hand from his arm and slipped sideways past her. Archer made a beeline for Maria, who held a large tray over her head despite her ballooning pregnant stomach.

"Maria. Let me get that for you." He took the tray from her and set it down on a nearby table. "You shouldn't be lifting that much. How are you?"

She smiled but moved to pick up the tray again. "I'm fine, Arch. Besides, I have to work."

"You must be due any day." He tried to do some quick math in his head from the last time he'd spoken to her. The young waitress had to be at least nine months pregnant. "Aren't you—"

Maria patted her belly. "Three days overdue already. Little one doesn't seem to want to go anywhere. But I do have to work." It was well known at the marina that Maria was going to be a single mom. She'd never been seen with a boyfriend, and if anyone knew who the father was, they weren't saying. And Maria had been equally tight-lipped about it. It wasn't any of Archer's business anyway. But Maria was his friend, and if no one else was there to take care of her, he would.

"If it's Joe you're worried about, don't. I'll take care of him if he gives you any trouble for taking a break." As if he needed more reasons for the dockmaster to dislike him. "You shouldn't be working right now. Sit down. Don't you have a break coming?"

To his surprise, Maria did sit. She couldn't have been too scared for her job and really, it was no secret that Maria had Joe wrapped around her little finger. For whatever reason, he would do anything for that girl, and everyone knew it. There was no way he'd get upset with her for sitting down, at least, not really.

"Okay, I'll take a break," Maria said. "I didn't realize how—oh." Her hands flew to her belly.

"Are you okay?"

She nodded but didn't speak.

"Maria?"

He didn't have a ton of experience with this type of thing, but he also wasn't an idiot. Archer glanced around to look for someone who could help. His gaze locked on Joe, who was already watching them. His eyes flicked to Archer, and in that moment Archer could see the concern in Joe's eyes. And something else: was it love? Not that Archer would know the look of love if he saw it. Besides, it didn't matter. What mattered was the woman in front of him, who was clearly in labor. Or if she wasn't, she was experiencing some other pregnancy-related issue that Archer was clearly not equipped to deal with.

"Arch? I think...I think..." She grabbed the collar of his t-shirt and pulled him down to her so he'd be able to hear what she was trying to say. "I might be..."

"I got it, Maria. Don't worry." He stood, carefully prying her fingers from his shirt. He had no idea what he was going to do, but as it turned out, the second he looked up again and his eyes met Joe's, he didn't have to do anything else.

Joe must have seen the look of panic on Archer's face and understood exactly what was going on. He nodded, and made his way quickly across the crowded room to Maria's side.

"Is she...?"

Archer nodded. "I think so. I mean, it's not like I know much about these things but it sure seems like..."

His words were lost as Joe knelt next to Maria and took her hand in his. "It's okay, baby. I got you."

Baby? Archer raised an eyebrow and glanced quickly between them. It wasn't the time or place for questions, but all of a sudden a lot of things made sense. He took a quick scan of the room for Joe's wife, Heather. The last thing they needed right now was a jealous wife, although that would explain a lot of things, too.

"I'm going to take her to the hospital." Joe stood. "If anyone asks, tell them...heck, tell them whatever you want. I'm going to be a father."

Archer watched in some sort of shock as Joe put a tender arm around Maria's shoulders and with the young woman leaning on him for support, slowly made his way to the door. By this time, they'd attracted a bit of attention from some of the guests, but from the looks of it, Joe didn't care one bit. He was totally focused on Maria and the baby that was so clearly his.

Everything made sense now. No. Archer scratched his head and glanced around for Joe's wife, who still hadn't been spotted; it really didn't make any sense at all. But at least it wasn't his problem to figure out.

He needed another drink.

One look toward the bar and Brooke, whom he'd left standing there, and Archer decided it might be safer to try his luck getting a drink with a waitress. He didn't need Brooke thinking something was going to happen between them. Sure, she was nice enough and all, but she wasn't Cass. Not even close.

She'd gone outside to escape the crowds, and the air conditioning. It was funny how only a month ago, the Panamanian heat had been oppressive and stifling and now, Cass preferred it to the air conditioning that was there for the comfort of the tourists.

The air was heavy with the scent of the orchids that grew on all the palm trees and the distant smell of diesel from the fuel docks. It was a comforting scent that Cass had quickly come to associate with Shelter Bay Marina, and the closest thing she'd had to a home in years. At least a home where people cared about her and not just a closet apartment where she got her mail and paid her bills.

Strange as it was, the marina and its random mix of people, along with the *Cassiopeia* with its cramped spaces, just might be the best place she'd lived since she was a child in Seattle, looking forward to weekend sails with her dad. Only this time, her comfort had nothing to do with her father.

Despite the fact that he was the reason she was there, and she was living on his boat...nothing. And she'd keep telling herself that, too. Just like she'd had to tell almost everyone in the Dockside Inn, who'd known her dad before his disappearance. She was different. Panama was different. So far, everyone had accepted her with open arms. Everyone, except one.

Her eye caught a sliver of movement in the dark of the patio. Over by the pool, someone sat and watched. It wasn't unusual for the parties to spill outside, but generally, people didn't have a habit of hiding. Unless...

Cass moved quietly over to the pool area, expecting to catch Archer, more than likely with that brunette he'd been with at the bar. Not that it bothered her, at least not that she'd admit to him. In fact, it would be good if he moved on with someone else. Even if it made her stomach sick to think of him with another woman, his hands on...no. She wouldn't even think about it, but she did need to see for herself. It was a twisted logic, one she knew she'd regret, but she kept moving anyway.

Only it wasn't Archer in the shadows; it was a much larger figure and he was smoking, his back to her.

"Samson?"

Figures. It would be the last person she wanted to talk to. At least, she was the last person he would likely want to talk to. Ever since he'd discovered that Roger Cutler was her father, Samson had kept his distance. He'd barely said two words to her, and she got the distinct impression, the few times he'd been forced to speak to her, he'd rather not.

"Cass. What are you—"

Whether he wanted to talk to her or not, she needed to ask him a few questions, and trapped in the corner of the pool deck, he was her captive audience.

"Just the man I wanted to talk to." She pulled up a chaise lounge chair, effectively blocking whatever exit he might have had that didn't involve jumping in the pool and swimming for it.

"Cass, I really—"

"I'm sure you're a very busy man, Samson, with a boat to scrub and lines to untangle, but surely you can give me a few minutes of your time?" She flashed him what she hoped was her most disarming smile. "We haven't really had a chance to know each other. I was hoping we could talk."

The man took a deep drag on his cigarette and exhaled long and slow before he answered.

"I'm not sure I have much to say to you, Cass. I didn't know your father."

"What makes you think I want to talk about him?" The blatant lie bristled her, but she wouldn't let him see it. Besides, she had a very hard time believing he didn't know anything. A very hard time. "I just wanted to get to know you, Samson."

She was full of shit, and they both knew it. So far, her charm and Archer's introductions had helped her meet most of the regular cruisers at Shelter Bay, and everyone had been more than welcoming and friendly. All except for Samson.

"Not much to know." He wouldn't meet her eyes.

"Tell me about your charter bus—"

"You'd like that, wouldn't you?" With a speed Cass wasn't sure he was capable of, Samson sat up with a lurch and ground his cigarette out on the pool deck.

"I don't know what—"

"You think I don't know that you and that Canadian mountain man are starting up a charter business to take all my customers away? Word travels fast, young lady. And if you think for one minute that I didn't catch wind that you were on the *Seaduction* for a free ride to learn everything you could about how to run a charter right, just so you could swoop in and steal my business, think again. I've heard all about it."

Cass sat back as if she'd been slapped. What the hell was

he talking about? She had no interest in stealing his business. The only thing Cass cared about was paying her debt and keeping her boat. That was it. She hadn't given any thought to stealing Samson's business.

Maybe that was the problem?

"Samson." She tried to meet his eye but he wouldn't look at her. "That's not what I'm doing."

"The hell it's not." He puffed up his barrel chest and glared at her. Even in the dark, he was an intimidating man and Cass reflexively scooted back on her chair. "That's exactly what you're doing. Not only are you setting up another sailing vacation business in an already small market, you're partnering up with that hippy woman on the island, aren't you?"

"Josie?"

She wasn't sure how Samson had heard about their plans, and although they weren't secret, the idea that somehow it had gotten back to the other sailor bothered her.

"Of course, Josie." Samson stood and glanced around, clearly looking for a way out. "Figures, you'd team up with her. I suppose you have some sort of surf-and-sand package figured out."

They did, but it didn't seem like the right time to mention it.

"Samson, sit down. Please." She stood so she'd be at slightly less of a disadvantage. In an effort to calm him, she held out her hands, but his sneer only grew deeper and more sinister. He really was pissed, and there was nothing she could do about it.

"You're a sneaky, conniving bitch without any regard for anyone else."

Again, Cass felt as if she'd been slapped. She wasn't any of those things. What she was doing wasn't about harming anyone else—it was...her thoughts were distracted by what he said next. Words that almost took her to her knees. "The apple doesn't fall from the tree, does it? You're just like your two-timing, back-stabbing asshole of a father."

She stumbled and took a few steps back, which gave Samson the escape he sought. He was almost off the pool deck when Cass's brain caught up with what his words meant and it was long past time she called him on it. "I thought you said you didn't know my father."

She didn't think he would, but Samson froze and turned around. The smirk on his face told Cass exactly how he'd felt about her dad. Still, she needed to know what Samson knew. It might give her a lead, a clue, anything that could tell her what happened to him. A man didn't just disappear, leaving everything behind, if he was okay. Despite what Josie said and what Cass agreed with, Roger didn't have a *traveling spirit*, not one that would lead him to wander away from everything and disappear. Not completely. She held her breath as she waited for what Samson would say.

The distance between them only made the large man look more intimidating, but when he opened his mouth, all he said was, "Oh yeah. I knew him alright," before he turned around and walked away.

She wanted to call after him and make him come back to tell her what she needed to know, but she hadn't the strength. Instead, she collapsed back into the chaise chair and dropped her head in her hands.

For the first time since she'd arrived in Panama, Cass was alone. Even before she'd met anyone in Shelter Bay, she'd had the benefit of the unknown. Now, with her father presumed dead somewhere, Josie on an island miles away, a room full of people who were relative strangers, and the only man she really did want by her side pushed into the arms of some willing bimbo, Cass was truly alone.

The release of the emotion she'd been holding in for the

last sixteen years took her off guard, and the tears slipped freely down her cheeks.

She sat by the pool and cried, exhausting the build-up of tears until finally she laid back on the chaise and listened to the party only a few feet away. Every once in a while, a group would spill out onto the patio, laughing and talking, making plans to get together again soon, or even later that night.

Cass listened undetected and felt strangely detached from the happenings. Until she heard a familiar voice. A voice that, despite her best efforts, made her stomach flip.

Archer.

"It's been a great night."

And then, a woman. "It doesn't have to end."

Her voice was low and throaty, and there was no mistaking her intention.

In the silence that followed, Cass was tempted to sit up on her knees and peek over the low fence that surrounded the pool to see who Archer was talking to, and why they were no longer talking.

But she couldn't do that. She'd be seen for sure and after the big lecture she'd given Archer about just being friends...no. There was no way she could move. She'd have to sit there and wait. And hope they didn't move toward her. She shuddered. There was no way she could sit silently by and wait for that to happen.

"That was nice." Archer's voice again, followed by a female giggle.

Cass wanted to gag. Seriously? What self-respecting woman giggled after what was no doubt a kiss? From Archer, nonetheless. If she wasn't currently eavesdropping on the situation, she'd go smack the woman upside the head.

But she wouldn't. Because she didn't care. Archer could see whoever he wanted. Kiss whomever, and...she settled back in the chair and tried not to listen.

The girl was talking again. “You should see what else I can do.” Another hair-raising giggle that made Cass want to scream.

“I have an early morning tomorrow,” Archer said, and Cass wanted to cheer. “I think I should—”

A silence again. Well, not really a silence. More of the tell-tale lip smacking and low groans that tended to accompany a kiss from Archer. For at least the tenth time, Cass tried to convince herself she didn’t care.

“Come with me,” the girl said. “I want to show you something.”

If Archer protested, Cass didn’t hear it. There was nothing but silence after that, except for the muted strains of music that escaped the Dockside Inn, where clearly the party was only firing up, instead of dying down for the night.

She bit her bottom lip and slid farther down in the chaise. She would not cry. Even if she hadn’t just exhausted almost half a lifetime of tears, she refused to cry over a man.

It wasn’t worth it.

And that’s what she was going to keep telling herself. At least until she believed it.

Chapter Fourteen

BY THE TIME he'd gotten back to the boat, it was dark. Not even the little cockpit light they left on for safety was on. Normally he'd find it suspicious, but under the circumstances—circumstances that included Cass—nothing was suspicious.

He climbed aboard, watching his footing as best he could. On a boat, there were no end of things you could catch your toe on or trip over, and that was in the light of day, never mind the black of night.

"Cass?" He half whisper-yelled because although he didn't really want to wake her up, he did. He wanted to talk to her, to debrief about the situation with Maria and Joe, and...well, hell. He just wanted to see her. He'd tried a number of times throughout the night to find her and be with her, but she either hadn't wanted to be found or she was having so much fun laughing and talking with the other cruisers, she just hadn't wanted to be found by him.

"Cass?" he said again, this time a little louder. "Are you up?" He stumbled into the cockpit and got his answer.

She sat across from him, her legs tucked under her and her head propped up on one arm.

Instantly, his body tensed and fear shot through him. "Cass, are you okay?" He reached for her hand or her leg or someway to touch her because he could tell she was upset and there was something about this woman, something that physically hurt him when she was hurting.

"No." She jerked back, out of his grasp. "I mean, yes. I'm fine. I was just..." She let the words trail off and she turned away. But not soon enough for Archer to notice, even in the dim light, that she'd been crying.

"You're crying?"

"No." She turned around with such vehemence and indignation that it flared in her eyes. "I don't cry. Not over anyone or anything, and definitely not over you."

"Me?"

"What?"

"You said me." He felt like smiling, like breaking out into a cheer or something, but somehow he was smart enough to know that wouldn't be received well. But he also wasn't going to let it go. "You said, you would definitely not cry over me. And not that I would ever want to give you a reason to cry, but...why would you say that? Did I do something—"

"You didn't do anything." There was a long sigh in the dark before she added, "At least not anything you shouldn't have or that I'd given you any reason to think you shouldn't have. Because you can do whatever you want and I shouldn't give you any reason to think you shouldn't do whatever or whomever you want."

Ah, there it was.

"Cass, I didn't—"

She pulled away from him again. "I don't want to hear anything. I told you, it's not my business and I don't care. And like I said, I don't cry."

Archer had to bite his tongue to keep from laughing. It was

cute to see how much she was so obviously trying not to care about him, and how clearly she was failing.

"You do care."

"Shut up." She looked away and Archer grinned.

He reached over and flicked on the small cockpit light, which illuminated the space with just enough light so he could make out her features.

"It's okay to care."

"If I did."

"Cass." He tried without a lot of success to keep the laughter out of his voice. "It's okay."

"No, it's not." She turned around again, a wildness in her eyes. "I mean, it would be if I did. But I don't. We're friends, Archer." She said the words, but there was no conviction behind them, and he knew without a doubt that she didn't even believe herself when she said it.

"We're more than friends." He touched her then and she didn't pull back. She let his touch linger on her skin. The heat that came from her body was second only to the fire he felt when he touched her and there was no doubt, Cass felt it too.

"Archer, I—"

"It doesn't matter." And it didn't. It didn't matter what excuses she was going to come up with about why they couldn't be together. What reasons she'd built up in her head for staying away from him, or any of the other bullshit she'd managed to convince herself of. He didn't care about any of it. The only thing Archer cared about was the woman in front of him, looking so heartbreakingly beautiful that the urge to pull her in his arms and kiss her until her smile returned to her gorgeous face and never again dimmed was so strong, it was a physical ache.

He put his hand on her cheek and stroked small circles with his thumb, until she closed her eyes in a sigh. Archer leaned in until his lips were a whisper away from hers. "It doesn't matter what you're going to say because I don't care. All I care about is you." His words were slow and soft; he let each one sink into her soul before he spoke the next. "And right now." As he spoke, his thumb traced her lower lip and a sigh escaped her. "And this moment."

When he kissed her, and finally had that contact his whole body had been craving for weeks, Archer thought he might implode. The connection between them was so much stronger than it had been before. Where there was animalistic attraction before, there was care and tenderness with an underlying heat that burned dangerously beneath the surface. He lost himself in the taste of her: sweet, yet somehow spicy, too.

Finally, despite any objections or arguments she could make, she was right where he wanted her, where he needed her, and he didn't plan to let go.

With Archer's lips on hers, his arms around her, and the press of his hard chest against her breasts, Cass could no longer remember why she'd been fighting the connection between them. Deep in her mind, there was a reason, she was sure of it, but with the heat of his touch flowing through her, she couldn't remember a damn thing. Her only focus was on him, and losing herself in the only thing that she knew would feel good. It was too damn hard to be worried about what was right and what she should and should not do when all she wanted to do was this.

A sigh escaped her and it sparked a memory in her. Something she needed to remember. The girl. Outside the Inn. Not all that long ago. She'd made the same sound, and Archer had —she put her hands on his chest and pushed him back, using all the willpower she had left.

"I...I can't."

"You can." He reached for her again and she turned her head to avoid meeting his lips that she might not be strong enough to resist the next time around.

"No." She shook her head. "I can't. Not after...no." The words tasted bitter on her tongue. How could she even think about being with him right after he'd been with another? It didn't matter how her body responded to him, how he made her feel. She couldn't. She wouldn't. She'd lost herself briefly in the moment, in feeling sorry for herself because of her situation, how things went down with Samson, with everything. But she would not lose her self-respect. She jumped up to put space between them and left the cockpit, headed for the bow of the boat.

Archer was right behind her. "What are you talking about? Aren't we past all of this? Haven't we exhausted every reason we shouldn't be together? Dammit, Cass. Look at me."

She couldn't.

"Cass." Archer's voice was stern, steady, and she could tell he was trying his best to keep it even. No doubt he was pissed. But let him be pissed. She wasn't the one who went off with someone else. Not that she had any right to be angry. Because she didn't. "Look at me," he said again. So she did.

"You were just with...that girl…it's not right. I can't."

There, she'd said it. She'd made it clear that she was some sort of jealous woman who couldn't handle the thought of him being with anyone else, even if they weren't together and she had no claim on him whatsoever and she'd more or less told him to leave her alone. Perfect.

Cass braced herself for Archer's response. He'd probably run screaming in the opposite direction, because what man wanted anything to do with a jealous lunatic? None she knew of. And if he didn't run off, he would at the very least laugh or tell her she was crazy.

But he didn't do any of those things. Instead, Archer

smiled—a slow, sexy smile that made her insides do violent flips—and he reached out for her hand again.

God, she needed that connection between them. She didn't realize how much she craved it.

He laced his fingers through hers and squeezed. "Listen to me when I say this, Cass. Because I'm only going to say it once."

She nodded mutely.

"Nothing happened between me and Brooke."

The woman's name struck her hard. A line of jealousy jolted through her body, and something else: a sense of familiarity, as though she should know the name. She swallowed hard and pushed away the feeling, focusing instead on Archer's next words.

"I walked her safely back to her room and I said goodnight. Not only did nothing happen between us, nothing was ever going to happen with her, Cass."

She wanted to believe him. She searched his eyes in the darkness, but couldn't see anything in the shadows, lit only by the moonlight.

"Archer, I—"

"Enough."

And then his arm was around her and his lips were on hers, and it was enough. It was more than enough. Everything she needed to know was in his kiss, in the way he held her and made her feel safe yet totally at risk for falling in love, all at the same time. He was heat and danger and total sanctuary all in one.

She wrapped her arms around his neck and let him kiss her deeply, thoroughly, and so completely she felt as if she would drown in him if she didn't hold on tight.

Somehow, without breaking their kiss, he lifted her and she wrapped her legs around his waist; he carried her back to the cockpit, where he laid her down and slowly removed her clothes, piece by piece.

There wasn't much privacy on the dock, surrounded by other boats, but neither of them cared. The only thing Cass could focus on was the beautiful man above her who had totally consumed her from the moment they'd met.

If she let herself, she could have thought of a million reasons she shouldn't be doing what she was doing. A million reasons it was a bad idea to let herself go. And a million more ways she could be hurt. She dismissed them all.

In the half light, Archer's hard chest gleamed: all ridges, hard planes, and tight muscle. She ran her hands down him; her fingers slid over every valley and line until they reached the waistband of his shorts. Without hesitation, she plunged her hands inside and circled his hard length, eliciting a groan from somewhere deep inside.

He flipped her over so she straddled him, her hands still firmly wrapped around him; only now, she was in control. Impatient, she shoved his shorts down, freeing him completely from the confines of his clothing.

His hands cupped her breasts, kneading them while his thumbs stroked her nipples into hard points that ached with need.

"Archer, I—oh, God."

"Don't tell me to stop, Cass." His voice was deep, throaty, and heavy with a need of his own.

"Never."

Archer's only reply was to wrap his hands around her hips, lift her and settle her back down on top of him, filling her completely.

She closed her eyes and let her body adjust to the size of him before she began a slow rhythm that slowly worked her body into a fever.

Cass opened her eyes and looked straight into his. This

time, even in the dim lighting, she could see everything she needed to. There, reflected back at her was everything she felt inside. It should have made her happy, should have filled her with peace and contentment. Instead, it scared the hell out of her. Cass closed her eyes and forced any and all negative thoughts from her head, all the *should have*'s and *supposed to*'s that tried to invade her brain. Instead, as she rode her way to completion and a climax that shook her to her core, Cass focused on only one thing: the man beneath her and inside her. And that was enough.

It was more than enough.

Chapter Fifteen

THE NEXT DAY, Cass should have felt concern, or remorse, or regret for breaching that boundary with Archer.

She didn't.

When she rolled over in her bunk where they'd finally crashed, spent from another love-making session, she saw Archer, one arm tucked under his head, the other sprawled out as if reaching toward her, and all she felt was happy. The type of pure happiness she couldn't remember feeling before. Or if she had, it had been so long ago, it was only a distant memory.

Propped up on one elbow, she watched him, using the opportunity of his deep sleep to study his magnificence. And he was magnificent. Never the type of woman to fawn over men or ogle a hard body, she could still appreciate one. And man oh man, did she appreciate Archer's fine form. Chiseled from long hours outside, not stuck in the gym, he was firm in all the right places. His abdomen tapered into a perfect *V*, disappearing below the sheet. Cass's entire body thrilled at the thought of what was beneath that thin piece of cotton and the pleasure she'd already wrought from it.

It was a bad idea to get involved with someone she worked

with. Or more specifically, someone who worked for her. But she couldn't care. There were too many rules to follow and she was done following any of them. She was starting a whole new life in Panama, on the *Cassiopeia*, and with that came a whole new set of rules. So far the only rule she had—the one she'd made up at some point last night when she had Archer's hands on her, his mouth on her, tasting her, kissing her, bringing her pleasure—was to do what felt right. Follow her gut and do what feels right.

The only rule she was going to need in her new life.

And at that moment, at least for the moment, what felt right was Archer.

She leaned over and placed a kiss on his belly, looking up as his eyelids fluttered open to watch her. She trailed kisses up his chest, neck, and along his strong jaw until finally she took his lips in hers and kissed him slow and sensually.

"Good morning."

He caught her head before she could slip away. "It absolutely is a good morning," he affirmed. "And what a perfect way to wake up. Although, I can think of an even better way." His grin was sinful and her body reacted accordingly.

With a strong arm, he pulled her over so she was on top of him and pressed her against his length. "Now this is exactly where I want you." His hands slid down and grasped her ass. She could feel his desire pressed against her belly.

It was so tempting. And when she kissed him again, her body told her loud and clear what it wanted, but it was getting late and unfortunately for her libido, what she wanted to do and what she had to do were two very different things. At least for the time being.

With more resolve than she knew she had, she pushed her hands against his chest and away from the body she knew would bring her so much pleasure if only she had the time.

So much for her only rule. Do what feels good would have

to wait. Mentally, Cass added a second rule: don't forget the goal. And right now that goal was to pay off her debt and keep her boat.

"We have our first charter today, remember?"

Archer rolled to the side and rubbed a hand across his face. "Is that today? Already?"

She used the moment to jump up and yank a tank top over her head. If she didn't get out of bed, and away from his naked body soon, she wouldn't have the resolve to do it at all.

"We have time." Archer held out his hand. "Come back to bed."

"We don't and, I wish." After she pulled a pair of shorts from a drawer, she tugged them on, too. "We have to do well today. It's like a test run. Two sisters. Two days. We can do this." She tied her hair back in a ponytail and looked at Archer, who watched her closely. "We have to do this."

He would have preferred to spend the day in bed with Cass next to him, on top of him, underneath him, or really, in any variety of combinations, but she was right: they had to run a successful first charter. Hell, they had to run a successful charter every time, but the first one would set the tone. It was important to Cass, and that made it important to him.

It surprised Archer how much it mattered to him. Never in his life had he been in the situation where he wanted to do something for a woman. Sure, when he was a teenager, it was all about doing something for a girl, so he'd get what he wanted. Usually resulting in some time wrapped up in a blanket under the stars by the lake. But this was different. The only expectation he had for helping Cass was to help Cass.

The thought both surprised him and scared him a little bit. But it also made him smile, so after he pulled her back into the bed for one last kiss and the promise of more to come, he reluctantly hauled himself out of bed and prepared them a quick breakfast.

They spent the morning putting the last-minute touches on the boat, tidying up and making sure everything looked perfect. Shortly before noon, Cass declared the boat ready to go and just in time. He pulled his teal blue polo shirt that Cass had given him to serve as a uniform over his head and joined her in the cockpit, where she was going over a checklist.

"I think everything's ready." She looked up from the paper and smiled at him. It was a nervous smile, but it was easy to see the excitement behind it, too. Finally, after all their preparation, they were about to do this.

Together. The fact that she'd finally relented to their relationship the night before just made it that much better.

"It's going to be great, Cass. Don't worry about a thing." He leaned over and kissed her chastely on the forehead. Anything more and they'd be late for their pickup. "Who are the guests?"

She glanced down at the list again, flipped through a few pages and looked up. This time, a small frown creased her brow. "Bridget Truit, and her sister, Brooke."

Archer froze. Brooke? Seriously? It had to be a different Brooke than the one he'd more or less rejected the night before. No. Not more or less. He had rejected her. And she wasn't too pleased about it.

Of all the guests who could possibly come aboard, what were the odds that they'd have *that* Brooke? Fantastic. Archer let out a long sigh and looked up to the sky before he remembered himself and the fact that Cass was inches away from him.

"Sounds good." He forced a smile, which resulted in Cass giving him a strange look.

"Is there something wrong?"

He shook his head. "Why would you ask?"

She narrowed her eyes at him, clearly not fooled. She likely remembered the name, too. "Is it going to be awkward for you?"

"Why would it be?"

"You know why."

Her eyes challenged him, as if he had something to hide, which he absolutely did not. And he needed her to believe that. "There's no reason it would be awkward, Cass. I told you, nothing happened."

She smiled, but it didn't reach her eyes. "I believe you. But still..."

"I know." He pulled her close then, kissing her thoroughly before he released her. "I meant what I said. It's going to be great. Don't worry. While you go get them, I'm going to run and grab some ginger flowers for their room. A nice touch, don't you think?"

She nodded. "Sounds good. I'll meet you back here in a few minutes, okay? And it's game on."

"Aye-aye, Captain." He snapped to attention and saluted her; she gave a quick frown, followed by a shake of the head before Cass laughed and jumped down off the boat to head to the dock.

He watched her go, admiring the strength in her stride, the confidence in her shoulders as she bravely set off to begin this new chapter in her life.

Damn. She was amazing. In every sense of the word.

Brooke.

She knew it sounded familiar. When Cass heard Archer say the name the night before, she knew it. She just hadn't put it together. No. The truth was, she hadn't wanted to.

All she'd wanted was him. She'd been so lonely, so totally alone and there he was, not with the beautiful woman from the bar after all, but with her. She'd believed him when he'd said nothing had happened between them. Believed him because she'd wanted to. No, she'd needed to.

And she still believed him. She'd seen it on his face. It wasn't the look of a man who had anything to hide, and that's what mattered to her. It didn't matter whether Brooke had been all over Archer, or whether her mouth had been on his. That's all it was. All it would ever be. Because he didn't want Brooke. He wanted Cass. A thrill went through her body at the idea of it, because she wanted him, too, and despite every single reason they shouldn't be together, she simply didn't care anymore.

Any nigglings of little doubts could stay squashed deep down, because nothing could ruin this day: Waking up in Archer's arms, ready to take out their first charter. The charter that would signify the start of her new life. It was a good day.

Cass quickened her pace and hurried up the dock to the restaurant, where she was scheduled to meet Brooke and her sister, Bridget. It was their first charter and sure, it could have been under better circumstances, but she wasn't going to let that bother her. It didn't matter who her guests were; it was going to be a success.

There they were. It was easy to tell they were sisters, with their matching thick, black ponytails and long white legs that would no doubt be burned to a crisp their first day in the sun out in the islands. Their duffel bags rested at their feet and they must have heard her coming, because they turned as one.

Twins.

Cass swallowed down the irrational surge of jealousy that slammed into her. Not only was Brooke beautiful—with breasts even she could appreciate bursting out of her top, red pouty lips, and jade green eyes that, even from a distance, Cass could tell were profoundly piercing—not only was Brooke all of those things, but there were two of them.

"Hi." Cass forced a cheeriness into her voice, suddenly wishing she'd done something a little extra with her hair or at least put on a swipe of makeup. "You must be Brooke and Bridget." She held out her hand. "I'm Cass."

"Captain Cass?" One of them, Cass would bet it was Brooke, laughed at her own joke.

"Yes. I'll be your captain."

The other girl rolled her eyes and shook Cass's hand. "I'm Bridget. Don't mind my sister. She thinks she's hilarious."

It was then that Cass saw the friction between them. The way they held themselves just slightly apart, their bodies leaning away instead of toward each other.

"I *am* hilarious." Brooke extended her hand and Cass maintained her smile. It would be an interesting few days, that much was certain.

"Are you both ready to head out for the islands? I'm excited to show you the San Blas." Cass picked up their bags and gestured with her head for them to follow. "When you see them, you'll know what I'm talking about, but the San Islands are truly paradise. In every sense of the word."

"Are there men out there?"

With her back to them, Cass couldn't be sure which of the two sisters asked the question, but the next statement told her everything she needed to know.

"Because there was a very yummy man here last night and I—"

"It's not all about men, you know?"

"You would not be saying that if you hadn't been such a party pooper and come down to the bar last night, because I'm telling you..." Brooke made a noise that left no room for doubt what she was telling her sister and who she was telling her about.

"Then why is it you came home alone?" Bridget retorted. Cass was grateful the sisters couldn't see her face, especially when Bridget added, "And don't think I didn't hear the way you were complaining about some man not knowing a good thing when it was right in front of him. Or something to that effect."

Cass stifled a laugh and a blossom of happiness burst in her chest. Not that she'd needed confirmation that Archer had turned Brooke down, but it was nice to hear it.

"What do you know?" Brooke retaliated, and Cass tuned out as she continued to make her way slowly past the restaurant. She'd have to pull herself together before she got back to the boat. It was bad enough that she'd been worried about having jealousy issues with the guests, but she'd better be careful not to alienate any of them either. Even if it did seem that Brooke might be a slightly difficult guest.

"Cass?"

A voice from the restaurant caught her attention; she spun and almost ran into the sisters, who were right behind her.

"Sorry, I—"

"Cass?" A woman she'd never seen before appeared at the door of the restaurant. She was tall, with the lean build of a runner. Her tanned legs peeked out from a short sundress; a backpack was over her shoulder, and her long, thick hair was tied out of the way and flung over her other shoulder. "You must be Cass." There was a hint of hopefulness in her voice and something else, an undercurrent of desperation or sadness. Cass instantly took a liking to her.

"I am." Cass nodded, unable to shake the woman's hand. "Were you looking for me?"

The woman nodded. "Yes. I heard you were going out on a charter today and I was hoping you had an extra room. I'd even sleep on deck if you don't have the beds. I just...I need...I really need to get away from here for a few days."

Something in the woman's voice appealed to a deep understanding within Cass. She glanced behind her at Brooke and Bridget, who watched the scene unfold with a vague look of disinterest. "I am taking out a charter." She dropped the duffels at her feet and ran a hand through her ponytail. "We're actually just heading out."

"Oh, I'm glad I caught you then." She glanced around Cass to address the sisters. "I know it's a lot to ask, and you're on holidays I assume. But I..." She looked back at Cass. "I'll pay you. If it's okay with your guests, I mean." Her voice shook and for a moment, Cass thought the woman was going to cry.

Cass didn't have the heart to say no out of hand. It was clear the woman was desperate. She looked instead to Brooke and Bridget. It was the latter who said, "It's fine with me." She shrugged and smiled sympathetically at the woman, who still hadn't introduced herself. "It might be nice to have someone else to talk to besides my sister."

Cass swallowed her smile as Brooke glared at her. Not to be outdone, she nodded as well. "The more the merrier."

Relief flooded the other woman's face and spontaneously, she pulled Cass into a hug even though it was the sisters who'd given the final consent. "Thank you so much. You have no idea how much I appreciate it. I really do need to get away from here for a few days."

"It'll be fun." Cass smiled and did a mental calculation to see whether they had enough food on board. Archer would have to be creative with the supplies, but surely it could work. And if the sisters didn't want to share a bed, which she was pretty sure would be off the table, Cass would happily bunk with Archer and give up the extra bunk. Besides, it would be nice having another woman along, who hadn't either put the moves on Archer, or look like the carbon copy of someone who did.

"I can't believe I haven't introduced myself yet," the

woman said as they once again began to walk down the dock. "I'm Heather."

Cass stiffened. "Heather?" She realized a moment too late that she'd spoken aloud.

"Yes. Joe's wife." She confirmed Cass's fears. She was the very same woman Archer had just confessed to actually sleeping with. Nausea rolled in her stomach. They hadn't even left the dock yet, and already her first charter was turning out terribly.

"Well, soon-to-be ex-wife," Heather spat out the words. "But men are the last thing I want to think about right now."

Cass kept walking, a sinking feeling in her gut. "Me too, Heather. Me too."

Chapter Sixteen

FOR MOST OF THE DAY, he'd managed to busy himself with tasks that kept him below deck and out of the way of the women. Because the last place he wanted to be was with the women. It was safer for him below. Hell, it would be safer for him if he were being dragged behind the *Cassiopeia* in a dinghy. When he'd returned from the jungle with a handful of ginger flowers to decorate the rooms with, he'd only had to take one look at Cass to know something wasn't right.

And it had only taken a second more, when Heather had appeared in the companionway, with her long, tanned legs and thick mane of hair, that Archer knew exactly what the problem was. Here, he'd been worried about Brooke and the flirting he'd likely have to endure when the real danger lay in the dock-master's wife and his own stupid honesty. If he'd only kept his mouth shut for a few more days...but it was too late for that now and it's not as if he'd done anything wrong, either. That had happened before he'd even met Cass. Hell, it was before he knew she was Joe's wife. It had been one time—okay, twice—and it had ended as soon as he'd discovered the truth. He didn't, nor did he ever, want anything to do with a married woman. It wasn't his style, and even if Heather hadn't been married, it never would have been anything serious; it wasn't like that with her. It was fun, a good time. That was it. It was nothing like what he had with Cass.

Not. Even. Close.

Still, that knowledge didn't seem to matter to Cass. Even if he did have a chance to explain it all, Heather was just the insult to the Brooke injury, and he was going to have to ride it out. Everyone had a past. It was just that his was literally staring at them in the face. There was nowhere to go on a boat. Nowhere to hide, besides the galley. And he'd stay there as long as he could.

"Archer."

Damn. That didn't take long.

But it wasn't the voice that made his gut tighten with desire. Not even close. It was Brooke. She'd squealed like a little girl when she saw it was him on the boat. The night before, they hadn't gotten around to talking about what he did for work, or what she was doing in Panama. Normal conversation skills had gone completely out the window, it seemed, in favor of flirting and trying to get him into bed.

What was next? The way things were going for him, he wouldn't be surprised to see all his ex-girlfriends show up next.

"Archer? Are you down here?"

Oh hell no. He did not need that woman getting him alone in the galley.

"I'm just coming up." He grabbed the platter of fresh papaya and mango that he'd just sliced and moved quickly out of the galley. But he wasn't quick enough. Brooke was already down the companionway ladder and reclined suggestively against it, her large breasts spilling out of her pink bikini top.

"I thought I'd find you here." Her tongue snaked out between her lips and slowly licked the plump flesh of her bottom lip. It was a move he'd normally find seductive. Hell, she was a good-looking woman; there was no denying that. But it wasn't Brooke's pouty lips that made Archer's blood grow hot in his veins, but Cass's sinful smile that made him want to take her and do dirty things to her. Something about that woman in less than two months had completely spoiled him for any other. And it scared the hell out of him.

Not that he would say anything to Cass. He wasn't stupid. And he'd been around enough women to know when to keep his fool mouth shut. That time was now. There was way too much going on for him to confess any feelings to her. Especially when they scared the hell out of him.

Besides, he wasn't going to say a damn thing about anything until he knew for sure that what he was feeling wasn't just the aftereffects of some very hot time between the sheets.

"Did you hear what I said?"

Archer forced himself back in the moment and the problem at hand, which was a very sexy and very persistent woman who stood only inches from him with her hands in a very close, very precarious position. Brooke definitely had the advantage over him. With his hands full, and in the tiny space, there was nowhere for him to go and she knew it.

He shook his head and focused. "No, I'm sorry." He tried for casual, because he was also smart enough to know that if he turned her down out of hand, she would be very unhappy and Cass's future depended on the success of the charter. Samson's advice when he worked on that very first job about flirting with the female passengers came back to him. He wouldn't do anything, or say anything to put it in jeopardy. But he sure as hell wouldn't do her either. No matter how persistent she was. That would put all kinds of other things in jeopardy. Namely, things with Cass. "I was just thinking about what kind of drinks would go well with this little snack."

Shift the focus to alcohol. It was a strategy that just might work. That is, if he had a good read on Brooke, and he was pretty sure he did.

"Let me check." To his relief, Brooke removed her hand from where it was about to *accidentally*—yeah, right—brush against his crotch and with two perfectly manicured fingers, picked a piece of papaya up and sucked it suggestively between her lips.

Maybe it would have been better if she'd just touched his crotch. Either way, his dick stiffened in response to her. Hell, he'd have to be dead inside not to respond physically to a woman like Brooke. But physical response or not, that's where it ended.

He looked away and swallowed hard. "It's pretty good, isn't it? Panama's finest."

"I think you're Panama's finest." She traced a fingertip down his cheek, leaving a sticky trail of papaya juice after her.

He laughed then, an action that definitely wasn't her desired response. "Sorry to disappoint, but I'm Canadian, born and raised." He winked to soften the blow of her failed seduction. "If you'll excuse me, I should get this up to the deck."

She moved aside and without wasting a moment more, Archer deftly climbed the steep stairs and emerged above deck. Dodging Brooke's advances would definitely make the next few days interesting, but it wasn't anything he couldn't handle. He put the tray down on the small cockpit table and his eyes locked on Heather, who watched him with a sad smile. A smile that told a story of not only who she was and what she'd been through, but also of what she'd thought she'd had, and lost. He could see in her eyes that there was more there, too. When he'd been with her before, Archer had been able to sense her sadness, what he now knew must have come from her deep unhappiness with her life and her situation with Joe. And he knew for at least the time that they spent together, he'd been able to give her a reprieve from that. When he looked at her across the table, he could see that in her eyes, too. A hopefulness. A hopefulness he knew shouldn't be directed at him.

Before she could say anything, he stood and turned so quickly he almost ran smack into Cass. Because she had that effect on him, he smiled at her instinctively, but the look on her face told him she'd also seen the way Heather had looked at him.

"Cass." He reached for her.

She hesitated a moment and he thought she'd say something, anything to let him know it was okay. And then she smiled, a smile that didn't quite reach her eyes, and forced a cheeriness in her voice that he knew she didn't feel.

"We're about an hour away from the anchorage," she addressed the group. "Why don't you all come enjoy the delicious snack Archer has so thoughtfully prepared for us? The time will pass quickly."

And just like that, she was gone. Back to the helm to navigate and stand watch for ships while he looked around at the women who'd surrounded him, helping themselves to a bite to eat as if they were all circling their prey.

Cass knew she was being unreasonable. There was no reason to be upset with Archer for the way women reacted to him. For goodness' sake, she *was* one of those women. Still, she couldn't shake the jealousy. Especially with Heather. The woman seemed fragile, broken somehow, and Cass hadn't missed the way she looked at Archer, as if there was salvation for her in his arms.

She focused on the horizon, unwilling to watch her guests any longer. Not long and they'd be in the anchorage, and she'd be able to dispatch them for some fun in the sun.

Her cellphone chirped in her pocket. Cass pulled out the

welcome distraction to see a message from her best friend. It had been a few days since she'd heard from Angie. Probably a good thing, because Angie always seemed to want to know more about Archer and why Cass wasn't sleeping with him. Her best friend could not seem to understand why Cass was keeping him at arm's length, especially when she'd told her how good the sex was. For Angie, it was an easy equation: Hot Guy + Great Sex = Love Match.

For Cass, it wasn't that simple. And it wouldn't be for Angie, either, if she had even a fraction of the history with men that Cass did.

Still, she glanced at the text and smiled.

Please tell me you gave in to the hot Canuck.

She knew she shouldn't, but Cass needed a reason to smile and just thinking about how the message would be received by her friend thousands of miles away in England made her smile.

What if I did?

Cass hit Send and waited.

She didn't have to wait long.

Details!

She tucked her phone in her pocket. She'd let Angie stew on that one for a little while.

After the snack, all the women made themselves comfortable on the boat. They stretched out to catch some sun or watch the ocean go by as they completed their sail into what, for Cass, was becoming a familiar little grouping of islands. They dropped anchor and Brooke and Bridget immediately dove in to the water, eager to cool off. Although, Cass was pretty sure Brooke was really just eager to show off her bikini.

To his credit, Archer didn't even glance in her direction. Cass smiled secretly. She knew she was being childish. She also knew Archer was trying extra hard to prove to her that he wasn't interested in the other women. And she believed it. She really did. But then why was it so hard for her to show it?

She blinked hard when she realized she was staring at Archer. Her phone vibrated incessantly in her pocket. No doubt Angie wasn't pleased with the way she'd left her hanging on the details. Angie could wait.

"Cass?"

Heather stood next to her, a bag in her hand. "I was wondering if I could get you to take me to the island? I need to stretch my legs a little."

The other woman looked lost and beaten down somehow. Cass had heard rumors and rumblings about Heather and Joe's relationship, but nothing concrete. She wondered whether Heather's husband knew she was on the boat. Or even whether he cared.

"Absolutely." Cass gave her a warm smile. She shouldn't like the woman. She should be jealous that Archer had slept with her, but despite that, Cass knew they hadn't shared the same connection that she had with Archer. And there was something about Heather. She was pretty sure they could be friends under different circumstances. Maybe even under the circumstances they were in. Now that she was over the initial shock, Cass wasn't jealous. Instead, she felt an overwhelming desire to protect Heather. To pull her into an embrace and let her know everything would be okay.

"You know what?" An idea popped into Cass's head. "I'll get Archer to drop the dinghy and take everyone to the island. You can meet Josie. I think you'll like her. She's very...insightful."

Heather's smile was grateful. Yes, she'd definitely benefit from a chat with Josie. There was something about the island woman; she'd be able to see through whatever was bothering Heather.

As an afterthought, before she turned away to find Archer, Cass asked, "Heather, do you mind me asking if you're okay?"

Cass nervously smoothed back her ponytail. “It’s just that, you know...you look really sad and—”

“You didn’t hear?” Heather shook her head and laughed in disbelief.

“Hear what?”

“Seriously? You weren’t at the bar last night?”

“I was. I was just...” She trailed off, not wanting to talk about or even think about it. “I was kind of preoccupied.”

“Me too.” Heather half laughed, half snorted. “It was fairly distracting watching my husband’s lover go into labor with his child.”

Cass almost choked on the air she was breathing. “What?”

The disgust fell from Heather’s face again, leaving only the sadness behind once again. “Can I give you a piece of advice, Cass?”

She nodded dumbly. What else could she do?

“Don’t fall in love.” Heather closed her eyes, disappearing into her memories for a moment. When she opened them again, they were so sad and full of pain, Cass could feel it for her. “You’ll only get hurt.”

She blinked twice before she focused on Cass’s face. Saw her as if for the first time. Her smile was forced. “What am I saying?” There was a forced glibness in her voice. “Don’t listen to me. As long as you fall for the right one, everything will be fine.”

Cass rolled her words around in her head. An image of Archer’s face flashed in her mind. “And how do you know if he’s the right one?” She didn’t realize she’d spoken aloud until she heard the words.

Heather reached out and squeezed her shoulder as if she were much older and wiser, when really, she could only have a few years on Cass. “That’s the real question, my friend.” The sad smile returned. “You don’t.”

Chapter Seventeen

HE'D GIVE HER SPACE. It was the only thing he could do. Particularly when Cass had all but forced Archer to take the guests to the island, with strict instructions to introduce Heather to Josie.

"She needs to meet her," Cass had said. "She *needs* it."

He'd tried to tell her then about what had happened with Joe and Maria and the baby, but Cass shook her head and smiled secretly, as if she already knew everything there was to know about the situation. And maybe she did. Maybe Heather had told her everything. Maybe not. But Archer did as requested—launched the dinghy and obediently took the women to the beach—shaking his head the entire way.

If there was one thing he did know about women, it was that he didn't know anything at all.

Maybe he'd sneak in a visit with Josie, too. Lord knew he could stand for some of the woman's wisdom to rub off on him. Maybe then he'd be able to figure out what the hell was going on with Cass. He'd tried to slip her a secretive kiss before he'd left, but despite the fact their guests wouldn't have seen a thing, she'd turned away at the last minute, offering him her cheek and a smile.

A friendly smile.

No, he'd never understand women.

"What's there to do here?"

Archer shook his head, banishing thoughts of Cass for the time being and focused instead on Brooke, who was currently pouting as she tried to hold herself as primly as possible on the side of the rubber boat as it bounced through the waves. It was only a short boat ride, and the dinghy wasn't known for its comfort, but it wasn't as bad as every jerk and bounce that Brooke was exaggerating.

Archer tried to hide his smile.

"Palm trees and the most beautiful white sand beaches you've ever seen," he replied with a smile.

"That's it?"

Heather flashed Brooke a look, but turned away. It was her sister, Bridget, who reached out and smacked her arm. "What else do you need? Were you expecting a mall or something? Perhaps somewhere to get your nails done? Seriously, Brooke. What the hell is wrong with you?"

"What the hell is wrong with you?" The sisters glared at each other in a showdown. "Is it so bad that I want to go on holiday my way? Isn't it bad enough that you dragged me down to this...this..."

"Paradise?"

Brooke snorted. "If you call this total seclusion paradise."

This time, Archer didn't even bother to hide his grin.

"I do," Bridget said with a sneer. There didn't seem to be any love lost between these twins. He'd be interested to know their story, except he seemed to have enough stories to keep straight these days. Women were complicated and the only story he was even attempting to decipher was Cass's.

"It's really a beautiful island," Archer said in an attempt to keep the peace. "There's an amazing coral reef off the back side and if you're interested, I'll go get the snorkel gear from the boat and you can—"

"I'm not snorkeling." Brooke crossed her arms over her chest before they hit another wave and she had to hang on.

"Suit yourself, but it's like a whole other world down there." Archer killed the engine and pulled it up so it wouldn't drag in the sand as they approached the beach. He deftly hopped over the side and grabbed the line on the front of the boat, pulling it with the waves, up the shore.

The women clambered out and gathered their things.

"Meet me back here in an hour," Archer said. "Unless you want more time. It's not a big island; I'll find you."

He watched and waited as the women walked away, all in different directions. He'd partly assumed Brooke would turn around and try to get him alone again, but she seemed fairly preoccupied with the sand, and picking her way through it. No doubt, she didn't want to step on any unseen or imagined sea creature. Archer fought the urge to laugh. What a woman like that was doing in the remote islands of Panama, he'd never be able to figure out.

For a minute, Archer considered pulling the dinghy up on the beach and going for a small walk himself, but he'd been right when he'd told the women it was a small island. And if he wanted to be alone, it was probably better to go across the bay to a completely different island, which wouldn't be hard considering there were a few more nearby. But his eyes locked on the *Cassiopeia*. It was a magnificent sailboat, with the backdrop of the teal Caribbean Sea and the equally gorgeous, yet different shade of blue sky. But what was even more breathtaking was the woman who stood on the bow, her blond hair flowing behind her as she looked out to sea. Away from him.

He knew she wanted to be alone. Needed to be alone. But

when he got back in the dinghy and headed back out into the bay, there was only one place he wanted to be.

The minute the passengers left the boat, Cass breathed a sigh of relief. To be fair, given who the passengers were, it could be going a lot worse. It wasn't that bad at all. It was just the stress of the first charter and everything that had happened with Samson. Never mind Archer. She breathed in a lungful of the hot, salty air. Yes, things could definitely be better. It would *have* to be better. And it would be; she just needed to get her head on straight and stop letting her feelings about everything else invade her thoughts. What was important was her business.

She watched as Archer made his way to the beach with the women, dropped them off and headed in the dinghy across the bay before she headed below. She needed to do something she'd been putting off for more than a month. Her father's room had become hers. It wasn't the largest bunk on the boat, but that was part of the reason she'd chosen it. Her charter guests would like the big room, even if *big* was relative on a boat, and without many belongings of her own, it didn't make sense for her to take the room. But that wasn't really it either. If she was honest with herself, there was something about the smaller room that spoke to her. It was the only bunk on the boat that felt *lived* in.

It had been her father's room.

There weren't many personal touches, aside from some *molas*, the traditional embroidery work of the Kuna Indians, tacked on the wall: A few drawers of clothes that Cass had already packed up and put into one of the storage holds. A row of books that lined the shelf behind the bed.

It was the books that drew her now. She'd done little more than scan the titles up until now. She hadn't had much time to read, and when she did find a few minutes to relax, it had been with cruising guides of the area and maps. Hardly relaxing, but definitely required reading. Cass trailed her hands along the spines of the books. Mostly they were true crime books or the suspense novels she remembered her father reading, but it was one book that she homed in on. It was different than the rest. Familiar.

As she reached for the book, she hesitated and her chest tightened. Cass let her hand hover in the air, inches from the leather spine. Next to sailing, it was one of the most vivid memories of her father. The book sat on a shelf in the living room and it was an unspoken rule that only he could handle it. *The Adventures of Winnie the Pooh*. A children's book, but with the special leather cover, and the thin pages, it transformed the stories of A. A. Milne into something more. Particularly when they were read by her father. She'd curl up on his lap in his overstuffed easy chair and he'd read to her about the silly stuffed bear and his friends.

After her father left, she'd looked for the book, knowing if it was still in place on the shelf that would mean her father would be back. It was gone. She hadn't seen it again.

Until the first time she'd set foot in the room that was his. Her eyes had gone to it at once, as if it were a beacon calling her home. If he hadn't taken the book, did that mean he was coming back? He'd taken it once. Surely he'd take it again. Cass swallowed hard, blinked once to clear the memories from her vision, and reached forward until her fingers touched the book.

The immediate feeling that she was doing something wrong, touching something that wasn't hers, flooded through her, but she shoved it away and picked up the book. Just feeling the weight of it in her hands caused emotions she didn't even know she was capable of to roll through her. She sank onto the bed and slowly opened the cover.

She would read it. She knew she would. But not yet.

For the moment, it was enough to hold it and let the pages slide through her fingers. She'd never understand how he could simply walk out of her life the way he had, but over the last few weeks, just by being on his boat, living in the space he lived in, doing the things he had done, something inside Cass had shifted. She no longer felt a deep pain when she thought of him. A pain that had morphed and shaped into anger over the years.

Now when she thought of him, it was with regret and more than a little sadness. The change had happened gradually, but it was definitely happening. Her fingers slipped across each page as she casually thumbed through. She didn't even look at the words on the page, lost in her memories, until she turned a page that felt different.

Very different.

Cass looked down, and turned a few more pages until the source of what she'd felt was revealed. A photograph fell out into her lap. Gently, she set the book aside and picked up the photograph. A breath caught in her throat when she turned it over and saw her father's face stare back at her and a younger version of herself, tucked under his arm as they sat on their sailboat. Cass remembered the day the picture was taken. Her dad had finally let her handle the boat on her own. She'd begged him all summer to let her pilot the small sailboat across the sound but he wouldn't relent.

"You're still too young, Cass. What if a gale blows in, or a larger ship?" He shook his head, and tugged his cap onto his head. "Not yet."

"Then when?" She tried never to whine around her father; he didn't tolerate it well. But after almost an entire summer of being rejected, she couldn't help it and her pre-teen attitude slipped out before she could catch herself. "I know I can handle it, Dad." She'd straightened her shoulders and tried to look as mature as she could manage. "I've been working hard all summer. Nothing will go wrong. Besides, even if something happens, you taught me well. I can handle it."

There must have been something in her voice, or maybe it was the argument she'd provided at the last minute, because he hadn't said no out of hand. Instead, he ran his hand over his stubbled chin and nodded once before he said, "Okay, I'll think about it."

It was progress. Big progress.

For the next few days, Cass kept quiet, waiting for him to make his decision. And then he had.

Another sailor had snapped the picture right after she completed the journey all by herself. She'd known something was different that day when they headed to the docks. There was a different feel in the air, and her father had been humming to himself. She'd held her breath in hope; when they got to the docks and prepared the boat, her father looked in her eyes and handed her the lifejacket she always wore. "Go ahead, kiddo. I'll be right here."

"You're serious?"

He'd only nodded in response before he turned away and walked to the end of the pier, where he sat on a crate and watched her. Cass couldn't be sure, but she knew in her heart that he hadn't moved an inch the entire time she was gone. He'd sat and waited for her, staring out at the water until she became a speck in the distance, and then once again reappeared.

As she looked at the picture now, all the memories from that day rushed back.

While she was in the relatively safe and familiar bay where she often practiced solo, she was confident, handling the boat with ease. Even once she maneuvered out into the open water, and the wind picked up a little, filling the sail and heeling the boat over so she was riding high on the pontoon's edge, she was in her element. It wasn't until she made it to the other side and the turnaround spot where she'd been with her father many times before that a flicker of anxiety set in. The wind had picked up and pushed the little boat faster than she was used to. And all the way on the other side, she could no longer see the bay and the marina where her father was. It was the first time she'd been all alone on the sea.

"I can handle it." She repeated the words she'd used on her father only a few days earlier. "I can handle it." The mantra continued in her head; she kept a tight handle on the lines and pushed the growing ball of fear down as she maneuvered the boat back across the open water. The knot of tension in her shoulders eased when the marina and the shadowy shape of her father came into view. He'd been there the whole time. She knew it.

He hadn't left her.

When she got close enough, her father hopped up and started to cheer. He'd yelled and hollered, attracting the attention of everyone else in the marina, and cheered her all the way into the slip, where he immediately hopped into the boat and pulled her into his arms.

"I'm so proud of you, kiddo."

All the anxiety and fear evaporated and in that moment, all Cass felt was happy and loved. Someone called their names and they turned in time to have their picture taken.

It had been the best day of her life.

Her father left four days later.

Chapter Eighteen

THE ONLY PLACE Archer wanted to be was back on the *Cassiopeia* with Cass. But he also knew it wasn't the best move. At least not for the moment. When it came to things between them, something held her back and despite all his efforts, he couldn't seem to figure out what the hell it was. Not for the first time, he thought about calling his friend Samantha back home. She was more like a little sister to him, and she might have some advice about what was going on and how he could break through whatever walls Cass was determined to set up for him.

He dismissed the thought, just the way he had every other time it had popped up. If he called Sam about a woman, she'd get all excited and knowing Sam, would definitely read more into the situation than there was. Hell, he wasn't even sure what the situation was. Only that he wanted more than anything to spend time with her, make her laugh, and erase all of her worries and fears. There was no way he could explain that to Sam, or anyone else for that matter, not without using the one word he didn't want to.

Love.

It was ridiculous. Sure, he had strong feelings for her, but love? That was crazy. No. There was no way he was discussing Cass and whatever was going on between them with anyone. Not until he had it sorted out in his head a bit more. And he couldn't do that while they had guests on board. He rubbed his hand through his hair, his other hand on the throttle as he picked up speed, and headed back out into the bay, away from the beach.

There were a few other boats anchored besides the *Cassiopeia*, probably cruisers who lived the winter months on their boat. He waved at one as he zipped by and his gaze caught sight of a large catamaran entering through the reef into the anchorage. *Seaduction*. Perfect. Samson hadn't said much to Archer since the one time he'd worked aboard, except to let him know that if he helped Cass, there would never be another chef job for him aboard his ship. There'd been enough animosity in that one comment that Archer had steered clear of the other man ever since he'd made his choice.

And it was an easy one to make. He had nothing against Samson, but if there was a choice to make, he was definitely choosing Cass. He navigated the dinghy across the small bay, carefully avoiding the reef, as he headed toward one of the other islands. Despite what he wanted to do—which was board the *Cassiopeia*, pull Cass into his arms, and kiss her until she couldn't breathe before he made love to her under the heat of the sun—he steered the dinghy to one of the other tiny islands.

The best thing he could do was make sure the charter was successful, and Samson's arrival only served to remind him of that fact. Cass had a lot riding on this first charter; he wouldn't let her down. From past visits to the area, Archer knew where the local Kuna Indian fishermen could be found, and if he put in a request for fresh lobster, they'd be sure to give him the first choice, which would mean a feast aboard the *Cassiopeia* for everyone to enjoy.

It hadn't taken Archer long to find the small group of Kunas. Using his rudimentary Spanish, which got better every day, he explained what he was looking for and they promised to deliver the finest lobsters they could find. He wandered away from their small settlement after he purchased a cold beer to enjoy as he walked down the beach. He still had time before he needed to pick up the women on Barbecue Island, and even if they were finished with their small expedition early, Archer would be able to see them. The anchorage was small, which made it one of their favorite places to visit while Cass and Archer were figuring out the boat over the last month. They'd come to know the tiny islands that dotted the landscape, both alone and together.

Despite the fact that Archer loved to be with Cass, boats were a small place to be, particularly now that they had guests aboard. He might as well take advantage of the opportunity to stretch his legs and absorb the peace and quiet, because something told him that when he got back to the boat with the women, the time for quiet would be over.

Archer took his time walking the beach. For a while, it was sandy and calm. Easy walking. But as he circled the backside, he had to pick his way over rocks and fallen palm trees. With no reef to protect the windward side of the island, the surf crashed against the shore, demonstrating a much wilder side of the sea.

It was getting late by the time he rounded the tip of the island and headed back to where he'd tied up the dinghy on the beach. He'd have to hurry to pick up the women and get back to the boat before the fishermen arrived with the lobsters. He hadn't mentioned his plan to Cass, mostly because he'd formulated it on the fly, but if she wasn't prepared to accept the lobster, and pay them for their trouble, the fishermen might go to the next boat in the bay and Archer's plan would be ruined.

Across the water he could see a group of people, likely the sisters and Heather, waiting for their pickup and he rushed to the tree to untie the boat. Only the boat wasn't there.

He must have gotten the wrong tree. Peering into the sun, he scanned the beach. Only there was no dinghy to be found.

"What the hell?"

He jogged over to the Kuna settlement; the Indians were still out, likely in search of the lobster, and there was no one at the hut except for an elder woman working on her *mola* embroidery. No dinghy.

Crime in the San Blas Islands was virtually unheard of, and he'd only been out of sight for a few minutes; no one would have taken his boat. So what happened? Growing increasingly worried, Archer ran back to where he knew he'd left the boat. Sure enough, there were the marks in the sand from where he'd pulled the boat up. And next to them…another exact marking. There'd been another boat.

He scanned the bay and the sailboats anchored. It was rare, but not totally unheard of, for another cruiser to *borrow* a dinghy. But his boat wasn't tied up on any of the sailboats; it was floating free. Abandoned. And it was quickly headed to the opening of the bay, which meant it was either going out to sea or would ram up on the sharp coral reef.

"Dammit."

Cass held the picture for a few more moments. Tears blurred her eyes until she couldn't see the face that was both so familiar and completely foreign to her after so long. It was ridiculous. For sixteen years after her father took off, she'd barely cried but ever since being in Panama, Cass felt as though she could cry at any moment. It was crazy. And more than a little annoying. It was also telling of the connection her father, and now she, had to this place.

With an ache in her heart, Cass stuffed the picture in the book before she shoved it back on the shelf. It didn't change anything.

She used the bathroom, splashed some water on her face and readjusted her ponytail before she headed back up on deck. She had a job to do, and she couldn't let emotions of any kind get in the way. Archer should be bringing her guests back aboard soon and she wanted to be ready for them. Maybe get the kayak launched and pull out the snorkel gear and—

What the hell was Archer doing?

Her attention was caught by the sight of Archer running along the beach of a totally different island than he was supposed to take the women to. She looked quickly over at Barbecue Island and saw Brooke, Bridget, and Heather standing on the beach, obviously waiting for him.

"You have got to be kidding me?"

Archer caught sight of her, yelled her name and gestured with his arms. With her eyes, she followed his outstretched arms and… "Shit."

Her dinghy floated, caught in the current, and headed to the mouth of the bay.

She looked back at Archer and fought the urge to yell some obscenity at him. How could he be so neglectful? A lost dinghy was definitely not a situation they could afford at the moment. Especially with their guests currently stranded in the hot sun.

With the current carrying the boat, there was no time to launch the kayak, so Cass peeled off her polo shirt and shorts, silently giving thanks for the bikini she always wore under her clothes, and dove over the side to rescue her dinghy. Cass was a strong, sure swimmer, and the current was in her favor, so it didn't take long for her to catch up with the runaway boat. She hefted herself aboard and immediately set to starting the engine.

Only it didn't start. She pulled hard again on the starter. Nothing.

After a quick adjustment, Cass made sure the engine was in neutral and tried again.

Still, nothing.

"What the hell?" She stood and scanned the dinghy, looking for something, anything that could explain what was going on with the dinghy. The boats were never reliable, but usually with a quick adjustment, Cass could make it work. But none of her usual tricks were working this time.

"Cass!"

Archer yelled from the beach, but she didn't bother to look over. It's not as though he was going to be able to help her from the beach. It was his fault she was in the predicament she was. And with a quick look to her left, she was in a predicament. The water darkened, signifying the reef was getting closer. And quickly, too. She knew from the little experience she had that the reef in the San Blas came up quick and hard. It wasn't as serious as grounding her sailboat, but she could easily do damage to her dinghy or the engine if she didn't do something fast. Cass took one more glance over to the reef and jumped into action, grabbing the anchor bag. It was always attached to the front of the boat, in case of just such an emergency, so she pulled the rope that freed the anchor and tossed it into the water. It connected with the sandy bottom and the chain pulled hard on the small boat before it made contact with the sharp reef.

The anchor gave her a second to stop and assess the situation. The current here was fairly strong, but not too strong for her to paddle. She scanned the bay for other boats in the area, but there were only a few. The closest was *Seaduction* and something told her Samson was not going to be much help.

With no other choice, Cass unstrapped the paddles from the bottom of the dinghy and secured them onto the sides. As soon as she was in position, she pulled the anchor up, plopped down and pulled hard on the paddles. Fortunately, she was strong enough to keep her boat off the sharp coral and propel herself through the bay to the far tip of the island where Archer waited to catch the boat.

"Good work. I don't know—"

"How could you lose the boat, Archer?" she snapped at him as she hopped out of the boat.

"What?" With his muscles flexing, he easily hauled the boat up on the beach and pulled the engine up to examine it. But instead of setting to work on the situation at hand, he crossed his arms over his tanned chest and stared at her. "You think I lost the boat?"

"That's actually exactly what happened." He was so damn good-looking, she tried not to look directly at him. She was mad, really mad, but she couldn't figure out why exactly. Boats floated away; it happened. It probably wasn't Archer's fault. Not really. But she couldn't stop herself from raising her voice. "It was floating out to sea, Archer. Do you know what would have happened if I hadn't noticed when I did? It would have been gone. Gone. And then what? How would we have gotten our guests off Barbecue Island? How would we have done anything for the rest of the charter? And do you really think I have the money to buy another boat? I realize this isn't your problem; it's mine. But it would be nice if you cared just a little that there is more at stake here than just a stupid dinghy." She wound up and kicked the rubber boat, which was harder than it looked.

Ouch. Cass bit her lip so Archer wouldn't notice. Too late.

He smirked and didn't even try to stifle the chuckle. "Are you done?"

She nodded.

"Good. Feel better?"

She nodded, but it was a lie and they both knew it. Her little outburst was about a lot more than a runaway dinghy and they both knew it.

Archer turned his attention to the engine and it only took him a matter of seconds to see that the hose from the fuel tank had been disconnected. He tightened it in place, primed it, and pulled the cord. The engine fired up at once.

Cass shook her head. "That was it?" She should have checked for that. She could have saved herself a lot of time and effort if she'd only bothered to look. Or more specifically, knew to look. "I should have—"

"You didn't know."

"But I should have." She ran her hands through her wet ponytail and turned away. "These are things I need to know. I can't expect to be able to—"

"Stop." Archer turned her around and silenced her with a look. "Don't talk like that. I won't even let you finish that thought and you shouldn't even think that way. You're doing a great job with all this, Cass. And that hose should never have been knocked off. It wouldn't have just happened on its own. Especially since it wasn't like that when I tied up the boat."

"You tied it up?"

"Of course I did. You didn't honestly think I just left it on the beach for the ocean to pull out to sea?"

She looked away. She didn't know what she thought anymore. About the boat or about Archer or about anything. Her thoughts were way too confused and there was way too much going on for her to focus on anything. Especially with Archer's bare chest so close to her.

"Cass?" His fingers touched her cheek and traced down her jawbone; thrills tingled right to her core. Her body betrayed her mind and she turned her head just as his lips met hers.

She let herself fall into the kiss, into the security and heat and danger he represented all at the same time. But it didn't last long enough; when Archer pulled away, she instantly wanted his lips back on hers.

"We should go get our guests," she mumbled before he could see the uncertainty on her face. It was all too much to think about right now, and there were definitely more pressing matters than whatever was or wasn't going on with Archer.

Chapter Nineteen

THE NIGHT BEFORE, after getting their slightly sunburnt and agitated guests back aboard the *Cassiopeia,* Archer had been kept busy making what felt like a never-ending stream of rum punches to help them forget about the annoyance of being stranded. Of course, Brooke put up the biggest fuss about it all, but it was nothing a little alcohol couldn't fix and soon Brooke was just as mellow as the rest of the women, enjoying the happy hour.

It was late by the time Archer had finished cleaning up the dinner dishes for the quick pasta dish he'd ended up making after the Kunas didn't come by with the promised lobsters. It hadn't been the feast their guests would remember, but with enough rum, hopefully it wouldn't matter. What did matter was that fun was had by all, and that would help Cass leave a good impression. That's all that mattered.

Cass.

He'd been looking forward to getting her alone again and getting another taste of those lips that would hopefully kiss away any doubt or confusion or whatever it was that was going on in her head, but by the time he finished with his duties, she'd long since snuck away to her room. As much as he wanted to join her, it didn't feel right. She'd put up a wall of some kind and although he couldn't explain it, it was definitely there. *For now.* He'd get to the bottom of it, but not at that moment. He'd back off. *For now.*

Instead, Archer had spent the night in the cockpit and slept under the stars, which meant he was up with the sun and back in the galley to prepare breakfast and mimosas for the ladies when Cass emerged, looking sexy as hell in her tight tank top, khaki shorts that made her legs look impossibly long, and her blond hair tied up in to her usual ponytail.

"Good morning." Archer poured her a cup of coffee, which she took with a shy smile.

"I didn't mean for you to sleep—"

"It's fine." He waved away her concerns. There didn't need to be any more awkwardness between them. "I needed the fresh air and you looked like you needed some space."

"About that—"

"You don't have to explain anything to me, Cass." But dammed if he didn't want her to. "There's a lot going on and the goal right now is to make this the best damn charter in Panama, right?"

She looked for a minute as if she was going to say something else, but then she swallowed hard, and nodded. Her smile was forced, but he wasn't about to call her on it. "That's right," she said. "And we will, too."

Archer turned to the bowl of banana pancake batter and gave Cass a moment to sip her coffee. Something was definitely going on with her and it had a lot more to do with than just the women who were on board. He just needed to get her alone and make her talk, because he'd never before met a woman who made him care the way she did and he'd be damned if he was going to sit back and let her push him away that easily.

"About that." Cass spoke up and Archer turned, his spatula in hand.

"About what?"

"Making this the best damn charter in Panama." He nodded and let her continue. "We need to move today. I was thinking about what happened yesterday, with the dinghy, and I believe you that you tied it up."

Archer bit his tongue.

"It had to have been sabotage."

"Wait. What?" Archer flipped a pancake before it could burn and turned to Cass again. "How did you get to sabotage so quickly? That's a bit extreme, don't you think?"

"No." She shook her head. "Not at all. It's Samson. It has to be."

"I don't know..." But even as he disagreed, the idea took shape in his head. Samson was a lot of things, but would he really go to the lengths of sabotage? That was a lot, even for Samson. But then again... "Do you really think so?"

Cass nodded, her mouth set in a firm line, and told him about the conversation they'd had at the Dockside Inn the night he was preoccupied with Maria and Joe. When she was done talking, his rage for Samson simmered just under the surface. How dare he try to intimidate Cass?

He turned and tended to his griddle for a moment, giving himself a moment to calm down and let the idea of sabotage roll around in his head while he worked on breakfast. It did make sense. After all, he *had* tied the dinghy to the tree and there'd been that other set of marks in the sand. Plus, it was no secret that Samson was less than pleased about Cass's new business venture, especially now knowing about their run-in. "Maybe you're right." He put a fresh pancake on a plate and handed it to her but Cass shook her head. "You need to eat." She picked up the pancake with her hand and rolled it.

"So you agree?" she asked with a mouthful. "It was sabotage?"

"It *could* have been sabotage." He was pretty sure that's what it was, but it wouldn't help to add fuel to Cass's fire about it at the moment. Even though it did seem more and more as though it was what had happened.

"Whatever." Cass swallowed her breakfast with a gulp of coffee. "Either way, I'm not interested in being anywhere around him. As soon as everyone's up, we're pulling up anchor."

"Aye-aye, Captain." He gave her a mock salute and she laughed, the exact response he was looking for. While she was still smiling, he leaned forward and pressed his lips to hers. When she didn't immediately pull away, he slipped one hand behind her head and kissed her deep. It wasn't exactly what he would have liked, but it would have to do.

"Well. Good morning."

Archer jumped back a step and looked to see Bridget and Brooke in the galley. Bridget had a knowing grin on her face, while her sister reflected the opposite emotion. Archer just shook his head. The sooner they could wrap things up with this particular charter, the better. "Who's hungry?"

Archer's kiss had felt good. Better than good. It had felt like more, which was why Cass was so glad the sisters had chosen the moment they did to interrupt them. She was trying so hard to keep a distance with Archer. Why? Her feelings scared the hell out of her and finding the picture of her and her father only cemented the fact that she didn't need one more man in her life who was going to leave her as soon as things got real. She couldn't let her feelings for Archer become anything more than they were. Besides, he was a distraction at a time when she needed anything but. No. She definitely didn't have time for any feelings for Archer.

And there were definitely feelings.

Cass excused herself as soon as was polite and headed above deck to get the boat ready to sail. The idea had stuck with her all night and she just couldn't let it go. It wasn't just the loss of the dinghy that was suspicious, although that had been enough. Archer had said something about arranging for a lobster dinner as well, but the Kunas hadn't come by with the promised feast. The Kunas were savvy business people, and it wasn't like them to give up a big sale like that. Unless a better deal had come along. Cass's brain spun with the possibilities that there was more to both the lack of lobster *and* the runaway dinghy. Sabotage. It was a strong word, but she really couldn't come up with anything else.

And there was only one name she could associate with it.

Samson.

Cass busied herself with the lines, organizing and tidying the deck in preparation for moving. It wasn't a big sail, but still there were a lot of things that needed to be tidied and put away. Especially with another three women on board. She gathered up a handful of towels and was about to throw them through a hatch below deck when a boat caught her eye. Specifically, the *Seaduction.* It didn't appear to be anchored where it had been the night before. Unless, of course, Samson had put out way more anchor chain than was necessary. But with a catamaran like the *Seaduction*, he could go right in close to shore because it drew a lot less depth. And that's what he did. But then why was the *Seaduction* almost as far out as they were? It was strange.

More than strange. She shook her head and tried not to care. Why should she care? It was Samson, after all. He'd only ever made things difficult for her. It wasn't her business if his boat had moved.

Unless…

Cass closed the back hatch where she'd been storing the snorkeling equipment and watched the *Seaduction* for another moment. It definitely wasn't a long anchor chain. In fact, the more she watched, it was clear that the boat wasn't anchored at all.

"Crap."

Cass jumped into the cockpit and grabbed the binoculars she kept there. A quick scan of Samson's boat turned up nothing. There didn't appear to be anyone on board, at least not above deck, and the dinghy wasn't there. She scanned her gaze to the nearby islands, where she spotted Samson's dinghy and farther into the island, a cluster of people sat on the sand. Morning yoga. *Perfect. They'd never notice their boat was drifting.*

"Archer!"

There was no real choice. Not for Cass anyway. As much as she didn't like Samson, she couldn't in good conscience sit back and let something happen to his boat. No way. And by the look of things, if she didn't do something soon, the big catamaran would be on the very same reef she'd almost been up against the day before.

"Arch—"

"I'm right here."

Cass turned and almost smacked right into his hard chest, he stood so close. She squeezed her eyes shut momentarily and inhaled deeply before she snapped her eyes open.

"It's Samson's boat." She pointed despite the fact that Archer had already spotted it. "We have to—"

"Absolutely." He was already in motion, grabbing a coil of rope and jumping into the dinghy. There was no time to yell down to their guests; besides, they'd figure it out soon enough.

She followed Archer's lead, jumped into the dinghy and within seconds they were zipping across the bay toward the runaway *Seaduction*.

Cass didn't have much experience captaining a catamaran, let alone a large one like the *Seaduction*, but the basics were the same and after tying up the dinghy, Archer went to the bow to deal with the anchor chain, while Cass fired up the engine. To her relief, there was nothing complicated about the boat and as soon as Archer yelled back that he was ready and had the anchor aboard, she slowly motored the boat back up into the bay and away from the dangerous reef. And just in time, too.

They managed to get the big catamaran back into position, close to where it had been anchored the night before. Archer dropped the anchor, and Cass pulled back gently until the boat was secured and she was sure the anchor had caught. It was unusual for the anchor to pull on such a sandy bottom, but one thing Cass knew about boats was that nothing was for sure and you couldn't take anything for granted.

When they were sure the boat was safe, Archer got back into the dinghy and started the engine. "He still hasn't noticed." Archer pointed to where Samson and his group were still in what had to be a zen-like state on the island under the palm trees. "It's a good thing, too," Archer continued. "It would probably really screw with his final shavasana if he saw you behind the wheel of his boat."

Cass couldn't help it; she burst out laughing at the idea of a wound-up Samson, fresh from his yoga practice, red in the face at the sight of Cass on his boat. "How do you even know what a shavasana is?"

She took his outstretched hand, allowing him to help her into the boat. Only, when she stood in front of him, he didn't let her go the way she'd expected.

"You don't think I know my yoga?" He spoke softly, but there was an undercurrent of something else in his words as he held her close. "I'm very in touch with the world around me, you know?"

She shivered at his words, and the meaning behind them.

Archer held her closer in response. She expected him to kiss her then. She wanted him to kiss her. Despite her uncertainty, despite her questions. Despite *everything*, she wanted him. That much she knew.

She was open to him. If Archer was to kiss her right then in that instant, he knew everything would be okay. He leaned forward, reached out and slipped his hand over her bare skin. The feel of her beneath his fingers sent a shot of desire to the core of him. "Cass." He pulled her gently, coaxing her closer in the boat. His lips brushed hers. Just a brief glance, but enough to get the salty taste of her. So close that it was almost impossible they weren't kissing, he whispered, "Whatever else is going on here, you need to know that I—"

"Kiss her already!"

The call from the direction of the *Cassiopeia* had the opposite effect and the moment was broken. Cass took a quick step back, stumbling and falling to the side of the rubber boat. She laughed and shook her head. "I guess we have an audience."

Together, they looked over to where Brooke and Bridget stood on the transom of their boat, laughing and cheering. Archer couldn't help it; despite the rush of frustrated desire he was experiencing, the whole thing *was* funny. And the fact that Brooke was laughing was huge because it meant that maybe she'd back off him with her predatory ways. At least for a bit.

Archer gave her a quick and chaste kiss on the forehead and took control of the throttle. "To be continued," he said, his words laden with meaning.

They zipped back to the boat, where they retold their story to their guests and instead of pulling up anchor right away to move the way Cass wanted to, Archer talked everyone into a celebratory mimosa. Because after all, it might still be early, but they'd just pulled off a boat rescue and for their guests, any occasion was one to celebrate.

One drink turned into two, at least for the women, and soon they were settled in for the day, jumping off the side of the boat into the ocean, swimming and calling for snorkel gear so they could explore the nearby reef.

"It doesn't look like they're in a hurry to pick up anchor." Cass shook her head, but didn't look overly disappointed as she settled into the cushions in the cockpit.

"It'll be good to stay for a day." Archer held up the jug of mimosas and Cass shrugged in response, which he took as a yes. "Besides, didn't Josie say something about doing a trial run for a night on shore? Maybe these three would be a good opportunity to give it a shot?"

Archer's motives were twofold. There had been discussion of merging the sail and shore trips, and there was no time like the present to give it a go and work out the kinks. Besides, even with all the chaos of the day before, Heather had come back from her visit with Josie markedly different. She seemed more relaxed and at peace with her demons or whatever it was that was troubling her. And Archer had a pretty good idea that those troubles circled largely around her husband and his new girlfriend.

"Heather would probably really like that." Cass seemed to read his mind. "She really seemed to connect with Josie. I'm not sure about the sisters." She glanced to the water, where Brooke and Bridget were currently snorkeling together. "They do seem to be getting along a little better. And Brooke is actually snorkeling." She shrugged. "It's worth a shot. Maybe I'll take the boat over later and work it out. And I guess that means that we'll have the *Cassiopeia* to ourselves."

And that was the other ulterior motive Archer had. He wanted some time alone with her. No, he needed some time alone with her. Never before had a woman gotten under his skin the way Cass had. She might be trying to push him away, but he had enough experience with his friends back home and watching them navigate their relationship dramas that he knew whatever was going on with Cass had nothing to do with him, and everything to do with her. He also knew he wanted to be by her side as she figured out what that was.

Chapter Twenty

IT HAD BEEN EASIER than Cass thought to get the women to agree to the shore portion of the trip and Josie was only too happy to pull it together last minute. It was becoming very clear how prepared the other woman had been and Josie's enthusiasm was infectious. She'd obviously been preparing and planning for what had been her dream for far too long.

Bridget and Heather had been an easy sell, and as expected, Brooke put up a bit more fuss when it came to leaving the comfort of the boat to sleep on shore, but it was short-lived when she saw the cozy sleeping accommodations Josie had prepared. The promise of a sky full of stars and the gentle sound of the waves washing up on the beach to lull her to sleep was all it took to convince her. Cass had been prepared for a bit more objection, but she wasn't going to look a gift horse in the mouth. The second the women were settled, she took her leave and headed back to the *Cassiopeia*.

And Archer.

Definitely Archer. It was time to get back to her one and only rule for her new life: Do what feels good. And being with Archer felt good. More than good, it felt *right*. She also knew he wouldn't wait around forever for her to figure things out. The last few days had been so intense and a roller coaster of emotions in so many ways, that if she wasn't careful, she'd screw up the one thing that was going right for her.

With a renewed determination, she navigated the dinghy faster over the bay toward the *Cassiopeia*. But as she grew closer, and the boat turned in the wind, she slowed up. There was another small boat tied to the back. Samson.

She had no reason to be intimidated by the man. Especially now, but it didn't stop her pulse from quickening and all her defenses to be up as she neared the stern. Archer was there to grab her line and tie up the tender. "Samson's here," he said unnecessarily.

Cass asked him a question with her eyes, aware that the other man was only a few feet away. Archer nodded and smiled. "He comes in peace," he whispered in her ear and gave her a quick kiss on the cheek before he led the way up onto the deck.

"Samson." Cass forced a cheeriness she couldn't bring herself to feel into her voice. After all, this was the man who'd less than twenty-four hours ago had tried to sabotage her business.

The other man rose quickly to his feet and extended his hand. "Cass." His grip was powerful, but there was kindness in his eyes she hadn't seen in a while, and something else. A dose of humility, perhaps. "I'm sorry to intrude on your charter."

She shrugged. "They're on the island."

"Right." His gaze drifted over to Barbecue Island. "With Josie."

She nodded, although they both knew it was unnecessary. "What can I help you with, Samson?" She didn't have time for formalities and small talk. The sooner she could figure out what Samson wanted, the happier she'd be. Especially if it meant getting him off her boat.

"I'm not trying to take up any of your time," he said. "I was telling Archer here," he nodded at Archer, who'd come to stand next to her, "that I just wanted to stop by and thank you for saving the *Seaduction* yesterday." *So he did know they were the ones who'd helped him out?* Not that Cass needed validation for what they'd done; they would have done it for anyone, and would expect the same type of treatment in return. It was the unwritten sailor's code. You helped each other out. It's just what was done. Her father had taught her that right along with her basic knots when she was a kid.

"We would have done it for anyone." She could feel Archer stiffen slightly next to her, but she knew despite his feelings for the man, Archer wouldn't hesitate to do it again. That was one of the things she loved about him. *Loved.* The word rang in her mind and she had to force it out so she could focus on the conversation she was still part of.

"That's the thing," Samson was saying. "I know you would and that's why I really need to apologize." He dipped his head and looked at his feet. "I'm not even sure if you know this, but I've been a first-class jackass."

"Oh, we know it."

Cass reached out and put her hand on Archer's arm. She appreciated his protectiveness more than he probably even knew, but she could also recognize that Samson was trying to humble himself and for a man like Samson, that wasn't an easy thing. She gave him an encouraging smile. Archer shook his head, but she could feel him relax under the weight of her hand. At least a little. It would have to be enough for the moment. "Why don't we all sit down?"

Once they were all settled, or as settled as they could be given the tension in the air, Cass was ready to hear the apology. She could have let him off easy, knowing how difficult it must be for him to sit across from her and admit he'd been a jerk, but she deserved an apology, and she'd be damned if she was going to let him off the hook without one. "So, Samson." She focused her gaze directly on him, surprising herself with how she no longer felt intimidated by him. It wasn't all that long ago that he made her a little nervous. No longer. "What was it you were saying earlier?"

He coughed to clear his throat and to his credit, got right to the point. "I need to apologize, Cass. I'm not proud of my behavior."

"What behavior would that be?"

Cass shot Archer a look, but turned to wait for Samson's answer. She, too, was interested to hear what he had to say.

"I shouldn't have released your dinghy."

She knew without looking at him what type of reaction that would get from Archer, so Cass put her hand on his leg in a preventative measure. It worked, but what she hadn't counted on was the charge she felt with her hand on his bare skin. She had to force herself to stay in control and focus on the conversation. "The dinghy?"

Samson nodded. "I'm sorry. It was childish."

"It was dangerous," Archer interjected. "Cass could have been hurt when she swam for it. And stranding our guests out in the hot sun…that was more than childish, Samson. It was—"

"I know." Samson held up his hand to stave off anymore of Archer's attack. "I wasn't thinking straight. I was just—"

"Thinking about hurting us? Hurting Cass?"

"Archer." She squeezed his thigh and forced him to look at her. "It's okay." She stared deeply into his eyes, willing him to understand that it would be okay. She didn't feel threatened by Samson anymore, and he needed to realize that. Finally, Archer blinked and nodded slowly. But it wasn't until he sat back that Cass released her breath and looked back to Samson, who waited and watched their exchange without expression. "I accept your apology, Samson."

He nodded, relief evident in his eyes. "It won't happen again. I know now there's room for all of us in the San Blas. I don't have to be the only charter company in town."

"No." She shook her head and laughed a little. "You don't. There's enough tourism for all of us. In fact, I think we can only help each other instead of hurt, don't you think?"

Samson smiled then and laughed a little. "You're so much like your father, Cass."

His words hit her like a blow and she sat back hard in her seat. *Her dad.* Despite what she knew, it was the first time Samson had actually admitted knowing him. She'd always known that he had to know something, but the admission was huge. Bigger than huge. The knowledge that Samson knew *something* was still there like a cloud hanging over them.

She couldn't look at him and suddenly the cockpit was too small. She leaned back, trying to get a lungful of fresh air, but the heat was stifling. From somewhere beside her, she heard Archer say something to her, but his words didn't permeate her brain. The boat tilted and her stomach flipped and rolled.

"Cass!"

She heard Archer's voice and felt his hands around her waist as he hauled her up and to the side of the boat, where she emptied the meager contents of her stomach.

Archer rubbed her back and sat by helplessly while Cass was sick. He'd seen the change in her so quickly he'd barely had time to react. It didn't take long and she rocked back on her heels until her back was pressed up against the side of the boat. Color slowly returned to her face, but before he had a chance to really assess it, she buried her head in her hands.

"Are you okay?"

She nodded, but didn't look up.

"Cass?"

"I'm fine," she mumbled. "Just so embarrassed."

A rush of affection washed through him. Here was this woman who had proved over and over again that she didn't need looking after, but dammit if that's not exactly what he wanted to do. No matter how strong she was, Archer wanted nothing more than to pull her into his arms and protect her from anything that would threaten to wipe that beautiful smile off her face.

"You have absolutely no reason to be embarrassed." He reached up and smoothed her blond hair back from her face. His hand lingered on the back of her neck. "I'm just concerned. What happened?"

She looked up then and opened her mouth to say something, but Samson chose that moment to appear next to them with a bottle of water. "I hope it's okay, but I found this in the galley. Thought you might…"

"Thank you." Archer took the bottle from him with a nod and shot him a look that had the desired effect of sending him back into the cockpit.

"Here." He unscrewed the cap and handed her the bottle. "Drink this."

She did as she was told and drank deeply. When she finished, she wiped her mouth with the back of her hand and looked at him. "I honestly have no idea what happened. I've never had that happen before. It was just like all of a sudden I couldn't breathe. I couldn't think. I couldn't do anything."

"Sounds like a panic attack."

"It wasn't a panic attack." Archer tried not to smile when Cass reached over and smacked him. "Why would you say that? I've never had a panic attack before. That's crazy."

She tucked a strand of hair behind her ear and moved to stand, but Archer put a hand on her knee. He tried to ignore the silky smooth skin beneath his fingers. "Sit for a minute."

She glanced at him, but didn't object. "It's okay, Cass. You've been under a lot of stress. Maybe it was just something Samson said. About your dad maybe?"

Cass shook her head, but he could see he'd hit a nerve. "It's not…okay, well, maybe it is." She dropped her head into her hands again. Archer wrapped an arm around her and pulled her into him. She didn't cry, but she did allow herself to be held, a small detail Archer was thankful for because he knew her well enough to know she'd be angry if she broke down in any way around Samson. It was bad enough she had the panic attack or whatever it was.

He gave her a few moments and then pulled away gently. "Good?"

She nodded. "Yup."

Archer stood and gently pulled her to her feet before he helped her back into the cockpit, where Samson waited a lot more patiently than he would have expected. He jumped to his feet when they came near.

"Cass, are you okay? You went all white and—"

"I'm fine." She held up her hand and managed a weak smile. "Really. I don't know what happened, but thank you for the water."

"Of course."

The men waited to sit until Cass was settled, a detail Archer was fairly sure irritated her—at least a little bit.

"I hope I didn't say anything to upset you." To his credit, Samson looked suitably concerned and Archer allowed at least some of his dislike for the man to subside. "I did want to talk to you about your father, though." He paused and glanced at Archer, who looked at Cass to assess how she might feel. "If it's okay?"

She nodded. "You guys both need to stop looking at me like I'm going to break. I'm fine. Whatever that was a minute ago, it's done. I probably just haven't had enough water today or something." She shot Archer a look, and he tried not to laugh. "I mean it. I'm fine."

He did his best to stifle his laugh. Cass ignored him and turned her attention to Samson again. "What did you want to tell me about my dad? I thought you said you didn't know anything?"

"That's the thing…"

Archer's protective instincts kicked in again and the familiar dislike for the man returned. If he'd been screwing with Cass on something as important as information about her father, Archer couldn't be sure whether he'd be able to let the man continue to sit across from him. He tensed in his seat and put his arm protectively around Cass.

Samson cleared his throat and ran his hand through his scruff of hair. "I wasn't totally honest with you before."

No shit. Archer had to bite his tongue.

"I knew your dad." Cass nodded. She knew that already. Archer willed the other man to tell her something of value. "In fact, we were good friends at one point. We sailed together, drank together…even worked together." His face took on a faraway look as he obviously got lost in a memory. "But then it all changed."

"Why?"

"Your dad met Josie," he stated simply.

"And you couldn't be friends anymore?" There had to be more to the story than that. A love triangle maybe? Was it possible that Josie and Samson were an item?

"It's not what you think," he said, reading Archer's mind. "There was never anything between us. Josie and Roger were always…" He laughed and shook his head in memory. "They were something else. I don't even want to use the word soulmates because that's not quite it. Not enough. It was more like, two pieces of the same person. They just worked. Ya know?"

Cass didn't say anything but unshed tears shone in her eyes.

"I do know," Archer half whispered, not taking his gaze off her.

Samson nodded. "At first, we were all friends but it became clear that I was just getting in the way. I'm not proud of it, but I was jealous. Not that Roger had Josie, but that she had him. We were going to build a business together but then they started talking about their ship-to-shore idea and..." Samson shook his head and forced a smile. "It doesn't matter. Things changed and that's just the way it was. But that's not what I came here to tell you."

There was a change in Samson's tone they both recognized. Cass sat up straight next to him, and Archer adjusted his arm around her. He had a feeling she was still going to need his nearness.

"Do you know what happened to him?"

There was a hope in Cass's voice that Archer hadn't heard before. Something had definitely shifted within her, whether she knew it or not: somewhere along the line, her indifference toward her father had morphed into something that looked an awful lot like concern.

"I don't," Samson said. "Not for sure. But I have a pretty good idea." He exhaled long and slow before he spoke again. "Right before Roger disappeared, he came to me for money."

"Money?"

The other man nodded at Cass's question but continued with his line of thought. "He asked me for ten thousand dollars."

Archer let out a low whistle. "That's a big chunk of money to ask for."

"Exactly. And I didn't have it." Samson squeezed his hands together. "Even if I did, I'm not sure I would have lent it to him. I mean..."

"It's fine." Cass let him off the hook. "Why did he need the money?"

"I'm not sure. I didn't ask."

Archer had a hard time believing that he wouldn't have even been a little curious about why his buddy needed so much money, but he didn't bother to say anything. It wasn't an important detail. Not at the moment anyway.

"A few days later," Samson continued. "There was a cargo ship headed for Columbia that came through the canal. The captain was looking for crew. Next thing I knew, Roger was gone. I always kind of thought he might have been on that ship."

Next to Archer, Cass sagged in her seat. "He ran away?"

"You don't know that, Cass." Archer could see her face closing up, the anger—or worse, indifference to her father—returning again. "We don't know why he needed the money. It might not have been—"

"It doesn't matter." Cass shook his arm off and stood. "Thanks for letting me know, Samson. It's more information than I had before. Not that it matters."

"Of course it matters." Archer stood and tried to grab her arm, but it was too late. She'd already walked away. He let her go for the time being. She needed time to process and when she was ready, he'd be there for her. Of that there was no doubt.

Chapter Twenty-One

CASS SPENT what should have been a night to celebrate and squeeze in some much-needed alone time with Archer restless. He didn't push her to talk, and for that she was grateful, happy just to be in his arms, the hard heat of his chest pressed up against her back as she tried to find sleep. But sleep was elusive and when the first rays of the rising sun finally, mercifully snuck their way through the window, she slipped away and sat on the back deck to watch the sun come up over the ocean.

It was the most peaceful part of the day, a time she used to enjoy when she was younger. The promise of a new day before her, full of possibilities, was empowering and somehow had always made her feel more connected to her life. When was the last time she'd watched the sun rise? It had been too long. Way too long. She wrapped her arms around her legs and dropped her head so her cheek was pressed against her knees as the sun rose higher, bringing the heat with it. A pelican flew in front of her vision, dipping low to skim along the flat sea before it rose again.

Cass let the moment fill her, and only once she felt at peace did she allow herself to think of her father again and the one thing that troubled her the most about what Samson had told her.

He ran away.

Just when she had started to feel connected to him, to his boat, to the life he'd had in Panama—the life he'd chosen over her—she discovered the truth. He'd really had done it again. Despite what Josie thought about Roger leaving, Cass had believed—had *wanted* to believe—that he hadn't left again. It didn't even make sense, but for some reason, it was easier for her to believe that something else had happened to him. But after Samson's confession, it was clear. Her father had run again. He'd left everything behind and run away, not caring about the broken hearts and shattered lives he left in his wake. As much as Cass hated it, and she did, hers was one of those broken hearts. Again.

The sound of her phone beeping in her pocket brought a smile to her face. It could only be one person and somehow even from thousands of miles away, on a completely different continent, her best friend always seemed to know when she needed her. Cass pulled her phone from her pocket and looked at the screen.

My life is boring. Tell me something exciting. How's the Canuck?

Cass laughed and shook her head. Angie's life was anything but boring. It had been Cass's life that was boring. At least up until recently. She had to admit, things had definitely taken a turn for the more exciting in the last few months. Not that she would trade it for the monotony that had been her existence in Seattle, but it might be nice if things were a little calmer.

. . .

He's good.

She typed and then as an afterthought, added,

REALLY good.

That would make Angie happy. But as soon as the smile spread across her face, it was gone, replaced by the reality of what was really bothering her.

My dad is an asshole.

She hit Send and waited.

But Angie didn't reply with a text. Instead, her phone rang in her hand. Answering it, Cass put it to her ear.

"He's alive?"

"Hi, Angie." Cass smiled at the sound of her best friend's voice. It had been too long since they'd actually spoken. "You didn't have to call."

"To hell I didn't. What's going on? Did you find your dad? Is he alive? What happened? I can't believe after all—"

"He's not alive," she cut her off. "Well, he might be. I don't know." She shrugged and considered the possibility for a moment. He could just as easily be alive as dead. It had just been easier to assume he was dead, but with the new information… "It doesn't matter," she said after a moment. "He is or was an asshole."

"Cass…" Angie let her thought, whatever it might have

been, trail off. It wasn't very often that Angie was rendered speechless.

"It's fine, Ang. I'm good." It was a lie and they both knew it. "I guess I was just hoping that after he left me, he'd changed. And you know what?" She didn't wait for an answer, but gazed out over the still calm sea before she continued, "Just being here on his boat surrounded by everything he loved...I felt closer to him. It was strange."

"I don't think that's strange at all, Cass."

"Of course it was strange." She couldn't sit any more. The pent-up energy she'd been feeling all night had started to take its toll. There was nowhere to pace on a boat, but she tried her best. "I've barely thought of him in years, let alone felt connected to him, and dammed if I didn't start to—it doesn't matter. I don't feel that way anymore. I'm done."

"You're done?"

"I'm done. I can't give him another minute of my time and energy. I refuse to waste another thought on what may or may not have happened to him." She looked toward Barbecue Island, where Josie was busy entertaining guests in what was supposed to be her dream with the very man she was writing off. It was all so screwed up. She looked away. "I'm done, Ang. I'm moving on."

"I don't know, Cass. I don't think it's so easy."

"Of course it is. Why wouldn't it be?"

Through the phone line, Cass could hear her friend exhale slowly. Something she only did when she was trying to figure out what to say, or how to say it. Even thousands of miles away, she could picture Angie biting her tongue and measuring her words so she didn't set Cass off. Which only meant one thing—Cass wasn't going to like what she was going to say when she finally said it.

"Cass, I—"

"Don't."

"Don't what?"

"Don't tell me that I'm being dramatic and oversensitive and that I should learn to accept the type of man he is and always has been and that I can't spend the rest of my life worrying about why he left me."

There was a silence on the other end and for a second, Cass thought maybe the call had been disconnected. "I wasn't going to say any of that," Angie said after a moment.

"You weren't?" She stopped pacing and sat down hard. "Then what were you going to say?"

"I was going to tell you to trust what you're feeling."

"But I—"

"You know exactly what you're feeling."

Dammit. How did she do that? Angie always knew what to say to cut through her bullshit. But this was one time when Cass really didn't know how she was feeling. She scanned the horizon, letting the silence between them stretch out. When it came to her father, she was angry, disappointed, frustrated, and… confused. It didn't add up. It didn't feel right.

Isn't that why she'd really had so much trouble sleeping the night before? None of it added up. Yes, her father was a leaver. Or at least he had been. But would he really leave this?

"Cass? Are you still there?"

She nodded and then quickly said, "I'm here. Just thinking."

"Any conclusions?"

She nodded again and a flash of color caught her eye as Archer appeared on deck. There was one more thing she'd have to trust her feelings on. A smile tugged at her lips and she turned away to finish her conversation with Angie. "Not yet," she said into the phone. "But I think I have some good ideas."

The sail back to the dock was uneventful and quiet, just the way Archer liked it. The women spent the time napping and reading when they weren't busy chatting about their night on shore. By all accounts, it was a night enjoyed by everyone, even Brooke. Archer had to hide his knowing smile every time the woman jumped in with some story about the food or how comfortable the hammocks were, or some other detail that only a day ago she was bemoaning. The lure of paradise was hard to ignore, even for a girl who was used to having all the comforts of a five-star resort. There didn't seem to be a better endorsement for the *Cassiopeia* charter business.

They docked the boat easily. Archer jumped ashore to tie off the bow, before he ran to catch the line Cass threw him off the stern. It was seamless, a far cry from their earlier fumbling attempts as they'd learned how to handle the boat. The fact that they'd worked through so much together in such a short time wasn't lost on him. After the last line was tied off and he climbed aboard again, he walked straight to the helm where Cass was shutting down the engine, and heedless of who might see or what they might think, he pulled her into his arms, and kissed her quickly yet thoroughly.

"What was that for?" She laughed a little as she pulled away. "We still have guests, you know." She didn't sound annoyed when she said it, which also spoke volumes about how far their relationship had come in such a short amount of time, but there was a trace of the cutest blush on her cheeks.

"I don't think anyone saw." He winked and turned to head down to the galley, but before he did, Archer turned and added, "But even if they did, I don't care. Because sometimes you're just so damn kissable, it's all I can do to keep my hands to myself."

This time, the blush on her face was real. And that's how he left her, standing at the helm and looking sexy as hell, totally flustered by both his words and his kiss. With a smile on his face, Archer headed down to the galley to clean up. He'd promised the sisters he'd carry their bags back up to the hotel and restaurant, and they'd gone ahead to start figuring out what they were going to do next. Brooke and Bridget were discussing their options and much to his surprise, even contemplating a longer stay out at the island with Josie. As for Heather, he wasn't sure what she was going to do. He couldn't imagine that she'd return to the restaurant with Joe and his new girlfriend and baby, but she probably didn't have a lot of options. He snuck a glance across the salon to where she was packing her bag. She didn't seem overly stressed about running into Joe; in fact, she looked downright blissful.

Archer left the dishes and moved through the boat to talk to her. "Hey."

She looked up and gave him a small smile.

"I was going to take the sisters' bags up the dock. Do you want me to take yours, too?" He gestured to her small backpack and realized how lame it was as he was doing it.

She smiled. "I got it, thanks."

"Look, that's not really what I wanted to ask you." Archer scrubbed a hand over his face. He was pretty sure he might regret butting in, but he had to say something. She stared at him, waiting. "I just wanted to make sure you're going to be okay. I mean…with…are you sure you want to go back to the hotel?"

Heather managed a smile but it didn't reach her eyes. "I don't really have a choice, do I? I mean, it'll be okay for now. I'll figure something out."

Archer racked his brain. He didn't really have any options to present to her; it's not as though there were a lot of places to stay in Shelter Bay. Only the one, really. "Maybe Samson could take you back out to the islands?"

This time Heather's smile was real, if a little sad. She shook her head. "No, Archer. As much as I'd love to spend more time with Josie, I need to deal with this. I can't run away forever."

Archer opened his mouth to say something, but there was nothing he could offer. For whatever reason, he felt protective of her. Perhaps it was because of her unfortunate situation, or that she reminded him of his friend Samantha back home. Whatever it was, he wanted to help her and it wasn't in any way romantic. There was only one woman he held any of those feelings for. There was nothing he could say. He pulled her into a quick hug. "If there's anything—"

"I know, Archer. Thank you." She slipped out of his arms and wiped her eyes quickly. "It means a lot to know that I have friends in all this."

"You do."

She smiled again. "And I just might take you up on that offer." She turned to grab her bag and slung it over her shoulder. "Josie was telling me about a friend of hers in Bocas who runs a jungle B&B. She said she might need some help for a few months. And even if she doesn't..."

Archer nodded knowingly. It was a place to go. He could understand that. And from what he'd heard, Bocas del Toro on the other side of Panama was definitely a place to go. Very different from the peace and tranquility of the San Blas, Bocas had more of a party reputation, but he'd heard there were some magical places tucked into the mangroves as well. He'd been curious to check it out himself. "Well, you never know." He led the way through the salon and grabbed the sisters' bags as he went. "Maybe Cass and I can arrange a charter out that way and deliver you?"

"Things are going well with her, then?" She smiled before she led the way out into the sunshine. "You two seem kind of...close."

He tossed the duffel bags to the dock and scanned the boat behind him to look for Cass, who was nowhere in sight. He thought for sure she'd be there to say good-bye. "We thought we were doing such a good job keeping it a secret." Archer laughed. They might have tried to be secretive at the beginning, but they'd both failed miserably, and everyone knew it.

"Why bother?" Heather took Archer's offered hand and hopped from the boat to the dock. She turned and looked at him still on the boat. "When you fall in love with someone, I mean, really in love, you just have to go with it, Archer. Anything less is an injustice to what you could have. And you'll never know what you could have until you allow yourself to open up completely."

Archer let her words roll around his head for a second. Finally he nodded and grinned. "You're a wise woman, Heather."

"Of course," she laughed and shook her head, "who am I to give love advice, right? Look at my screwed-up life."

He put his arm around her shoulder in a quick, affectionate squeeze. "Something tells me you'll be fine." And he meant it, too. He didn't know much about her, but from what he could see, she was a strong woman and this thing with Joe, whatever it was, it was only a minor setback. She'd come through the other side and it would be a brighter future when she did. But he didn't tell her that, not yet. She'd need to see it for herself.

Archer took another quick scan for Cass. Maybe she'd gone up to the restaurant already. No matter; he'd find her. "Come on, Heather. I'll walk you up."

The second the sisters had left the boat, Cass did too. Despite what she'd tried to convince herself of, she couldn't let it go. Not yet. She was going crazy with unanswered questions and she needed some answers. No matter what they were. She'd waited until Bridget and Brooke were set up in the bar with a drink and slipped away to find Joe. As it turned out, she got lucky and found him in his office instead of doting on Maria and their new baby girl. She shook her head and felt a twinge of sadness for Heather, who no doubt was going to have to deal with the drama of her cheating husband in a very real and likely very public fashion. But she couldn't let herself think about that too much right now. She needed answers and Joe was her best and perhaps only option at the moment. She needed him on her side, and if that meant playing neutral even though she would absolutely choose Heather's side, she would. At least for the moment.

"Knock, knock," she said as she walked into his small office. So much had changed from the last time she'd stood there. Had it only been a few months ago when she'd arrived in Panama with no idea how her life was about to change? *Wow.* "Do you have a minute, Joe?"

He looked up from whatever paperwork he was poring through on his desk, and blinked at her a few times, as if trying to place who she was. He looked tired. No. Tired didn't quite cover it. He looked flat out exhausted. Chewed up and spat out kind of exhausted. The type of exhaustion that could only come from the stress of being a new father for the first time in your fifties with your new, considerably younger girlfriend, while your wife was still trying to absorb the news. There was no doubt about it, Joe had a lot on his plate. And she was about to put more on it.

His eyes finally cleared; acknowledgment of who she was registered on his face. "Hey, Cass." He scrubbed a hand over his scruffy chin. "How was your first charter? Everything go okay?"

If he knew Heather was on the trip, he didn't say anything. She smiled. "It went pretty well. We had a few hiccups, but Samson and I worked them out."

That brought a smile to his face and he laughed. "I had a

feeling there might be some trouble from that end of things. I'm glad to hear it's okay." He narrowed his eyes. "They are okay, right? You don't need me to handle anything, do you?" As if he didn't have enough to worry about? "Because I'll totally take care of it if you need me to. I mean, I kind of owe you."

Cass frowned. "You owe me?"

Joe's face morphed into a state of distress, and he aged another few years in front of her eyes. "Heather."

"Right." Cass nodded. *So he did know where his wife had been the last few days.* She wasn't usually the type of person to use someone else's distress to her benefit, but this wasn't a usual situation and she needed all the leverage she could get. "Well, I don't need any help with Samson, but I do need a little help. If you're not too busy," she added as an afterthought. "I know you must have a million things going on and I don't want—"

Joe silenced her by holding up his hand. "Anything, Cass."

She took another step into his office and leaned against the wall. "Things with Samson are fine," she said. "At least I think they are. As a peace offering, he actually gave me some information about my dad that might help me figure out where he went."

Joe perked up a little in his chair. "I knew Samson knew something. I've always known it."

Cass ignored him and continued. "Anyway, he said something about my dad wanting to borrow money. Do you know anything about that?"

Joe stuck the end of his pencil in his mouth and chewed down. "No," he finally said. "He didn't owe me anything. That came later." Cass nodded and tried not to roll her eyes. "What I mean," Joe added, "was that he was always up to date with his dock fees and he never carried a balance. In fact, he was rarely even on the dock here. He preferred to anchor out. It always kind of struck me as kind of strange that he put the *Cassiopeia* on the dock before he took off."

The words *took off* rang through her head but she chose to ignore them. "What do you mean, he anchored out? Why would he put the boat on the dock if he was taking off?"

"That's what I'm saying." Joe stuck the pencil back in his mouth and Cass had to fight the urge to yank it out. "It never made sense. If he planned on taking off and leaving the *Cassiopeia*, which I could never understand, it wouldn't make any sense to leave her on the dock. It would have made more sense to drop her on an anchor in a bay somewhere. But that doesn't make any sense either…"

When he didn't continue right away, Cass prodded, trying to hide her annoyance at his slow responses. She tried to cut him a little slack for being an overtired new dad, but that bit of sympathy came with a whole host of other guilt issues because of Heather. She shook her head. There was no winning in this situation; she just needed to get her information and get out. "Why doesn't that make sense?"

Joe tipped his head back and let out a long, slow yawn before he continued. "If he planned on leaving, and he needed money, he would have sold her."

"Sold her?" She hadn't considered that. But of course. If he'd needed money, he was sitting on a big pile of it in the form of his boat. It wouldn't have made sense to just walk away without attempting to liquidate.

"The *Cassiopeia*."

"I know what you meant." Her response was much sharper than intended and she immediately felt bad. "I'm sorry, Joe. I know you're trying to help. There was one other thing that Samson said that I was hoping you could help with."

He nodded. "What's that?"

"He said something about a cargo ship from Columbia that

was looking for crew. It came through a few days after my dad asked him for money. And then he was gone."

"You don't think he was on—"

"I don't know what to think." And that was the truth. "All I know is that I have to start somewhere and this is the best lead I've got."

Joe didn't speak again for a moment. Instead, he stared at her with a strange expression on his face. She was just about to ask him what he was staring at when he finally opened his mouth. "I don't know what caused your change of heart regarding finding out about your dad, but I have to tell you, it's heartening to see your concern."

"Heartening?"

"Well, I have a little girl now and just knowing that there's a bond between—"

Cass held up her hand to stop him. "That's different."

"I don't know if it is."

"Trust me." She crossed her arms over her chest. "It is." She immediately felt bad about being short with him again. He was clearly excited about his new baby, as he should be, but excited or not, drawing a parallel between however he felt with his new little girl and the dysfunction that was her own father-daughter relationship wasn't something she'd be able to stomach. "Can you help me with this or not?" She needed to get out of there. The room started to close in around her; the heat smothered her and made it hard to breathe. "I just need to know if he was on the ship or not?"

"You think he was—of course." Joe nodded slowly. "That actually makes perfect sense. I don't know why I didn't think of it earlier."

"Like years earlier," she mumbled.

But he must have heard her because his face turned red. "Of course, there's new information now that makes it—"

"It doesn't matter, Joe. Honestly." She gave him the most genuine smile she could muster.

Through his exhaustion, he smiled back and Cass felt her annoyance melt away to be replaced by the affection she'd felt for the man originally. Despite his actions, he was still the same kindly man who'd welcomed her to Shelter Bay a few short months ago. He was a friend and she knew he'd help her.

"I'll do what I can, Cass," he said, reading her mind. "Maria's probably still nursing the baby and there's nothing I can really do to help with that. I'll look into it right away."

She could have cried with relief. Not that she had any answers yet, but somehow just knowing he was going to help her made her feel better. Closer to the truth somehow. "Thank you." She turned to go, but stopped in the doorway and looked back. "And Joe?" He looked up from his papers. "Congratulations on becoming a father."

Chapter Twenty-Two

ARCHER EXPECTED to see Cass at the restaurant, but she wasn't there. Brooke and Bridget were into their second drink, and claimed they hadn't seen her since they'd said good-bye an hour earlier, but still Cass hadn't shown up. He was starting to get worried when he headed outside the air conditioning to take one more look down the dock. Maybe she'd gone back to the boat and he'd missed her? It's not as though Shelter Bay was a big place, and normally he wouldn't be worried about it, but something was off with Cass that morning. No, something had been off with her since Samson's visit the night before. They hadn't had a chance to talk about it yet, but Archer knew that the information Samson had given her had only added to her stress instead of putting her mind at ease. Perhaps this was one of those situations when it was better off not knowing what had happened.

But Archer knew that wouldn't fly. Cass was the type of woman who once she set her mind to something, saw it through. That much he knew for sure.

A flash of blond caught his eye and he swung his head around in time to see Cass turn the corner by the pool. She was headed toward the yard where they kept the ships in dry dock to work on them. "What the hell is she doing?"

Archer broke into a slow jog. "Cass!" She either didn't hear him or ignored him. He had to think it was the former. "Cass!" He yelled again as he closed the distance between them. He put his hand on her shoulder and spun her around. "Where've you…" The question died on his lips when he saw the look on her face. "What's wrong?"

She shook her head.

"Cass?"

"Nothing." She shook his hand off her and took a step back.

Oh no. Whatever was going on with her and all the craziness with her dad, she wasn't going to push him away. Not going to happen.

"I just need a minute to—"

"No."

Her eyes flashed. "Pardon me?"

"I said, no." He crossed his arms over his chest and stood strong. "You do not need 'just a minute' to do anything." He knew he was pushing his luck with her, but he'd had enough of her tough girl act. When it came down to it, if it was bothering her, it was bothering him and he wasn't going to let her deal with something so major on her own. Whatever had happened between them over the last few months, he'd totally fallen in love with her and dammed if caring about her wasn't one of the side effects of that.

She matched him by crossing her own arms over her chest. "Oh yeah? I suppose you know exactly what I need then, do you?"

"As a matter of fact, I do." He uncrossed his arms and grabbed her hand, tugging her along with him. "What you need is to breathe. And the best way I know to do that is to go for a walk."

"It's a million degrees out, with a humidity index of a—"

"It doesn't matter. It's cooler in the trees." That was partly true. But mostly, it didn't matter how hot it was. What mattered was getting Cass out of her own head long enough for her to think clearly. And that quite obviously wasn't going to happen if they stayed at the marina.

She didn't stop walking, but she also didn't stop protesting or questioning him as they walked toward the rain forest. Shelter Bay was situated next to an old US Army base that closed over fifteen years earlier. Most of the buildings had fallen into ruins as buildings tended to do in the rain forest, but the roads remained, lending themselves to perfect walking trails through the lush growth of the jungle. Since he'd been there, Archer had spent hours exploring the trails and marveling at the vast array of wildlife that was so completely different from the Canadian mountains, yet just as soothing to his soul.

"I don't know, Archer." With her hand still in his, Cass stopped so abruptly he was yanked backward.

"You don't know about going for a walk?"

She shook her head and shrugged. The confident woman he knew vaporized as she looked at the jungle in front of them. It only took Archer a moment to figure it out.

"Wait…you haven't been in the jungle yet?"

"I've been a little busy."

"True." He kissed the back of her hand and gave it a squeeze. "You're going to love it."

"But there are snakes and jaguars and—"

"You'll be fine." He started walking again, and to his satisfaction, her feet moved along with his. "I promise, you'll be perfectly safe. Besides, don't you want to see the monkeys?"

"Monkeys?"

Archer stifled his laugh. He knew that would convince her. "Come on. I promised you I'd take your mind off your troubles and if it's going to take monkeys to do it, I'll deliver monkeys."

The last thing Cass wanted to do when she left Joe's office was go for a walk with Archer, but she didn't seem to have much choice in the matter. At least not as far as Archer was concerned. She didn't want to go for a walk. She wanted to stew. She wanted to think and she wanted to figure out the mystery of her father once and for all. She couldn't even figure out the exact moment when it had become important to her, but it had. It really had. And like Angie had said, she needed to trust her feelings. The whole problem was, she didn't know what she was feeling.

At least not when it came to her father.

She stole a glance at Archer, who was crouched down on the side of the small road and peered down at something. His t-shirt was stretched tight over his strong, solid back and as if he could sense her watching him, he turned and smiled. Her stomach did a little flip inside when he looked at her that way.

Yes, everything might be confused and messed up, and she might have a screwed-up way of showing it lately, but she was pretty sure she knew exactly how she was feeling when it came to Archer.

"Cass, come see this." He waved her over and trusting she would join him, turned back to whatever he was looking at. Intrigued, she squatted next to him and ran her hand down his back as she did so. He turned, giving her a sexy smile before he pointed to something on the ground in front of him. "See that?"

It took her a few seconds to see what he was talking about, but then she did: a parade of bright green pieces of leaf moving in a very quick and very long line.

"What the…is that…"

"They're leaf cutter ants."

Cass looked to the left and then to the right as she watched the ants parade through the dirt and carry their loads over rocks, twigs, and even down the trunk of a tree. "That's incredible. Look at them go."

"Cool, right?"

She nodded and stood, walking along the edge of the road, traveling their path with her eyes. She was so involved in watching the ants that when a low, guttural roaring sounded all around her, Cass jumped. "What the hell was that?" She walked backward so quickly, she bumped into Archer's solid chest. His arms wrapped around her, instantly holding her close. It took her a second to realize he shook slightly as he held her. It took her another full second to realize he shook from laughter.

Cass spun so she faced him, but he didn't release his hold on her. "What the—"

"Howler monkeys."

"Pardon?"

"They're howler monkeys." Archer laughed out loud and it was a good thing he held her so tightly because she might have tried to smack him. "They're up in the trees. I promise they won't hurt you. They're just establishing their territory. Although…"

"What do you mean, 'although'?" Cass narrowed her eyes at him.

"If they're close, they might throw fruit at us. Or worse."

"Worse than fruit?" Cass instinctively looked up, and when, a moment later, she realized what could be worse than fruit, she locked eyes on Archer again. "You mean—"

He nodded and laughed. "They're primates," he said. "Not exactly house-trained. But don't worry, they could be miles away. They're just really loud."

Cass opened her mouth to reply with a smart remark but it died on her tongue. Being held in Archer's arms, protected from the threat of the howler monkeys, real or perceived, a smile tugged on the corners of her mouth. "Thank you." It was all she could say. And when she stood on her tiptoes to touch her lips to his, it was all she needed to say.

"What was that for?" Archer asked when she pulled away. "Not that I need a reason for you to kiss me, because I certainly don't."

"Then don't question it."

She wiggled out of his arms and started to walk down the road again, following the path of a vibrant blue butterfly with her eyes. She didn't want to get into any deep conversations with Archer. She just needed to forget everything. Just for a few hours at least. She silently prayed for him not to push her, not to try to make her talk.

"I won't question a thing," he said as he came up beside her. "But I need you to promise one thing."

She stopped walking, watched the butterfly flit off into the jungle and gave Archer a nod. "Anything," she said, and genuinely meant it because in her heart she knew Archer wouldn't ask anything of her that she couldn't deliver.

"I know you have to go through this," he started. His hands traveled up her arms and squeezed them enough to center them both. "But whatever you learn, whatever you find out, promise me you won't turn away from this." His finger gestured between them but he didn't let her go. "There are a lot of things I don't know," he continued. "But I do know this." He paused and looked into her eyes so deeply she could have sworn he saw right into her soul. "What we have, Cass. What we're building here together…it's worth hanging onto." She bit her bottom lip and nodded slightly. "Whatever happens, don't push me away."

"I wouldn't—"

He silenced her with a finger to her lips. "Your dad, he made his choices and you might not ever know or understand why he made the ones he did, but you do need to understand that I'm not your father."

"I know that." She wanted to laugh it off, but his words resonated more than even she expected.

"No." Archer let the word hang in the air. "I need you to really understand it. I'm not your father, and I will not leave you, Cass. I am completely and totally falling in—no." He closed his eyes and shook his head sharply, just once. "No," he repeated. "I *am* completely and totally in love with you." His words sent a ripple through her, right to her toes. Something warm bloomed inside her and spread throughout her body, filling her completely. "You are under my skin in all the right ways, Cass Cutler, and that is certain. I need you to both understand and believe that. Promise me you'll try."

She nodded dumbly, unable to process the magnitude of what he'd just said.

"Promise me."

She looked into his eyes, and trailed her fingers down his jaw. "I promise." The words came out as a whisper, and immediately they felt inadequate. She should have said more. She should have told him that she loved him, too. "Archer, I—what was that?"

The moment was gone, her train of thought broken as a flash of movement from the treetops above them stole their attention. "It's a monkey!" Cass took a step back and pointed up to the trees to a spider monkey swinging through the vines above them. "Do you see it? It's incredible."

Archer laughed. "I see it. There's a few of them. See?"

She clapped her hands like a little girl and watched the monkeys use their arms and tails to cross overhead like acrobats. "It's the coolest thing I've ever seen. It's not at all like watching them in the zoo. Wow." She took a breath and tipped her head so far back she thought she might fall over. "Don't you think it's amazing? Have you ever seen something so incredible?"

When he didn't answer her right away, Cass turned around to see Archer, not watching the monkeys at all, but watching her instead. "No," he said seriously. His eyes pinned her. "I've never seen anything so incredibly breathtaking."

The way he looked at her sent a line of heat through her body, straight to her core. But it was the way he reached out, cradled her face in his hands and pulled her into him for a long, slow kiss that loosened a knot inside her she hadn't even known she had. Cass melted into his touch, and standing there, surrounded by the wildness of the jungle all around them, she couldn't remember the last time she felt so perfectly safe.

Chapter Twenty-Three

THEY MADE their way out of the rain forest, just as the sun started to dip below the horizon. Night came quickly in the jungle and despite everything Archer had said about being perfectly safe, there was no way Cass was about to spend any time in the jungle at night. Hand in hand, they left the wild behind and walked toward the glow of the restaurant. Strains of music slipped through the air toward them, and the scent of roasted garlic tickled their noses, reminding her just how long it had been since they'd eaten.

"Let's grab something to eat," Archer suggested, before she could.

"You read my mind."

He laughed. "No. I heard your stomach grumbling. Unless that was the howler monkey again."

She smacked his arm, but laughed along with him. "Well, maybe if my chef cooked me something, I wouldn't be so—"

He cut her off with a kiss that sparked a different kind of hunger in her.

Cass nipped his bottom lip and pulled back. "Point made." She smiled. "But I do think we both deserve a drink to celebrate our first official charter." She didn't mention that she was also hoping to run into Joe and see whether he had any news for her. She'd done her best to put everything out of her mind while they were walking and it had worked, too. In no small part because of Archer. She squeezed his hand. He was good for her; there was no doubt. But no matter how calming his presence was for her, it still didn't change the facts. Or the lack of facts, or whatever it was that was going on.

Either way, she was going to figure it out and put some closure on that chapter of her life.

The Dockside Inn was packed, but they managed to find a table by the bar. Archer went to get them drinks and Cass scanned the crowd for Joe. Of course, the chance that he was still around was probably pretty slim, considering he had a new baby to take care of. But she wasn't about to give up hope. He'd promised to look into it, and she had to believe him.

As the night went on, Cass had almost completely given up hope of talking to Joe by the time they finished their meals. Leaving Archer to chat with an older couple visiting from the Netherlands, she'd excused herself to take care of the tab when she saw him. Joe stood behind the bar, talking to one of the new waitresses. She moved quickly, determined to catch him before he could slip away.

"Joe."

He looked startled, but not entirely surprised to see her. "Cass. I'm glad I ran into you."

"You are?" She tried to manage her expectations, swallowing down the excitement that bubbled up inside her. "Does that mean…"

"Come on." He gestured to her to follow him outside, which she did. "It's so loud in there," he said as soon as they were next to the pool. "But business is booming and that's a good thing, right?"

She nodded distractedly. Of course it was a good thing; she

just didn't have the patience at the moment to talk about business. "Did you find out anything?"

Joe smiled, but it faded quickly. "I did, actually."

She held her breath. There was something in his voice. Something that worried her.

"You were right, Cass," he continued. "Your dad was on that ship." He produced a piece of paper from his pocket. "The HS *Calabera* was carrying a load through the canal and after they came through the passage, they picked up a few new crew members. It's actually pretty common for men to jump on the short hauls to make a bit of money. So if he needed money for whatever reason, it seems like a feasible thing to do. I mean…I don't know if I would do it, but…" He shook his head, as if remembering for the first time why they were standing there. "Anyway, I found your dad's name on the registry." He handed her the paper, which was a copy of the ship's roster. Her father's name was typed at the bottom of the crew list. "This was filed with customs and immigration when the ship checked out," Joe continued. "I have a friend who works…it doesn't matter. And honestly, it's pretty unusual to have an exact accounting of the crew on these types of ships. It's pretty transient, so there is a chance that your dad wasn't actually on the ship at the time when it…"

"When it what?" A wave of nausea washed through her. She knew without a doubt she wasn't going to like whatever he had to say next. "Joe?" she prodded. "When it what? What were you going to say?"

He pursed his lips together and shook his head slowly.

Warning bells went off in her head. She wasn't going to want to hear it, but at the same time, she needed to. Without a doubt in her mind, she knew that she needed to finish the story. "Joe?" Her voice was barely a whisper. "Please."

"I'm sorry, Cass. I really am, but the HS *Calabera* never reached her destination. There was a storm, and possibly a mechanical problem. I'm not sure exactly what happened, but she went down just off the coast. There's no record of any survivors."

Her knees buckled slightly, but she caught herself. For a moment, it sounded as if his voice came through a tin can, but then the fog cleared, and she stood strong in front of him, processing his words and exactly what they meant.

He was gone.

Her father was really gone.

"Cass? Are you okay? I'm really sorry that this is the news I had to give you. I was really hoping it would be better, that there'd be something…"

She tuned him out, his words becoming background noise to her thoughts. There was really no other news it could have been. She'd always known how the story would end. It was a feeling in her gut. But it wasn't until she'd arrived in Panama and spent time in his world that she'd both felt his presence and his absence so acutely. "It's okay," she said after a moment, interrupting Joe's rambling. "It really is. Thank you for this." She held up the paper and managed a smile. "It's exactly what I needed. Will you excuse me? I have something I need to do."

Joe nodded. She leaned over to give him a kiss on his cheek before she turned and walked down the dock, away from the restaurant.

Cass had been gone awhile by the time Archer finished talking to the Dutch couple. He was pretty sure he'd convinced them to try a short charter out to the islands, and he'd been hoping Cass would come back so they could arrange it, but she seemed to be totally MIA. He was just making his way outside when he saw her kiss Joe on the cheek and head down the dock.

What the hell? Where was she going now?

Archer pushed through the door and was about to call after her when Joe's voice stopped him. "Give her a minute."

He turned to the man who was more his enemy than anything else. "Pardon me?"

"Archer." Joe put his hand on his shoulder. "I just gave her some bad news. She might need a minute."

Archer's immediate response was to shrug Joe off and go after his woman. Especially if she'd just received bad news. She'd need him.

"She doesn't need you to get through this, Archer."

Rage flared through him, and it was all he could do not to punch the older man. "To hell she doesn't," he growled.

Joe shook his head, but didn't back down. "No. She needs to do this herself and I think you know that."

"You don't have the slightest idea what I know."

"I know you love her."

That realization stopped him.

"And I know you think I'm full of shit and you'd like more than anything to deck me right now."

Okay. Maybe the man had a point.

"I'm listening." Archer crossed his arms over his chest, but he did try to keep an open mind. Mostly. "What do you need to say?"

"This is a lot for her to process," Joe said slowly. "All of it, I mean. That girl has been through hell and back in her lifetime because of her father." Archer nodded; he couldn't disagree with that. "But she loved him. Probably more than even she will admit. Her memories…they aren't all bad."

"Of course they're not."

"But she needs to remember that. She needs to be at peace with him and with what happened."

Joe's choice of words cued Archer. "And what happened?"

He shook his head again and Archer had to physically

restrain himself from grabbing the other man and shaking him. "Just give her a minute."

"To hell with that. If you're not going to tell me, I'll ask her myself." Archer ran his hands through his hair. Why was he still standing there, listening to this philandering fool anyway? He didn't respect the man even a little; why should he care what his thoughts were on the woman he loved?

"I'm not going to stop you."

"That's right, you're not." Archer turned, ready to leave Joe and the nonsense he was spouting behind.

He was only a few steps away when Joe's voice stopped him. "Just love her, Archer." It was so full of remorse and concern and something that Archer couldn't quite identify, that for just a moment, for a completely unexplainable reason, he felt a little sorry for Joe. He paused, a sharp retort on his tongue, but swallowed it down, shook his head and went to find Cass.

By the time Cass got back to the boat, she'd had time to process the information Joe had given her. It hadn't been a surprise. Not really. She'd always known on some level he was gone. She'd let herself doubt that after meeting Josie and seeing the love they had. It was almost as if some part of her wanted to know that she wasn't the only one her dad loved who he'd left. That somehow it would be better if he'd also loved and left others. But there was a bigger part that knew that wasn't true. It had never been true.

He hadn't left. Not willingly.

But something had driven him to take the job on the ship. And that was the question that fueled her as she climbed aboard the *Cassiopeia* and headed straight below deck to the nav station. She retrieved the small wooden box that had sat there since Archer did as she'd asked and put it away weeks ago. She took the box and went into her bunk. Her eyes went straight to the shelf of books over her bed. One book in particular.

"Why did you need money, Dad?"

She pulled the book off the shelf and held it for a moment, feeling the familiar weight of it in her hands. She sat on the bed and shook the book open. The picture fell out in front of her. Cass put the book down next to her and picked up the picture, taking a quick second to run her finger over the picture of the two of them. "Come on, Dad. Tell me, what happened? What were you doing on that ship?"

Her eyes fell on the box. She was ten when she gave her father the secret lockbox. She'd visited a wood-carver with her Girl Scout troop and they'd been taught how to do simple carvings in the special boxes. Although the other girls had carefully constructed their own names on the lid, Cass had created the box for her dad. She ran her fingers over the rough letters and then slid down the side of the box to the secret panel the wood-carver had put there. It took a bit of force, the wood swollen from the humidity, but she slid the panel out. A small key fell out, and the tiny lock was exposed. Cass suspected before she put the key in the lock what she'd find inside, but she needed to confirm it.

She placed the picture in front of her so she could see it as she unlocked the box. She lifted the lid slowly to reveal a stack of money. Just as she'd suspected. She took the pile of bills out and flipped through them. Her mouth fell open. It was a lot of money. Most of the bills were hundreds or fifties. And with a stack that size, there had to be thousands of dollars in her hand. Tens of thousands.

She fanned through the money one more time. Her fingers stopped on a piece of paper tucked between the bills. Cass set the money down and unfolded the paper.

Her eyes scanned the figures and notes scribbled there and

when she was done, she read them again. The notes weren't very detailed, but they were clear. If the calculations were to be believed, there should be just under $30,000 in the box. At the bottom of the column of numbers was another number: 2,000, with the name HS *Calabera* written in brackets. That would have been the amount he would've been paid for his trip to Columbia.

So much money. And the reason why was printed just below the calculations. In her father's familiar angled, precise strokes was a sketch of an island: Barbecue Island. Josie's island. Only in the sketch, there were different buildings. The bed and breakfast they'd discussed together. A tear pricked at Cass's eye. Her breath caught in her throat as she realized just what it was she was looking at.

She was holding the dream in her hands. The dream her father and Josie had talked about, planned, and according to the figures in front of her, were almost ready to make a reality. He only needed a little bit more money. That's why he'd gone to Columbia.

He hadn't been running away at all. The knowledge flooded her with relief and she choked back a sob. "Oh, Dad. I knew it," she said to the photo. A tear dripped onto the paper and she quickly wiped it away. "I knew there was more to it."

"Cass?"

She hadn't heard Archer come in. Hadn't heard him standing there. She turned and wiped at her tears.

"Are you okay?"

She nodded and shook her head all at once. "Remember when you made me make that promise?"

"It was only a few hours ago." He took a step into the room. "I remember."

"Well, I'm going to keep it." She made a decision that all of a sudden became so clear and felt so right, she wondered how she hadn't realized it ages ago. "I'm not going to shut you out."

Archer nodded slowly, confusion written all over his face.

"Nothing makes sense, Archer. My dad left me and that sucked." She scoffed at her understatement. "But it didn't suck as bad as coming here and thinking he'd done it again to Josie. I can't even explain it. Part of me felt vindicated to know that he's a leaver and it wasn't just something that was broken in me that he needed to leave."

"Of course it wasn't you."

She held up her hand to stop him. She needed to finish her thought. "But even feeling that way felt wrong. It wasn't just that it wasn't fair to Josie, and it wasn't. But it didn't sit right with me. And I know it wasn't about me. He left me because of something inside him that he needed to find. It had nothing to do with me. I don't have to agree with his decision or feel good about it, because I won't. Not ever. But I do understand now that it was something he had to do." On some level she was aware that she was talking a mile a minute, but she couldn't stop. She had to get it all out while it made sense. Even if it only made sense to her. "When I got here and saw this boat, it all made sense. Well, some of it did. I could understand it. I felt connected to him. That's why his running away from Josie didn't make sense. But he didn't."

"What?"

"He didn't run away." Cass grabbed the piece of paper and thrust it toward him. "See? He wasn't running away at all. He was trying to make their dream come true." She watched as Archer's eyes traveled down the page and then back up again.

"What is this?" He shook his head. Confusion clouded his eyes as they moved across the bed and locked on the pile of money. "Is there really almost thirty grand there?"

She nodded.

"And the plan for the sea-to-shore bed and breakfast tours. Did Josie know about all this?"

Cass shook her head. "I don't think so. She would have said something. And she was so sure he left her."

"Do you know what this means?"

"It means a lot of things."

"It means you have enough money to pay off your dock bill, Cass." As soon as Archer said the words, words she herself had already thought, she knew it wasn't right.

"No." She shook her head and moved so she was only inches in front of him. "I can't do that."

His smile was soft and Cass could see in his eyes that he'd come to the same realization as she had. A very small detail that meant the world to her and confirmed something else to her. She had totally fallen in love with the man before her.

"I know you can't." Archer reached around her, retrieved the envelope and tucked every last bill back inside. "This is Josie's money." He voiced exactly what she had been thinking. Every dollar in that envelope belonged to the dream Josie and her father had worked to build. It wasn't her money and she wouldn't feel right spending it.

"I can't wait to tell her."

"That will be pretty amazing." Archer put his hands on her waist and held her tight. "But there's just one thing…" She tilted her head, listening. "I absolutely agree with you about the money. It belongs to Josie. But doesn't a part of you think you should use some of it to pay off your father's bill? I mean, to be fair, it's not your bill to pay."

That thought had crossed her mind. But she'd dismissed it immediately. She had to trust what she was feeling, it had been some good advice her best friend had given her, and Cass made a mental note to thank her next time she spoke with her. "I did think of that." She shrugged. "But I'm not too worried about it."

"You're not?"

She slipped a hand up Archer's back and shook her head. "No." She ran her tongue along her bottom lip, letting the love she felt for him fill her up. "I'm not. Because I've just started the most amazing charter boat business and I have the sexiest chef in Panama on my boat."

"Is that right?" His lips twitched up into a smile.

"That's right. And there's something else." Cass reached up and trailed her fingers down the side of his face to cup his jaw. "That sexy chef? If I pay off my bill, I'll have no legitimate reason to keep him here. And that will be a problem, you see, because I am totally and madly in love with him."

His grin was wicked and immediate. "Here's the thing about that chef." He closed the gap between them. "Bill or no bill, he's not going anywhere without his captain."

Without saying another word, she reached up, wrapped her arms around his neck and kissed the love of her life.

I hope you enjoyed your trip to Paradise!
If you can't get enough of Cass and Archer, download an exclusive bonus scene and see what happened on a return trip to Barbecue Island.
And next...Heather Holt is more than ready for a change of scenery, and a little piece of paradise tucked away in the jungle of Bocas del Toro seems like a pretty good place for a fresh start.
Join Heather in her Escape to the Sun. Read on for an excerpt right after this.

Escape to the Sun

Enjoy this excerpt from Escape to the Sun, the next in the Destination Paradise Series.

Heather Holt picked her way through the paper bags, empty bottles and…*oh no, was that a used…?* She didn't want to think about what else was under her feet on the crowded dirt road. The man at the airport told her it was Main Street, but it was unlike any main street she'd ever seen. And she'd been living in Central America for five years. It wasn't just the road that was dirty and littered. It was the very air she pulled into her lungs. It was heavy. Heavy with humidity, yes. But more than that. Heavy with the cloying scents of curry and fried foods, some type of blossoming flower that she couldn't pin down and… people. It was a dizzying perfume. One Heather was absolutely certain she didn't want to wear.

She tried to fight the growing sense of desperation. *No. Not desperation.* It was more like a terrifyingly crippling realization that she had nowhere else to go. For better or worse, she would be staying in Bocas Town in the Bocas del Toro archipelago on the west side of Panama. At least for a few months. Even looking through her veil of emotion, Heather feared she'd only seen a small part of the *worse*, and there was definitely no *better* in sight.

It's not as if she was new to the country or the people. But if she hadn't seen it for herself on a map that Bocas Town was part of the Panama she'd come to know and love, there's no way she would have believed it. Not that she'd come to know much of the country, living as a dockmaster's wife at a well-to-do marina just a few hours north of Panama City for the last five years. If she'd had anywhere else to go, she would have gone there.

As it was, all Heather had was a name—Mick. And the name of a bar—the Bitter End—scratched on a piece of napkin. It wasn't much. But it was all she had. She'd make it work.

It's not as if she had a choice.

The more she looked around at the mix of locals, backpackers who wished they were locals, and transplanted North Americans, who likely were some sort of mix of the two, the tighter the knot in her stomach pulled.

"Great idea, Heather." She mumbled the words to herself, but a passerby heard and tried to high-five her. She dodged him, but it didn't deter him any.

"Whatever it was, man, I'm sure it was stellar."

Stellar? It was anything but stellar. It was a gut reaction, last minute, completely foolish, act of a woman out of options. That's exactly what she was. A woman completely and totally out of options.

She'd been worse. And she'd be better, too. Just not today.

Heather straightened her shoulders and hitched her backpack higher on her back. Everything she owned, or at least, everything she wanted to own, was in that pack. She'd only had a few hours' notice when her friends Cass and Archer confirmed that they'd have room for her on their charter sailboat to take her to Bocas del Toro. Not that she needed much more. Everything back at the Shelter Bay Marina was full of memories of a different life. An old life. A life she no longer wanted anything to do with. If she was honest, it was a life she'd never really wanted. At least not with Joe. But it wasn't until he'd had a baby with one of his waitresses that she got the out she'd been looking for.

It didn't make her proud to think that she'd stayed in a loveless relationship because it was *easy*, but it was what it was and she couldn't go back and change it.

No. It was all about looking forward now.

Bocas would most certainly not be the cushy life of Shelter Bay, but that's why she knew it was going to be okay. No. It would be more than okay. She was more than ready for a change and a challenge.

Heather glanced down at the scrap of napkin again as if she hadn't memorized the details days ago, a full five minutes after it was given to her. She owed a lot to her friends, and the connections they had in the islands that had led her to that address on that napkin. What was waiting for her after she checked in with Mick, she couldn't be entirely sure. Although, she hoped her friends were right and it involved a bed-and-breakfast run by a woman who could use some help. More specifically, *her* help. Because that's why Heather was there.

Only a few weeks earlier, when she'd hopped on another charter with Cass and Archer out to the tranquil San Blas Islands, she'd met Josie, an eccentric old woman who, in one afternoon, had changed her life. Heather couldn't even explain it. She wished she could. But ultimately, it didn't matter because Josie had seen that she was lost and broken, and with only a few words, the older woman gave her hope. And at that moment, that hope looked like a beer shack with a broken surfboard hanging over the door, a scrawny mutt curled on the crumbling concrete step, and a crate full of empty bottles sitting next to him. *The Bitter End* was painted in block letters on the surfboard.

She looked at the napkin.

Back to the surfboard. It wasn't what she'd been expecting, that was for sure, but Heather had long ago learned to expect the unexpected. She stepped up, resisting the urge to pet the flea-ridden dog, and reached for the door at the same moment as it opened. The pumping beats of what sounded like Top 40 hits on a steel drum band spilled from the opening; a shirtless, golden brown man who looked as though he could have been riding that surfboard in a different circumstance, appeared. His back to her, the man walked backward down the stairs as he yelled back to someone inside. Instinctively, Heather stepped out of the way, narrowly missing the dog. Or maybe she didn't miss him, judging by the growl beneath her.

The man turned at the sound.

"Hey, Poco." He bent to scratch behind the dog's head. "You all right?"

"Excuse me?"

The man looked up, seeing her for the first time.

He was gorgeous, if you liked the rough around the edges surfer boy type with hard, tight muscles, golden skin, salt-tousled-curling-over-the-ears dirty blond hair, and an attitude to match. She swallowed hard.

"Did you need something?"

She did. She needed a lot of things. And judging by the way her body vibrated into a full-scale heat, he might just have exactly what she needed.

If only she had time for that. Heather cleared her throat. "Mick?"

"Depends." Looking up at her from his squat, his lip curled up in a smile so sinful, in any other instance there was no doubt she'd be in trouble.

Any instance where she didn't need a place to sleep that

night. Alone. She narrowed her eyes, fairly certain she wasn't speaking to Mick. "Where can I find him?"

He laughed and straightened. "It's like that, is it?"

"It's like, I need to find Mick." Heather crossed her arms, which only made Surfer Boy laugh again.

"Don't get all twisted up, sugar." He pointed behind him. "You'll find him behind the bar."

Heather twisted to look past the golden muscles in front of her. "This is a bar?"

"Of course. And a hostel. And…" His mouth twisted up in that damned sexy grin again. "Let's just say, this place lives up to its name."

"Its name?" She glanced around but didn't see any other sign telling her where she was.

"The Bitter End."

"What does that mean?"

"It's just like it sounds." Surfer Boy swallowed his laugh so hard he looked as if he might choke. "It's also a nautical term."

She didn't respond, unsure of what any of that meant. What any of it meant.

She didn't realize she was staring at him until he winked at her, flashed a smile that could only mean he came from money, and said, "Mick's inside."

"Right." She shook her head, embarrassed that he probably thought she was checking him out. It wasn't entirely untrue, but even if there was truth to it, she certainly didn't need him thinking that. Heather pulled herself together and squeezed past him through the doorway, careful to avoid both the dog, who'd returned to sleeping, and Surfer Boy, who made no effort to move out of her way.

He smelled like salt, suntan lotion, and sex. She couldn't help but inhale his scent, holding her breath to keep it in just long enough to push out the stench of the street but not long enough for her body to register the effect he had on her.

Too late.

He waited until she finally moved past him to let out his own breath. Damn, he didn't usually go for the fresh-off-the-plane backpacker type. Too young. Too idealistic. Too needy.

But that woman was different. Sure, she had a backpack, and yes, he hadn't seen her around. Bocas Town was a small place, and Ash knew everyone, including—no, *especially*—the ladies. The woman was obviously new to Bocas, she wasn't new to traveling. That much was clear by the slight wear of her clothes, as if they'd been kissed by the sea a few too many times, the scuffs of her pack, and the tan on her skin. He was willing to bet that tan probably didn't have a whole lotta lines if he looked close enough.

And he would be happy to investigate closer.

On any other day, that's exactly what he would be doing.

But not today. "Damn. Hey, Paco?" The dog lifted his head before tucking down again.

Ash shook his head to clear himself of the sight of her long, dark braid, and toned, tanned legs. It didn't totally work.

No. Not today.

He didn't get into town very often these days, and he'd felt the loss of companionship in his arms, as well as his balls. His dick twitched, needing attention. With one more look behind him at the now closed door, Ash shook his head. "Maybe later," he assured himself.

His trips to Bocas Town didn't come as frequently anymore, and although he usually had time to fool around and play for a bit, today he didn't. He'd promised Sherri he'd pick up all her packages, including the new caretaker of her jungle bed-and-breakfast.

He'd somehow become the self-appointed caretaker of

Sherri's bed-and-breakfast, and more importantly, of the older woman. She was like an eccentric old aunt who'd taken him in when he was new to Bocas and as lost as anyone else in what could only be described as the *Land of the Misfit Toys.* She'd recognized something in him that he couldn't even see himself. At least, not at the time. Sherri probably didn't even know it, but she'd saved him with the unconditional love she'd had no reason to give him. No reason beyond the fact that Sherri's heart was too big for her own good.

He'd do anything for her. Including missing a primo surf day to take the boat into Bocas Town to pick up anything she needed.

And that's just what he was going to do.

His flip-flops provided a thin barrier protecting him from the street. He hardly noticed anymore. Not that he noticed it much when he'd first come to Bocas four years earlier. The contrast between his ordered, all too clean life back in the States and the tousled mess of Bocas was exactly what he'd been looking for when he'd arrived. After time, as he slowly woke to his new life, the disorder and chaos around him, the pure opposition of his surroundings to his past, gave him comfort. He'd craved something different. Anything.

"Ash. Ash. Señor Ash!" The familiar high-pitched shriek Ash had come to know would be followed by Miguel's toothy grin, made him grin and was just about enough of a distraction for him to forget about the long-legged beauty. Just about.

"Hey, kiddo." Ash turned just in time to catch the small boy before he crashed into his legs. Miguel had the ability to pop out of nowhere and if Ash wasn't careful, he'd take him out. It'd happened before. But only once. As soon as he untangled the kid from his legs, he reached into the pocket of his cargo shorts and handed Miguel the peppermint he'd stashed there.

"*Gracias.*" He unwrapped the candy; it disappeared in an instant. "Help today, Señor Ash?"

“You know it, Miguel.”

Ash had sort of adopted the boy—or more likely, it was the other way around—only about a year before on a trip into town. He had a huge order from Sherri that required more than one trip to the boat, where he’d have to leave supplies unsupervised. That was never a good idea in a place like Bocas Town. Not unless you felt like paying for those supplies twice. The second time with a *local tax* attached. That’s where Miguel came in. For a small fee, usually the price of a sandwich or a bottle of soda, he’d happily guard anything for Ash. Or carry bags, or pretty much help out with whatever was needed.

As far as Ash was concerned, it was the perfect symbiotic relationship.

“Where we headed?”

Ash pointed up the street. Everything in Bocas Town was within a few streets. It was small, but the town managed to pack in a whole lot of trouble in such a tight space.

“The clinic?”

Ash nodded.

“What ya gettin’ there?”

He shrugged. “You know Ms. Sherri. Could be anything.” And it could have been. With Sherri’s place so far away from town and the clinic—as basic as it was—she liked to have a well-stocked first-aid kit for her guests. Just in case. Not that there’d ever been a case. Nothing more serious than a monkey bite, anyway. “Comin’?”

Ash didn’t need to ask. Miguel was right behind him like a crow picking up crumbs. Not for the first time, Ash wondered what Miguel’s home life was like.

Or whether he had one at all.

“All right, kid. We have lots on the list today. I’ll need all the muscle power you can handle.”

Miguel flexed his scrawny arms. His smile was so hopeful,

Ash would find him a whole afternoon's worth of work, even if he had to make it up.

The inside of the Bitter End was not at all what Heather expected. Not that she had any idea what to expect. But if it was a bed-and-breakfast she was looking for, the Bitter End was decidedly not that. Just inside the door was a small doorway with numbers labeled on a piece of paper tacked to the wall. She peeked inside and saw two rows of bunkbeds with backpacks, towels, and underwear slung over the frames.

Interesting choice for a bed-and-breakfast.

She followed the pumping music, lulled as if it was the Pied Piper leading her out of town instead of into what could only be described as a pit of pleasure. If your idea of pleasure was lounging around on hammocks and overstuffed chaise chairs, spending your day drinking and smoking all kinds of things. It wasn't hers. But maybe because she got her hard partying days out of her system many years ago. Now, Heather would settle for a good book and a quiet place to enjoy it. Far away from the pounding music.

She took another look around.

She'd signed up to run a bed-and-breakfast. Not a youth hostel. But things were a little foggy in Central America and there were more shades of gray when it came to things like this than there were colors in the rainbow. It wouldn't surprise her if she'd signed up, sight unseen, to spend the next six months slinging drinks to backpackers.

She would have sighed—or more likely, cried—if she thought it would do any good. But Heather had been out in the world long enough to know it wouldn't have any impact on the outcome. Besides, she was up for an adventure if need be. Anything that allowed her to move on.

Which was exactly why she was there and exactly why she was going to keep forcing her smile until finally it stayed put on her face, where it needed to be.

She'd do what she had to.

Especially if it meant staying in Panama and not returning home to her *I told you he was no good—you should have listened to me and stayed home* mother.

Heather dropped her hand on the plywood but it wasn't necessary. A glass of something red, sweet, and dangerous-looking appeared in front of her.

"Welcome, *chica.*"

Heather waved her hand to dismiss the drink. "I didn't order that."

"You didn't have to." The man's grin was toothy, warm and practiced. "It's on me. And you clearly need it. Name's Mick." He didn't offer his hand, a fact Heather was grateful for. It had been a long day, followed by a long week on Cass and Archer's boat, preceded by a long life. At least that's how it felt at that moment. She'd lived a lifetime in the last few months. A life she no longer wanted to live. "Drink, Heather. Then we'll talk."

He left her alone, another fact she was grateful for. She was halfway through the drink that was every bit as sweet as she expected it to be, and only half as strong as she needed, before she realized that he'd known her name.

She finished the drink, and then another that was placed in front of her before the man came back. This time he held out his hand, and she was ready for it. "Nice to meet you, Heather. Welcome to Bocas. Feeling better?"

"Was it that obvious?"

"Nah. You're okay. But Bocas Town can be a bit much the first time. But it's just the town."

That was an understatement. From the moment she left the serenity of Cass and Archer's sailboat, all five senses had been assaulted to the point of complete overload.

"Whatever you put in that drink helped."

"It always does. The rest of Bocas del Toro is...well, paradise," Mick said. "Wait until you get a chance to see it."

"I look forward to it." She slid the glass around the bar top. "How did you know who I was? Is it so obvious that I don't fit in?"

He laughed. "Sweetheart, you fit in just fine. *Everyone* fits in here. Look around."

She did as she was told and for the first time noticed the mixture of those around her. There were men, women, and people who could only be described as both, all ages and colors in a variety of clothing or in a few cases, not much clothing at all, scattered around the room. The mix was eclectic to be sure, but no one looked out of place.

"Am I right?"

"You are."

"Bocas Town is the Land of the Misfit Toys. Even if you don't belong anywhere else, you will here."

Land of the Misfit Toys. Perfect. She reached for her empty glass.

"How about a water?"

"Probably a better idea," she agreed. Whatever he'd given her had been delicious, but she could see how it could be dangerous. She drank half the bottle of water he placed in front of her before she finally asked, "You seem to have a good handle on things around here. Why do you need me?"

"You?" His eyes danced under the frayed brim of his San Francisco Giants cap. "Oh no, *chica*. I don't need you."

A flicker of panic lit in her chest. No doubt it would have burst into flames had it not been for the two magic red drinks currently flowing through her. "You don't need me?"

If this bed-and-breakfast deal didn't work out, where was she supposed to go? No doubt, Archer and Cass had already moved their boat, *Cassiopeia,* to their next destination. They had paying guests aboard and had only been doing her a favor bringing her to Bocas Town. *Without them, she'd have to—*

"You're thinking." Mick's friendly tenor interrupted the train of panic that was quickly picking up speed in her brain. "Another drink then?"

Heather shook her head. "No. But if you don't need me, I will need a—"

"*Chica.* I don't need you. But Sherri does."

"Sherri?" The train in her brain slowed slightly. "Who's Sherri?"

"The one who needs you." He wasn't helping. "At Casa del Sol. *Chica*, you didn't think you'd be staying here, did you?"

She could lie. There was no point. "I did."

"And you're glad you're not."

"A little." She laughed. The first real one in a long time. "Okay, a lot."

Mick winked, and the train slowed even more. He had that effect. "Sherri's place is a little piece of paradise. It'll be exactly what you need."

"And what is it I need?"

"I need to tell you?"

There was no point in answering him. He didn't need to tell her anything. At the same time, there was nothing he *could* tell her. How could anyone else possibly see what she needed, when she herself was blind to it?

"Sherri," she said the name again to clarify. "She needs my help?"

Mick nodded. "That's why you're here. I guess Josie wasn't too clear with the details."

There hadn't really been any details. Not that she'd asked for any.

"When I say that Sherri's place is paradise, it's not an exaggeration. It literally is. Or at least the Garden of Eden."

"Then it can't be nearby." She raised her eyebrows and Mick laughed.

"No. It's about a twenty-minute boat ride from here. Cut off from the world. People go there to unplug and hide."

"Hide? From other people?"

"From themselves, *chica*." Mick winked at her.

Perfect.

"So how do I get to Sherri's? She's expecting me?"

"She is. And I'm sure she's just as eager for you to get there as you are. Ash will take you when he gets back."

"Who's Ash and where is he?"

Mick shrugged. "Ash helps Sherri out with things. And honestly, there's no telling what he's gotten up to this afternoon. He probably had a list, but he'll be back by three. He likes to get the boat out there before the sun goes down. You're welcome to wait here. Make yourself comfortable." He pointed to a lounge chair on the deck close to the ocean, away from the business of the bar.

"Thank you." She hoped the weariness didn't show in her eyes, but it was false hope, because there was no way it didn't. She hefted her backpack up and grabbed the water on the bar. Just as she turned away, Mick stopped her.

"*Chica*?"

Heather glanced over her shoulder.

"Welcome to Bocas. You came to the right place."

"For what?"

"For everything."

"I've got what you need right here, Ash."

There was no doubt in Ash's mind that Sara had exactly what he needed in all the right ways, and without a doubt there was no one who filled out scrubs the way she did. His dick twitched just thinking about the curves that the thin piece of pink cotton was concealing. Ash had personal experience with those curves and those experiences were more than enough to deserve a replay. If it weren't for—

"I'm also free tomorrow night for dinner. Rumor has it Oscar got some fresh lobsters this morning."

If it weren't for that.

Sara was a nice girl. Despite the fact that she fell for his moves, she was a smart girl, too. She was in Bocas on some sort of work exchange, which made her dangerous. Because she was not like any of the other women Ash *dated.* Sara wanted more. She wanted Ash to take her out. She wanted to date.

Like all nice girls did.

Ash didn't.

Ash avoided nice girls.

Ash wasn't a nice guy.

"Ah, if only I could, Sara." He ran a hand through his shaggy blond hair and gave her a smile he knew was devastating. "But I have to get back to Casa del Sol. Sherri has a big order and a new manager starting today. She'll need a bit of help getting everything set up and you know how that is."

The girl didn't even bother trying to hide her pout. "Another time?"

"Of course," he lied.

The truth was, Ash could have a lot of fun with Sara if she didn't try to push so hard for a relationship. It was too bad, but there was no way Ash was going there. Not with anyone. *No matter how fun they were. Or how far their legs bent—*

"Ash, did you hear me?"

He hadn't.

"Sorry. My mind drifted."

"I bet it did." The mischief in her eye and the way she licked her lips almost made him change his mind. Almost.

"Behave." Not that she would. "How many boxes did Sherri order for me today?"

"That's what I was telling you. Her order today is quite large. You're going to need help."

"I have Miguel." He pointed to the boy, who'd been standing by, listening to everything with an interested ear. No doubt, the kid had gotten quite an education hanging out with Ash, despite his efforts to keep things as G-rated as possible when he was around.

"I think you might need more than Miguel for today's load." She shot the boy a doubtful look.

"Two strong men like us?" Ash nudged Miguel and they both flexed comically. "We got this."

Sara rolled her eyes, but he didn't miss the way her eyes traveled over his bare chest. *Damn, he should have found a T-shirt to put on.* Not that it would have stopped her.

"Wait here. I'll get your stuff."

When she returned moments later, wheeling a cart full of boxes and bags, even Ash had to admit it might be a little more than he and Miguel could handle. *What had Sherri ordered this time?* There was more than a few first-aid supplies on that cart. He mentally calculated the size and weight of each box, what each of them could probably handle and in the end, admitted defeat.

"I'll have Miguel bring the cart right back." He put one hand on it and attempted to glide it away from her. But Sara wasn't having it. She held firm, the cart jostling awkwardly between them.

"No can do, Ash." She shook her pretty little head, her mouth pressed into a line. "Clinic property."

He gave her his sexiest smile, but still she didn't relax her grip.

Ash knew when he'd been beat. "Okay, what will it take to let me borrow the cart?"

It was clearly the right question. She opened up; her lips curled into the smile of a woman who knew she was about to get exactly what she wanted. "A date. A real one."

Dammit.

He took a step toward her, reached out and tucked a strand of hair behind her ear before his fingers drifted across her cheek. "Oh, baby. You know you don't need to bribe me for a date." He leaned in, just enough so she'd feel his breath on her skin.

Just as he knew she would, her body trembled, a sigh escaped her lips, and her hand released the cart. Ash pressed his lips in a gentle, sweet, dismissive kiss and pushed the cart back to Miguel, who started down the street with it long before Sara knew what'd hit her.

Ash was already a few steps away when she called out after him. "Call me about that date."

"I'll have Miguel bring the cart back right away." He blew her a kiss. "Thanks, Sara."

He probably should have felt bad about using the girl's affections for his benefit, but she was a grown woman, and he'd been upfront with her from the beginning. She made her choices; he made his. It wasn't his fault if they didn't line up.

Besides, he didn't have time to dwell on her or the feelings she may or may not be having for him. Feelings that may very well include causing him bodily harm when she realized he had zero intention of taking her on that date. He still had more orders to pick up before he headed back to Casa del Sol and if he didn't hurry, he'd run out of daylight.

"Miguel, can you take this and load it in the boat? I'll meet you there."

"*Sí*, Señor Ash."

"You're a good kid."

The boy beamed and hurried off with the overloaded cart. Ash wished he could do more for the boy. He never asked what

Miguel's family life was like, but he had a sneaking suspicion there wasn't much of one.

Ash hurried through the rest of the list Sherri had given him and by the time he returned to the dock outside of the Bitter End where he'd tied up his boat, Miguel had almost finished up loading the supplies.

"Good job." He patted the kid on the head as he hopped into the boat with a practiced, fluid motion. "Almost ready?"

"*Sí*, Señor Ash. All done." He grabbed the last box and tucked it under the front seat. The boat was full. It would be a slow ride back if he wanted to keep the splash down.

"Good work, Miguel." Ash reached into his back pocket and pulled out a few bills. "You'll get that cart back to Sara for me?"

Miguel nodded. "I'll get the woman now."

"Right. The woman." Ash shook his head. "Wait. The woman?"

"*Sí*, Señor. *La mujer.*" His scrawny arm pointed toward the deck of the Bitter End and the same dark-haired beauty who'd tempted Ash to break his self-imposed rules.

Damn.

While he watched, she stood and stretched her arms overhead. Her T-shirt crept up just enough that he knew he'd be able to see a band of sun-kissed skin if he stood close enough.

Double damn.

Read the rest of Escape to the Sun NOW!

About the Author

Elena Aitken is a USA Today Bestselling Author of more than forty romance and women's fiction novels. The mother of 'grown up' twins, Elena now lives with her very own mountain man in the heart of the very mountains she writes about. She can often be found with her toes in the lake and a glass of wine in her hand, dreaming up her next book and working on her own happily ever after.

To learn more about Elena:

www.elenaaitken.com
elena@elenaaitken.com

www.ingramcontent.com/pod-product-compliance
Lightning Source LLC
Chambersburg PA
CBHW021233250626
47155CB00008B/2986